I0553365

A Dangerous Job

■ ■ ■

#14 in the Edgar Award-winning Dan Fortune mystery series

Dennis Lynds

(Formerly published as *Castrato*, by Michael Collins)

The characters and events portrayed in this book are fictitious. Any similarities to real persons living or dead is coincidental and not intended by the author.

© 1989, 2011 by Gayle H. Lynds 2007 Revocable Trust
The Gayle H. Lynds 2016 Revocable Trust

Cover © 2015 Gayle Lynds
Cover Design: Shannon Raab
Cover Photographer: Kesu01/iStockphoto.com

All rights reserved. No part of this book may be reproduced, or stored in a retrieval system, or transmitted in any form or by any means, electronic, mechanical, photocopying, recording or otherwise, without express written permission of the publisher.

A Dangerous Job e-book edition: 978-1-941517-26-0
A Dangerous Job POD edition: 978-1-941517-27-7

For inquiries:
Gayle Lynds
P.O. Box 732
125 Forest Avenue
Portland, ME 04101-9998
www.DennisLynds.com

For Kate and Deirdre,
with love, Dad

Acclaim for Dennis Lynds & His Novels

"A tautly crafted mystery." – *Publishers Weekly*

"The most ambitious of the series . . . engrossing." – *Kirkus Reviews*

"Finely honed prose, suspense, and bits of reflective philosophy . . . crackling with excitement." – *Library Journal*

"His best yet." – *San Diego Union*

"It's refreshing to encounter [Lynds's] uncynical, unjaded private detective Dan Fortune living happily in Santa Barbara with his lady friend Kay . . . [Lynds] combines superb characters and excellent plotting to produce an exciting mystery." – *Booklist*

"Engrossing and empathic." – *New York Daily News*

"Conspiracy never sounded so good." – *Inside Books*

"Gets you in the brain, in the heart, and in the gut." – *Mystery Scene Magazine*

"Here's a crime novel you can sink your teeth into . . . adventure and grit crafted from lusty language." – *Houston Post*

"Lively characters and experiences rarely encountered in the tough-guy mystery." – *Santa Barbara magazine*

"[Lynds] at his best. . . . powerful." – *Library Journal*

"A fast pace, interesting characters, and a finely crafted mystery . . . the book has an exciting climax." – *The Orlando Sentinel*

". . . filled with vivid description . . . a fast action plot . . . memorable characters." – *Asheville Citizen-Times*

"Like Ross Macdonald, [Lynds] writes vivid prose and dialogue *and* can plot a mystery." – *Ellery Queen Mystery Magazine*

"Collins has the ability to set in motion a sequence of events that moves with the inevitability of a huge boulder rolling down a mountainside." – *New York Times Book Review*

"A compelling novel of people with dark secrets." – *The Raleigh News and Observer*

"Briskly paced, tersely told." – *The Buffalo Evening News*

"A fast-pace thriller . . . a good book to read at one sitting on a rainy evening." – *Minneapolis Tribune*

"[Lynds] writes with firmness and intelligence. His style is staccato, matched to the action and tone." – *Washington Post*

"[Lynds] is in splendid form." – *The Detroit News*

"A gripping story." – *The Charlotte Observer*

"A novelist of power and quality . . . one of the major imaginative creators in the crime field." – Ross Macdonald

"Some of the rawest, most unencumbered mystery writing extant in the genre." – *American Library Association*

"Tough, believable." – *San Francisco Examiner*

"[Lynds's books are] filled with as much closely observed incident and detail as John O'Hara short stories." – *Wall Street Journal*

"Collins is the Costa-Gavras of the PI world . . . we might also call him the Captain Kirk of PI writers, boldly taking the genre where no colleague has gone before – and doing it so passionately that we can't help but sign on for the quest with him." – literary critic Francis M. Nevins, Jr.

"Lynds is a major contributor to the form, even a redefiner of it; whether or not he is ever given his just due, he should take satisfaction from the fact that he has written mystery novels of genuine distinction." – literary critic Richard Carpenter

Dan Fortune series, by Dennis Lynds, originally published under the pseudonym Michael Collins

Act of Fear, 1967
The Brass Rainbow, 1969
Night of the Toads, 1970
Walk a Black Wind, 1971
Shadow of a Tiger, 1972
The Silent Scream, 1973
Blue Death, 1975
The Blood-Red Dream, 1976
The Nightrunners, 1978
The Slasher, 1980
Freak, 1983
Minnesota Strip, 1987
Red Rosa, 1988
A Dangerous Job, 1989
Chasing Eights, 1990
The Irishman's Horse, 1991
Cassandra In Red, 1992

Paul Shaw series, by Dennis Lynds, originally published under the pseudonym Mark Sadler

The Falling Man, 1970
Here to Die, 1971
Mirror Image, 1972
Circle of Fire, 1973
Touch of Death, 1981
Deadly Innocents, 1986

Kane Jackson series, by Dennis Lynds, originally published under the pseudonym William Arden

A Dark Power, 1968
Deal in Violence, 1969
The Goliath Scheme, 1971

Die to a Distant Drum, 1972
Deadly Legacy, 1973

Buena Costa County series, by Dennis Lynds, originally published under the pseudonym John Crowe
Another Way to Die, 1972
A Touch of Darkness, 1972
Bloodwater, 1974
Crooked Shadows, 1975
When They Kill Your Wife, 1977
Close to Death, 1979

George Malcolm, private detective, by Dennis Lynds, originally published under the pseudonym Carl Dekker
Woman in Marble, 1973

Langford ("Ford") Morgan, ex-soldier, ex-CIA, ex-roustabout, by Dennis Lynds, originally published under the pseudonym Michael Collins
The Cadillac Cowboy, 1995

Other of his works include
science fiction novels, literary novels, mystery short stories,
literary short stories, short story anthologies, and poetry.

Table of Contents

SANTA BARBARA

1

Dianne hears about this young woman with two little kids and a pony who goes door to door taking photographs of other kids on the pony for proud parents. It's a bit she can use as a teaser for the female business consultant firm she reps, so she finds Nina Owen, makes an appointment to photograph her and the pony.

It's a new client and the budget is low. She goes alone with her camera. Nina meets her in a trailer camp on Punta Gorda street in the *barrio*. The pony is in back with a thin, silent boy and a small, chunky little girl. The freeway is ten feet away through a high fence.

While Dianne is setting up, a man appears. He's good looking, not tall but slim and lean in faded jeans and a heavy maroon corduroy shirt over a pale blue cotton turtleneck. He has a wide boyish smile under a macho mustache, good shoulders, and a lot of interest in her. He asks about her camera, what she's going to do with the shots of Nina and the pony. Billy's his name, he says.

"I do public relations," she tells him. "I've got a new client who advises women on business, and Nina's door-to-door pony is an eye-catcher for an ad aimed at women in business."

"Thought it all up herself," Billy says. Nina says nothing, holds the older child, the boy, on the pony.

"About how much do you gross, Nina?" Dianne asks as she finishes adjusting the camera.

"I don't know. You almost ready? I got to feed the kids an' groom Taffy."

"You don't have to hold the boy on the pony," Billy says. "It'll shoot better if you hold Taffy's halter, right Miss . . . Hey, I don't even know your name.

"Dianne," she says and returns his smile, aware that he's more than just interested in her. She looks toward Nina, asking silently woman to woman if this Billy belongs to Nina. But Nina doesn't seem to notice, interested only in getting the picture taking started and over with, and, later, in being paid. Once she has the fifty dollars Dianne agreed to, she takes the two children and Taffy and disappears into a ramshackle lean-to that seems to be where Taffy is housed.

"You always do your own camera work?" Billy asks as he helps Dianne carry her stuff out to her car.

She hears herself laugh and knows she is flirting. "Only when the budget is low,"

"Sounds like the countries I soldier for," Billy says. "Bring your own gun and uniform."

"What countries would that be? Aren't you American?"

"As apple pie, and my lips are sealed." He laughs too. She wonders why people laugh so in sexual skirmishing. He is still talking. "Let's just say it's always hot and everyone except us paleface mercs is kind of dark-skinned."

"What do you do when you're not soldiering, or advising Nina how to pose for pictures?"

"Hey, that'd be telling." He looks around like a secret conspirator. "Actually, I'm a bunco artist, but keep it quiet."

"Bunco?"

"Sure, the big con, the scam." He grins that boyish grin. "Hey, you want a tip? If you want to run a safe con game in Santa Barbara, a scam with no problems and no sweat, pull it off Friday morning an hour or so both sides of lunch."

"Why is that?"

"Anyone gets suspicious and calls the cops they get told to call City Hall. The fraud guy at City Hall's at lunch. So they call the public defender, only the whole office is closed for lunch. They try the Sheriff, the Sheriff don't have jurisdiction in the city. Better Business Bureau? Forget it, they get sent back to the cops. The detective squad this time. They send you to the D.A. Only D.A. Fraud is closed on Fridays, call back Monday! Half the town is ripped off before anyone's back from lunch!"

Dianne is really laughing now. Billy sees his advantage.

"Hey, how about we talk about it some more over dinner? Seven o'clock?"

She looks him over more carefully, from juvenile smile to good chest and slim hips and tight jeans. He's callow, yes, but he could be fun too. He talks big, and she wonders if he can follow up. Is he all hot air, or is there some power behind the smile? Then, he's so eager she's flattered. He could be a kick in bed, eager and boastful and gawky all at once. All need and drive and no technique. But that can be the best. She can teach him, guide him into what's best for her.

"Why not? Seven o'clock. Pick me up at my place, I don't like meeting in public. You have a car?"

"Hey, I'll be there panting."

They both laugh. She gives him directions and drives back to her office. The rest of the day she has doubts, but she knows those doubts. They are one of the prices you pay for being female in this society when you've agreed to do something a little daring, even risky. So after work she goes home and gets ready. Not too dazzling or too feminine. Tailored jeans and a silk blouse. Light blue and dark blue so that she doesn't look too eager. He probably won't even change out of his jeans, which is okay, he looks nice in them. She is ready when the bell rings.

But it isn't Billy.

And yet it is. She is puzzled. It is a taller man, and older, yet he looks very much like Billy. He wears the same jeans, the same kind of turtleneck under a plaid shirt that looks a lot more expensive than Billy's shirt. Viyella. Billy with more solidity and without the juvenile smile. There is nothing juvenile about this man.

"Billy won't be coming," the man says. "You can swing your cute little ass somewhere else."

He turns and walks away. Just like that.

"Your ass is kind of cute too," she says to his back. "What do you do with it when you're not babysitting Billy?"

He stops. "Don't you ever ask their last names, Miss Krasnowicz? Mine's Owen. Just like Nina's. It's Billy's name too. Shazzam, right? What a surprise. A married man. Not that they seem to care much, especially Billy, but I do."

"Why"

Now he looks at her. As if it wasn't what he had expected.

"They didn't say anything," she says. "Either of them."

He walks back toward her. "What the hell did you think he was doing there with Nina and the kids?"

"I suppose I didn't think. Do you always? Whatever your name is."

"Frank Owen," he says. "Look, I guess it's mostly Billy's fault, okay? I talked him out of it so let's just forget it."

Again he turns to go. He is taller than his brother, broader in the shoulders and chest while still lean. Not a slim man, solid hips, and she guesses he's eight to ten years older than Billy. He fills his clothes better, especially the jeans. A lot of man in those jeans, as the girls used to say in high school. His face is more mature, creased in long sun and wind lines, and more handsome. He doesn't need his brother's macho mustache, moves with more grace than Billy. A man not a boy.

"Tell me," she says, "does Billy really do all those things he implies? The soldier of fortune?"

He turns once more. She almost smiles. She knows he isn't going to walk away again.

"Some of them," he says.

"What about you? What have you done wild, Frank?"

She does smile, challenging.

"Mostly avoid your kind of broad."

"What is my kind of broad, Frank?"

"A ball-breaker. Someone who goes after the easy mark like Billy. Gets her kicks and cheap thrills second-hand from married men."

"And you get your thrills first hand, is that it? Step right up and take your thrills and kicks and whatever you want."

"Most of the time," Frank says.

They stare at each other.

"Why don't we have dinner and talk about it," Dianne says. "Someone in the Owen family owes me a dinner."

"With Billy you'd have paid your own way, probably his."

"All right then, I'll pay for the Owen I'm looking at. You interest me."

"Okay, so let's talk."

Frank crooks his elbow for her to take his arm. She laughs, gets her handbag, and they go out to his car. She is intrigued to see where Frank will take her, is sure that with Billy it would have been a chain with big drinks, if not a fast food joint. She has learned that where a man takes a woman to eat tells a lot about him. From the way Frank has acted she guesses a steak house. Somewhere Frank knows the owner and bartender, where they greet him by name. Perhaps Harry's Plaza Cafe or Gallaghers or Joe's on lower State.

He parks in a lot on lower State, but they do not go into Joe's. He picks The Chalkboard, a small French restaurant owned by a man who had been chef at The Grand Hotel over in Los Olivos. It is one of her favorite restaurants. He is a more complicated man than he seems. He likes good food, good wine. He's been around, is the way he puts it when she asks. She doesn't let him get away with that.

"Don't give me the dropout roughneck act."

"What act do you want me to give you?"

"How about the real one? College, work, cities."

"Marriages?"

"All of them."

He tells her his family came from Nevada, he went to Eastern prep schools. About the Marines, the colleges, the teaching, the marriages, the children. She tells him about the West Pointer she married immediately out of college, and the divorce six years ago. The acting and modelling, and how bad she was. She tells him about the talent agency and then the public relations jobs, the PR and ad agency she owns now, and how she has always hated her name.

"What's wrong with Krasnowicz? A fine old Polish name. The melting pot. What are you, a snob? You want to be a WASP, have blue blood, eat sandwiches with the crusts cut off?"

"You're a WASP."

"Bite your tongue. Owen is Welsh. I'm a dark, brooding Celt. No effete, pale-faced Anglo-Saxon."

He is amusing, charming, they have a good time. Then it is the end of that first dinner. They have coffee.

"Tell me about your wives," she says.

He tells her their names, where he lived with them, when he was divorced, where they are now, and where he is now—alone and teaching in a private school in Montecito. It is not what she wants to know and she knows he knows that, but it is a first date and he has told her much. They have laughed and been open. She goes home with him to the two rear rooms he rents in a house on Humphrey Road which he calls the slums of Montecito.

They go to bed. His body is all she had expected it to be, and she seems to please him. He is lean and hard and not at all skinny, and his ass and shoulders and back feel good in her hands as he thrusts and she holds him in her. His hands feel good on her back as he holds her under him so tightly she could not break out if she wanted to.

Later, she gets up and dresses. He comes awake, sits up.

"What's wrong?"

"Nothing's wrong. I'm just going home."

He lights a cigarette, lies back and watches her. "Why?"

"Because that's what I do, Frank."

"Always? Slam, bam, thank you Sam?"

"Not always." She slips on her shoes, stands. "I have my business to run. It has to be something more for all night."

He nods. "Okay. I'll drive you home."

"I already called a cab. I didn't want to wake you."

"I'll call you."

"I'd like that."

She leaves, not at all sure he will call, making herself not care as she has always done. She won't be a man's playgirl, not since Richard. She is a woman with a full life of her own. Yet she listens for the phone. Do men listen for the phone? They probably do, but she'll never really know. This time the phone does ring. He has L.A. theater tickets. His odd combination of convention and rebelliousness attracts her strongly. The educated freebooter, mental outlaw.

In bed that night they talk of men and women, of his wives, of Richard. It has been another good night, she is tired and sleepy but she will go home and he knows it. He has a sheen of sweat on his chest and belly, in the pubic hair where it has pressed against her wetness.

"It was a kind of dream with my first wife," he tells her. "We were going to be together forever, you know? Then it started to change. I was always doing what I didn't want to do. She had what she wanted. Husband, house, kids, friends. I needed more, something different. She couldn't be different. The second couldn't either. Maybe no woman can."

"Some can, but the man has to be different too. Richard was everything he was told to be, and he expected me to be the same. I was a sex partner, the comfort waiting back home. Women can't be just sex objects."

Frank lights a cigarette. "You *are* sex objects, there's nothing you can do about it except cut men's balls off so we won't need sex at all." He shakes his head. "You can refuse to be the sex object of a particular man. You can deny him and his needs. You can refuse to have any sex relation, but unless you create a world of eunuchs you're a sex object to *all* men."

"All right," Dianne says, as she gets up and starts to dress. "But I have to be a lot more to one man. If all he sees in me is what every other man sees, then I'm nothing to him. I may not be able to stop being a sex object to all men, but I can stop being just a sex object to *my* man."

She is dressed and comes back to the bed to bend and kiss him. She kisses his chest, his belly, the wet penis in its hair.

She leaves and he does not try to stop her.

The next days she does not listen for the telephone. She knows now he will call again. It is three days, she does not know where he is, but then he calls. There are no tickets this time, no courting dinner in a special restaurant. They go straight to his rooms and drink beer and make love. After, he tells her about his father.

"He killed himself when I was ten," he says in the dark, his eyes up to the ceiling, his hand touching her mound. "They'd been fighting, him and my mother. They'd fought as long as I'd been old enough to remember. He never *did* anything. Hunt, fish, cash the checks his brokers sent, drink and gamble, tell dirty stories with the boys, and chase other women. What kind of life was that for a man? A man was supposed to do something useful. A man was supposed to carve out a career, be *someone*."

His hand goes on slowly playing with her mound, her pubic hair. She says nothing, waits for him to tell it in his own time, his own way. It is, she senses, important to him.

"She never understood him. She would have to have been a different women. He hunted, and fished, and gambled, and drank, and flirted with every woman in town *because* he had nothing to do except make money, provide a husband for her and a home for me."

"Not Billy?" Dianne says, trying to be gentle.

"Billy wasn't born. I'm not sure he ever knew about Billy. Maybe he did. Maybe it was knowing about Billy made him climb up on South Gorge, sit there from noon to sunset, then light a cigarette and step off into the river two hundred feet below."

She waits and watches him as he lights a cigarette, smokes, puts his right hand back on her wet mound.

"Only it wasn't Billy. It was her. It was El Dorado. He'd never had a chance to go and find El Dorado. He'd never gone, and he suddenly knew he never would."

She doesn't know why, but that night she stays. That night she decides she will sleep there, and in the morning he is up first to make juice and coffee and his special pancakes. Thick buckwheat pancakes, the way his father had taught him to cook them over a campfire in the high mountains. He uses that exact phrase: ". . . over a campfire in the high mountains."

She enjoys the buckwheats. He is pleased. He doesn't have to be at his school until ten, watches her get dressed for work.

She says, "Why do I feel something just ended instead of beginning. Why do I feel I've betrayed myself? Why do I feel you're going to run screaming? Why do I hear a train whistle, a jet engine, see vapor trails coming out of your ass? Why do I have this sense of a vacuum where your chair is, an empty space?"

He eats the last buckwheat, carries his dishes to the sink, rinses them.

He says. "You're different. Maybe you're even different enough. I won't fake anything."

"Neither will I."

He nods. "I'll pick you up after work. We can talk."

"All right."

"It might really go."

"It might," she says, and goes out to her car.

2

The first shot blew the left front tire on the Tempo.

I rolled out and lay flat in the dirt road. A narrow road that curved upward to where the cabin had to be somewhere out of sight among the dusty old oaks and thick chaparral.

The second shot smashed the driver's window over my head. From the left. A statement—he had me if he wanted me. I could have run, but it would have taken too long to hide. All I could do was inch toward the car, hope to slide under before the third shot.

The sky was a clear, high blue.

Four turkey vultures and a red-shouldered hawk soared the late morning thermal currents.

But no condors.

The last wild California Condor was in the Los Angeles Zoo in a final attempt to save the largest flying land bird from extinction. They would fail, and *Gymnogyps californianus* would cease to exist because *Homo sapiens sapiens* needed gold, cheap land, baronial estates, and sport. Without *Homo sapiens*, the condor might have gone on forever.

Now there were only vultures and hawks. And me inching on my belly under the Tempo.

There was no third shot.

My professional judgment told me I'd been on my stomach as long as the sniper wanted.

I got up, dusted the dirt off with my lone hand, and walked on up the road. It curved in a switchback above itself, and the cabin was off to the left among native oaks, imported palms and pepper trees.

Invisible from below, it was almost as hidden from the narrow track that went on upward past it. Someone preferred privacy to the magnificent view of the coastal plain that had to be there through the trees.

A Jeep stood under the trees, one tire flat, a week's dust and leaves on it. I found where the sniper had parked off the road, saw his fresh tire tracks that went up the dirt road, not down. There was another way from the cabin back to Camino Cielo. The underbrush from the cabin to the road was too thick to show footprints, the dirt too hard.

The front door was open. Inside, someone had had a party. Maybe a week ago. Someone who was a lousy housekeeper, or had left in a hurry. Beer cans littered a bare table. There were two tequila bottles: one empty, the other half full. Junkfood containers, rancid french fries and moldy Chicken McNuggets, stale tortilla chips, and three dried up containers of salsa.

The rest of the cabin was bare and clean, in almost military order. A narrow cot covered with an army blanket. A single armchair and a side table. A neat row of paperback books, all in Spanish. A spartan bureau and some side chairs. A large radio with shortwave bands. The bureau was orderly with rolled socks, underwear, jeans, and shirts. The closet held work clothes, boots, a single expensive grey suit and black oxfords.

I walked around the house in widening circles to the edge of the steep drop behind it. The work boot lay at the edge, and the odor reached me on the light wind. It's not a smell you ever forget. I held to a branch, looked over and down.

It lay near the base of the drop fifty feet below, sprawled on large, jagged rocks in a barranca that hid it from the road. A short, thin shape in jeans, red cotton shirt, one work boot, black socks. Hatless, black hair matted. The stink of rotted flesh in the sun and heat.

I walked down to my disabled Tempo, got a rag from the trunk to hold over my nose and mouth, stepped warily through the brush and rocks into the barranca. It was rattlesnake country, and they came out in a hot April. On the body one leg was twisted and broken, one arm almost torn off. A large rock had fallen on the crushed head. The clothes said it had been a man, but the face was gone to putrefaction, vultures and small animals.

I searched fast to keep from gagging. Three dollars and change. The keys to the Jeep. A wallet with two credit cards, a California driver's license, and two fifty dollar bills. The credit cards and license were in the name of Hector Jantarro.

Back on the road, I put the spare on the Tempo, drove to San Marcos Pass and down to Cold Spring Tavern to call the Sheriff.

"Reporting a death. Dan Fortune, private investigator."

For a real New Yorker, if you have to leave the old neighborhood you might as well move across the country. Burned out of my old Chelsea loft, and my lady in California, the move to the coast seemed like a good idea. Sooner or later you have to decide what's important.

Her name is Kay Michaels, and we rented the house in Summerland six months ago. Long and slim, she likes to sit in black slacks and white sweater on the window seat in the living room where the sun lights the auburn in her hair. A model and sometime actress, she is good at the business end, represents other models in Los Angeles, and lived as long as I've known her in an apartment in the Hollywood Hills. When I came out, she sublet.

"We both start fresh," she said. "It's hard enough without having to adapt to where one of us has lived for ten years."

Only ninety miles north of Los Angeles, Santa Barbara is some of what New York is, everything New York isn't. Kay found a Spanish-Colonial style rambler with the red tile roof and white adobe walls. It has a tower for her office, an odd L-shaped living room of dark hardwood floors, three bedrooms, and a dining room through the kitchen. It's quirky, has no land, and if it weren't in Summerland we'd have paid twice the rent. It was her money until I went to work. Smalltime New York private detectives don't have money in the bank.

I paid my $100, passed the written test, and with my New York experience had my wall certificate and my paper license with the color photo. I had a permit to carry my old cannon—a lot easier in Santa Barbara than New York. I didn't have an office yet, but Dianne Owen found me through Kay.

"I've known her since she started to act," Kay said. "She's younger, but not much. Late thirties, she couldn't act worth a damn, went into the agency business. Talent, models, public relations. Now she runs an ad and PR agency here in Santa Barbara that handles mostly female businesses."

Dianne Owen was a small, compact woman. Curved and firm, maybe five-five and a hundred and ten. Black-haired and sturdy, with the pale skin of her Polish peasant ancestors.

"I think sometimes I married Frank because I wanted to be Owen instead of Krasnowicz. Got what I deserved, right, Kay? Two ex-wives, three kids he didn't live with, and I still married him. Two years after I divorce him I still worry about him."

She wanted me to find out what the ex-husband she still worried about, Frank Owen, was doing to find a missing brother.

"Billy Owen is a flake, Dan. Some of the people he knows are worse than flakes."

"How long has the brother been missing? Why is Frank worried?"

"No idea on either. And I don't give a damn about Billy, it's Frank. He's not as young as he thinks he is. Four days ago he came down from San Francisco, showed up at my house. He drops by any time he passes through. I say come on in, flop on my back and open my legs." She shook her head in wonder at herself. It was a model's head: black hair, blue eyes, high cheekbones and hollow cheeks. "This time he asked if I knew where Billy was. I didn't. He said Billy was supposed to meet him but hadn't, and hadn't been to work in three days. Now it must be a week."

"Billy Owen lives in Santa Barbara?"

"Over on the Westside with his wife Nina."

"You see a lot of him?"

"Not if I can help it. He comes sniffing around once or twice a month."

"Sniffing you?"

She shrugged. "A lot of men have to try for anything and every-thing in skirts. Part of their image of being men."

"Even if they're married," Kay said.

"Especially if they're married," Dianne said. "Especially their brother's ex-wife."

"Rivalry between them?"

"Not exactly rivalry."

"What then?"

"I don't know. I'm not a man. Something male."

That was when she told me how she had met and married Frank Owen over four years ago, and I agreed to see what I could do. He hadn't told her where he was staying, what he was doing to find his brother, or why he was worried. All she could tell me was that Billy Owen worked at Canton Construction and lived at an address on the Westside.

I started with the address. It was a rundown cottage set behind a larger house. Nina Owen was a small, silent woman in her early twenties. She stood in the doorway in worn jeans and a flannel shirt, a straw sombrero set on her long, dirty blonde hair. She wasn't sure how long her husband had been missing, and didn't seem to care that much.

"The foreman from Canton said he ain't been to work a week. He come with Billy's back pay, wanted to know if I knew where Billy was, what he was doin'."

"Do you?"

"Didn't even know he was gone anywheres. Like I told Frank, 'cause Billy ain't around it don't mean he's gone somewheres. Last time I seen him he was gonna cruise bars with Jantarro."

"Who's Jantarro?"

"Guy he works with. Lives up Camino Cielo."

"You know where Frank Owen is now?"

She rummaged in her jeans, came out with a crumpled scrap of paper. "He left me a number case Billy called."

The telephone number turned out to be the Seabird Motel. Frank Owen didn't answer his phone, wasn't there when I went. The city directory got me up to Camino Cielo and a dead Hector Jantarro.

Back at the cabin the patrol deputy and sergeant looked at my new papers, weren't impressed with my views, sealed off the whole area with yards of yellow tape imprinted endlessly with: CRIME SCENE— DO NOT ENTER. They examined the body—deputy sheriffs are also deputy coroners in Santa Barbara County—saw the big rock and the head wound, and immediately called for the coroner's detail, the major crime detectives, and the crime scene investigation detectives.

They took my statement, let me go. I called Dianne Owen, told her to get over to the Summerland house. Now I wanted to know everything about Frank and Billy Owen. Death makes a difference.

3

Dianne Owen sat in the bay window. The mountainous islands out on the ocean behind her looked so near at the end of winter.

"I knew," Dianne said. "But I married him anyway."

"Why did he marry you?" Kay said.

"Because he's better than he knows. That's why I'm scared, Dan. Scared he'll get in over his head because that's what he thinks he's supposed to do."

"Someone was there, kept me away from the cabin," I said. "But Jantarro had been dead a week, maybe more, and there's no sign of Billy Owen."

"Jantarro fell over that cliff?"

"The Sheriff seems to think so, they have to do an autopsy. There'd been heavy drinking. He could have been alone, the food and beer and booze all his for a couple of days, or there could have been a party. Since no one reported the death they think if anyone was with him they're too scared to come forward. Illegals or transients and long gone. That's what they told me, anyway."

"Don't you believe them, Dan?" Kay said.

"I don't believe them or not believe them," I said. "The big rock that crushed Jantarro's skull raises a question, but they've told me what's officially most probable to them right now." I looked back at Dianne Owen. "Billy Owen's wife isn't worried, why is Frank?"

"If Billy was in trouble, he'd tell Frank before Nina."

Kay said, "It doesn't sound like much of a marriage."

"A little worse than most, but not much. Most of the men I know can't really be close to women, only to other men."

"You attract the wrong kind of man," Kay said.

Dianne laughed. "Tell me something I don't know."

I said, "You better tell me everything you do know about Frank and his brother. From the top, their whole history."

She lit a cigarette. The smoke drifted in the room like a thin haze between her and us, filtered the sunlight and screened the sea and islands.

"How much does a third wife who didn't last long know?" She waved the smoke away from her face. "Frank doesn't talk a lot about his family, not sober, but I'll give you what I can."

Frank Owen's grandfather was a second-line railroad-cattle-silver baron around Reno, Nevada, in the Comstock Lode days, had Frank's father with his fourth wife when he was almost seventy. The old man got killed in a brawl with another silver tycoon when he was eighty-four. He left a lot of money to his last wife who was still under fifty and lively, so sent Frank's father, William (Buck) Owen, to schools in the East and Europe.

Buck Owen cut a swath in the East—the playboy from the wild west—and married an eastern belle who never understood him. He brought her west, stashed her in the family mansion while he hunted and fished, womanized, and committed suicide when Frank was ten. The mother took to the bottle. Frank was too much to handle on her own, so she sent him to prep school too. The power was gone with the death of the men, and she managed to spend most of the money.

Frank was kicked out of his prep school for affairs with a teacher and a town girl at the same time, finished high school in San Francisco, then walked away from his mother for good. He dropped out of various colleges, finally got a B.A. from The College Of Idaho with a major in Fine Arts but really in skiing. After that he did five years in the army, ending in Vietnam.

His mother died while he was in Vietnam. When he returned he settled what little estate there was left and then drifted for a year or so, with and without Billy. Somewhere along the line he married his first wife, Jennifer, picked up an M.A., taught art in some small colleges.

Jennifer's father was a dean at the first college. They moved from college to college and split after six years or so. Jennifer Owen got the two children. She remarried, Frank moved on. There was another wife, another child, more teaching, and finally Dianne. They lasted two years. After they split, he went on to a series of night jobs—hotel clerk, bartender, security guard. "He's a rambler and a chaser, a drinker and snorter, and it was fun for a year, but after that I had to get on with my life."

Billy Owen never knew his father. Ten years younger than Frank, he was born in San Francisco when the mother was there with her parents after the suicide. The mother wanted Billy near, so he went to public high school, neither dropped out nor graduated. Eighteen when the mother died, he enlisted in the Marines. Vietnam was over, Billy got into trouble in the Marines, was kicked out as unstable. He picked up a little carpentry, drifted doing day work until he met Nina Cansino and married her. He got bored with carpentry, Nina, his children, and took a job in Central America. As a security guard, or a mercenary, or a gun-and-drug runner, no one seemed to be sure. A year ago he returned to Santa Barbara, worked at carpentry again, then got the job at Canton Construction and worked up.

Dianne rummaged in her bag, came out with a snapshot she handed to me. "That's Frank's father and grandfather."

It was a modern copy of an old photograph from the early twenties. A big, bearish old man with a thick white mustache stood beside an already tall youth in his early teens. The old man wore a town suit of that thick, heavy material you see in photos of Teddy Roosevelt or The Wild Bunch—vest, heavy watch chain, western hat and boots. A man of substance and power who wanted the world to know it. He had cold eyes, a calculating smile, and a fly-fishing rod in his hand. The boy also held a fly rod, was more sensibly dressed in corduroys and a flannel shirt under a fly vest, but still wore a tie as if to show he was the son of an important man.

Kay said, "Do you still want Dan to find Frank, Dianne?"

Dianne Owen lit another cigarette. "Billy is half as smart as Frank, and twice as crazy. Uneducated and mediocre. That scares me. What he could get Frank into."

"And you still love Frank," Kay said.

"I married him, and I divorced him, but I don't want him hurt."

I said, "Why did you divorce him, Dianne?"

She thought about it. "Because I wasn't important to him. I wasn't a person."

After Dianne Owen had gone, I looked out at the ocean and distant islands, thought of the years of brick walls across airshafts, the grimy buildings and tenement fire escapes.

"What does she really want, Kay?"

"Probably Frank, but he's got to bend. Maybe this is the time he'll get bent enough so she can take care of him."

4

The horse trailer was parked behind the Westside cottage on a narrow dirt alley where the rear yard was fenced. In the yard, Nina Owen groomed the pony.

"They found Hector Jantarro dead," I said.

Two dark-haired children played silently between the manure droppings. A thin boy who shot marbles with himself, a sturdy girl brushing a doll as her mother brushed the pony.

"Billy could have been with him," I said.

"He's on one of his big deals. He'll show up in a couple days, a week, maybe a whole month if we're lucky."

A polaroid camera on a tripod leaned against the house. A pony saddle hung on the stall gate. She saw me look at them.

"Billy don't make a lot when he's on his own, don't hold a steady job too good. Kids like Taffy, parents likes pictures of their kids on Taffy. We goes around."

"The children go with you?"

"He don't give me no money to throw on babysitters."

The two children constantly looked up at the pony as if to reassure themselves it was still there. As Nina brushed and combed she seemed to forget me, any outsider. Only herself, the children and the pony.

"Why do you stay with him?"

She brushed the pony's sleek hide. "He just seen too many Coors ads, the Marlboro man. Sometimes it ain't so bad."

"What made Frank think he was missing before he came to you?"

She shrugged, brushed.

"Tell me about Billy and Jantarro."

"They knowed each other down in South America. Costa Rica or Honduras or someplace."

"Central America," I said.

She didn't react. Geography meant nothing. She lived in her isolated world of two children and a pony named Taffy.

"What was Billy doing down there?"

"Guard or somethin' for some American company."

"He told Dianne he was a mercenary, maybe smuggled guns in and drugs out."

"Not what he told me."

"What does Billy do for Canton Construction?"

"Calls himself a foreman, but that McElder's the only real foreman at Canton. Billy got to make himself look big."

"What else does he do?"

"Works out, does some karate. Shoots on a range. He's a lousy shot. He used to take me shootin', but I'm pretty good. My Daddy taught me, and I'd beat him so he stopped takin' me."

I got the addresses of the gym and the range. She didn't have to look them up, had been both places many times looking for Billy. "You want names and addresses of the bars he drinks in, try 'em all. Any place down lower State, or on Milpas, or out in Goleta an' Isla Vista. He ain't particular, likes Latino places so learns more Spanish."

She finished grooming the pony that gleamed like silk in the afternoon sun. "Some funny people come around asking for him."

"Funny?"

"Guys in suits don't ever smile. A real polite black lady had some kind of accent. Talked real soft and smiled a lot."

"When were they here?"

"The guys come a couple of days ago. The black lady was around just yesterday."

"Anyone else?"

"Only that McElder. He come around askin' where Billy was, brought money Mr. Canton owed Billy." She shivered, took the pony's halter. "He gives me the creeps, that McElder. Way he looks me over all the time." It was the strongest show of animation I'd seen from her. "You want to find Billy, you try the bars. Billy could sit in a bar all day."

She walked the pony toward its stall. The two dark, silent children gathered up their marbles and dolls and followed her.

The gym where Billy Owen worked out was off lower State Street. Billy hadn't been in for over a week, hadn't paid his last bill. The manager didn't know any particular friends of Billy's, the name of Jantarro meant nothing. Frank Owen had been in asking the same questions two days ago.

The rifle range was six miles out of town, dark and locked. There was a single building. It was locked. I saw no one inside through any of the windows, and there were no cars parked in the lot.

Back in town, I started with the bars on lower State, worked my way up to the corner of Anapamu. Most bartenders and some customers knew Billy Owen by sight, but none had any idea where he'd gone, or that he even was gone.

"He's not a regular," the bartenders said. "No way we'd notice if he didn't come in until it was maybe a year."

There aren't that many saloons in Santa Barbara. Cocktail lounges, wine and champagne bistros, but not plain bars where working men drink away the aches and insults, watch football, talk, achieve a kind of nirvana. I worked my way over to Milpas Street and the *barrio*. The Jalisco Cafe was a block off Milpas.

"Billy? Ain't seen him maybe a week."

"He say anything about where he was going or why?"

The barman looked around the room. "Hey, Sergio? Billy tell anyone where he was goin'?"

A swarthy older man playing a pinball machine in the rear shook his head without turning around.

"How about Hector Jantarro?" I said.

"Sergio?"

The older man shook the pinball machine carefully, gently, just enough. "Jantarro ain't been in. Same time."

"Jantarro's a loner," the barman said. "Don' talk to no one much 'cept Billy. You a cop from somewhere?"

It told me three things: he was wondering if maybe he had talked too much; he knew every detective in Santa Barbara by sight; and he'd been about to say something indiscreet.

"Private and local." I showed him my paper license with the crisp new photo in full color that made me look ten years older. "You figure Jantarro's a Mexican illegal?"

It wasn't a polite question, but he'd told me already.

"He stays low, don't mix or drink much, don't chase."

"Any friends beside Billy Owen?"

"No one I knows."

He looked past me at a shadow that stood at my shoulder in the dim daylight of the bar. A shadow not quite to my shoulder, hunched over and skinny, speaking to me but looking at the beer on the bar in front of me.

"I know about Owen."

Skin and bones in an ancient army overcoat. A collarless shirt, army fatigue trousers, scuffed combat boots with no heels left and little sole. Clothes that would have been too hot on anyone else. But it seemed he had long ago stopped feeling heat or cold from outside. In the eyes that stared at my beer there was only the internal need. What had brought the need, too much hope or too little, I couldn't know.

"What do you know, Mr.—?"

But he had already turned back to a table against the wall.

"His name's Jay," the barman said. "He drinks tequila and beer. Unless you got some dust on you."

"Not today."

I took the shot of tequila and the beer to the table. He looked down at them as if not in immediate need but trying to be sure of the night ahead.

"Got any blow?"

"What do you know about Billy Owen?"

He had yet to look at me. His hands didn't shake. He didn't twitch. But he was nervous. He looked around the bar. The place was empty of everyone but Sergio and the pinball machine, the barman who tried to cover his yawns, and two small men in work clothes and straw sombreros who spoke Spanish to each other as they fondled beers. As if he were watching for someone he didn't want to see. Or didn't want to see him.

"He soldiered for money. What d'you call it—mercenaries?"

"Where?"

"Somewheres down south."

"How do you know?"

He drank the tequila. "He's always shootin' his mouth off about all he done, the big deals 'n hotshot fightin'."

"Fighting for who?"

"Hell, who knows? Any o' those crazies."

"Then what good is it to me?"

"Him and Jantarro had something goin'."

"How do you know?"

"Jesus! You want it on fucking video tape?"

"Yes," I said, "but convince me."

His gaze was fixed on the door. "Last couple o' times in here him an' Jantarro got their heads together talking up a storm. I knows they met up somewhere when Owen was soldiering for dough, so they got to have somethin' goin'."

"That's it?"

He was getting desperate. "Christ, those guys fights for dough're into guns, drugs, hijackin', CIA crap, everythin'." He looked all around us. "I mean, I figure that Jantarro ain't even no Mex. From someplace else, you know?"

"Where?"

"I don' know, but I feels it." He looked at me. Eye to eye. "He ain't no beaner got wet hair."

The nervousness, and the sudden eye contact, told me he was telling me things he knew he shouldn't be telling. I waved to the barman for another round.

"Who else is interested in Billy Owen or Jantarro?"

He looked away. "No one."

The barman arrived with the two beers and a tequila.

"No one's been talking to you?"

"Me?" He drank his tequila fast this time. "Hell, no."

"And that's all you know?" I held a twenty folded in the palm of my hand, hidden from the others but in his full view.

"Maybe someone else who can help me?" I said.

He'd told me his guesses about Billy Owen and Jantarro. He might be taking a risk, but only he was involved. Now I was asking him to involve someone else. That way lay danger. In my hand lay a good night.

"Maybe Bello. He's the only guy I ever see Jantarro with more'n once. Besides Billy Owen, I means. He was a cop down Mexico, Bello. No one likes him much 'cept Jantarro."

"Where do I find Bello? He have a first name?"

"Aguado. Hangs most over to The Xochitl."

I gave him the twenty. He didn't thank me. He'd done what he didn't want to for the money. It scared him.

The Xochitl was a block down Milpas. This time I was the only anglo face and I wasn't welcome. Everything stopped when I came in. They didn't know when or if Aguado Bello would be in, or where he might be found, and they'd never heard of Jantarro.

5

Beyond the elevated freeway and the dusty back streets behind Milpas, were palms over the latest hotel monument to mediocrity. The gift of a TV-made millionaire whose taste was worse than his acting, it replaced a hobo jungle with cheap plastic elegance, created low-income jobs instead of low-income housing.

Canton Construction was a large fenced yard, with tall sheds for materials that had to be out of the weather, and a one-story frame office. Inside the office, behind a low railing, four women worked at computer monitors and keyboards. At the rear, three office doors were closed. There were straight wooden chairs in the railed entryway, and between the offices and the working women a large man sat at a larger desk.

"Mr. Canton?" I opened the gate in the polished railing. A growl stopped me. The dog lay under the desk at the big man's feet. A white dog with a blunt muzzle and powerful shoulders. Red-rimmed eyes and even more powerful jaws. A pit bull.

"He's out. Take a seat."

In the old-fashioned waiting area I studied the big man. I guessed he was the foreman Nina Owen said gave her the creeps. An even six feet, he easily weighed two-twenty. The burly, beefy type that seems fat and slow but is neither. Thick and sloppy, a belly and no neck, but as powerful as the dog at his feet.

He worked over papers on his desk, methodical but not slow, watched the four women, and now and again looked toward me. Slow turns of his bullet head to see if I was still there. The way I imagined a chain gang captain would have surveyed his prisoners at work.

"When do you think he'll be back?" I asked on his next look.

"You want to tell me what you want? Maybe I can handle it."

"Depends who you are."

The stare darkened. "General foreman. Name's McElder."

"I guess I can talk to you. The dog going to let me in?"

"You don't like dogs?"

The fixed stare into your face was his personality. The challenge. Overt aggression as much a part of him as the blue of his eyes, the thickness of his neck, or the speech without tone or expression.

"Not pit bulls."

"Afraid of them?"

"Afraid of their owners."

The women looked up.

"What'd you say your name was?"

"Dan Fortune."

"How'd you lose the arm?"

"Tank ran over it."

"You were in combat? Ever kill anyone?"

"Probably."

"How many?"

"I never counted."

He shook his head. "You ever kill anyone, you know. When, where, how many."

"You would," I said. "Not me."

The door opened, and a solid but not very tall man came in. In a tailored and fitted grey lounge suit that had cost a minimum of a thousand dollars, he strode across the entry area with the assurance of the man who owned the place. A white shirt with a thin blue stripe and a red and navy regimental tie completed the ensemble. When he opened the gate, the pit bull didn't growl.

I looked at McElder and saw his foot on the dog under his desk. The bull was trained to threaten unless restrained by the command of McElder's touch. To attack until signalled not to, so if anything happened to McElder the dog would be turned loose.

"This guy wants to talk to you," McElder said.

L. S. Canton looked back. He had dark brown eyes that took in my arm and old cords, blue work shirt and tweed jacket with elbow patches that really covered holes and knew instantly how little I was worth and how unimportant I was.

"About what?" he said to McElder.

"What do you want with Mr. Canton?" McElder said to me.

"About Billy Owen," I said. "And Hector Jantarro."

"You know where Owen is?" McElder said.

Canton said, "I'll handle it, Ken. Come on in, Mr.—?"

"Dan Fortune."

I opened the gate with the pit bull eyeing me, and me eyeing the bull. It didn't even growl, put its head back on the floor under McElder's desk. Canton and I went into his office. He pointed to a chair, hung his suit jacket on an old-fashioned hat tree from frontier days, and disappeared through a side door. I waited. He came back drying his hands.

"Wine at lunch goes through me like straight piss, but the lady insisted, and you don't argue with Montecito ladies if you hope to do business and maybe a little more, eh?" His blue striped shirt billowed as he sat behind his desk. Egyptian cotton so fine it acted like silk. "So. CIA?"

He examined me like a new car buyer, especially my empty sleeve. He was in his mid-fifties, soft around the belly.

"You expect the CIA to be interested in Billy Owen?"

"Why do you think I hired him? I know all about his past. I needed a guy could ramrod day labor that's mostly Mex."

"Tell me about his past."

"You know what I mean: the Marines, gun-running flights, training the Salvadorans, fighting with the Contras, the works."

"Owen tell you all that?"

He came forward in his chair. "You're not CIA, are you?"

"No."

"Cop then? Billy is in trouble somewhere."

"Private," I said. "You think he's in trouble?"

"Hell, I don't know. All I know is him and Jantarro left me up shit creek."

"You know what happened to Jantarro?"

He nodded. "The cops got here ahead of you. You working for the brother?"

"More or less," I said. "When did Frank Owen talk to you?"

"A couple of days ago."

"Was he looking for Jantarro too?"

"He didn't mention him."

"What did you tell Frank Owen, Mr. Canton?"

In his high-backed executive chair he fixed his gaze on my face in an imitation of McElder outside. "What I'm going to tell you. Jantarro didn't show for work about a week ago—make it nine days now. One, maybe two days later Billy doesn't show. That made us two men short on a couple of jobs—not that either of them was all that good, especially Jantarro. I only put him on because Billy asked me to, said he'd make Jantarro pull his weight. I never liked him. A bad-ass type, sullen and surly."

"You think they went off together?"

"I didn't at first. I figured Jantarro'd saved up his pay and headed back to beaner land. Most of them do that sooner or later. Billy was probably off on a toot. He's pretty nutty."

"What do you think now?"

"Now I don't know. The police say it was an accident, Jantarro blind drunk. But maybe Billy and Jantarro had something going that went wrong. Jantarro was lousy at the job, and Billy had been damn anxious for me to put him on."

"Something like what?"

"Haven't a clue."

I got up. "One thing kind of puzzles me. They were both off the job a week, but no one thought of checking Jantarro's house?"

"A flake and a wetback? Hell, Fortune, they come, they go. I only sent McElder to Nina Owen because I figured she could use the money. We didn't even have an address on Jantarro. Real sullen and secretive."

"Maybe he had a reason," I said.

I left him thinking about that. McElder was gone from his desk. No one else even looked up from their work. A tight ship.

Outside, as I drove out of Canton's gate. The sheriff's car was parked up the street under the elevated freeway.

6

It caught up to me a block along Montecito Street. A brief flash of its top lights and a low siren growl. I went to the curb. It parked ahead of me. No one got out.

I walked to it. The front door opened.

"Get in, Fortune."

Sheriff's Lieutenant Holley's uniform was as crisp as the night in Lompoc he'd asked me to forget the history of Rosa Gruenfeld and the Bannisters, and his voice was as cool as when he'd suggested I stay out of Santa Barbara County.

"You didn't take my suggestion."

"Things changed."

"How? Maybe you won't be on the first plane to New York."

He wasn't working out of the Santa Barbara offices, or he'd have known what I was doing. I took out my wallet, showed him.

"I live here now, Lieutenant. I'd like to live peacefully."

He sat silent in the low sunlight as the traffic passed us going to the freeway north. "You're on a local case?"

I told him about Frank and Billy Owen.

"How's Lee Canton involved?"

"They both worked for him."

"Both brothers? I thought one was from out of town?"

"Billy Owen and Hector Jantarro."

He was confused. "The wetback who got drunk and fell over his own cliff?"

"You're sure he fell over?" I said.

He looked like he wondered if a fresh start for me was such a good idea. "The report says it's open and shut. We don't like privates fishing for business out here, Fortune."

"Jantarro's dead and Billy Owen's missing. Maybe it's nothing, but Frank Owen's worried about his brother."

"The wetback had a party with other illegals and fell. If there was horsing around or fighting, they won't talk."

"From what I'm picking up," I said, "Jantarro didn't drink all that much, kept to himself, and might not have been Mexican."

"Picking up where?"

"Around the bars where Billy Owen hung out."

"You talk to our office?"

"Just got it this evening."

"Well, it's not my case, but tell them." He looked out at the home-going traffic headed to the freeway. "This Billy Owen have any con-nection to a woman named Elizabeth Martin? Maybe a man named James?"

"Not that I've heard so far. Who are they?"

"People we're interested in. You run into anything about them, give me a call, okay? Up in the Santa Maria office." He looked at his watch. "I have to get back. I hear anything about Billy Owen, I'll let you know."

"Thanks." I got out. "Martin and James."

"Keep it under your hat," Holley said, and drove off.

He had a long drive back to Santa Maria, and he hadn't been watching for me outside Canton Construction. Whatever he was do-ing he didn't want the Santa Barbara office to know. If it was some internal problem I'd keep clear, but if it was something Santa Maria just didn't want to share the credit on I could make Holley into a friend by going along.

I called the Seabird Motel from a phone at a gas station on Milpas. Frank Owen's room still didn't answer. It was twilight when I reached Summerland. Despite the freeway and railroad tracks that blocked most of it from the actual beach and sea, Summerland has that easygoing, raffish aura of all beach towns. The main street was wide and irregular, the parking haphazard, the grocery store unconcerned about bare feet, and the hamburger restaurant a local hangout.

Our rented house was high on a side street. I parked the Tempo behind Kay's green Honda, and had a strange sensation—I was glad to see her car there. It is not something a city man who has lived alone most of his life experiences.

I wasn't glad to see Dianne Owen's blue Subaru parked in front of the Honda.

They were in the living room, Dianne Owen on the couch, the windows behind her. Kay was a shade stiff in her chair, not glad to have Dianne there right now either. I took the Eames chair facing the couch and the windows and the view. Kay had bought it for me as her welcome-to-California present. Kay got drinks.

"Well?" Dianne Owen said.

She fidgeted in her gray flannel business suit. She didn't have the figure for a tailored suit, too small and curved, but the image was what counted. Free women didn't wear frills.

"Nina doesn't know where Billy is, and doesn't much care. Frank knew Billy was 'gone' before he went to Nina. Mr. L.S. Canton has no idea where Billy is. The police seem convinced Jantarro's fall was an accident, and no one around the saloons knows where Billy even might be. So far, Frank hasn't been in his room at the Seabird."

"Anchor Steam and Ballard chardonnay," Kay announced.

Dianne Owen looked at Kay, looked at me. Not so much disappointed as confused. Was I a lousy detective, or too busy to really work at finding Frank Owen?

"I'll pick him up, Dianne, that's not the problem. It's no good if I find him but don't know what he's doing or why."

"But you could be too late!" She took the wine.

"I could have been too late before I started, and so could Frank."

"You think Jantarro was murdered, don't you? You think Billy knows something about it. That means Frank could be—"

"I don't think anything except that Jantarro doesn't sound like a man who'd fall off his own cliff." I thought about it for a time, drank the good beer. "When I came out of Canton's, a sheriff's lieutenant was watching the place. We had a talk. He asked about an Elizabeth Martin and somebody James. They mean anything to you?"

"No. I mean, yes, I know who they are. I never met them."

"Who are they?"

"J. James is an investment counsellor based down in L.A. Elizabeth Martin runs his Montecito office."

"Do they have a connection to Lee Canton?"

"I don't know, Dan."

"What do you know about Canton?"

"What everyone else does."

"I'm new in town."

Kay brought two more Anchor Steams and another glass of the Chardonnay.

"The Cantons are an old family." Dianne drank, relaxed with the second glass. "Lee must be in his mid-fifties. His father, old Sam Canton, owns the Double C Ranch near Los Alamos. Twenty thousand acres from 101 to the mountains. That's a lot of real estate, even if it's only cattle and cauliflowers, so the Cantons have clout here, in Sacramento, in Washington. Lee was named for his grandfather's favorite politician: Leland Stanford Canton."

"He didn't like ranching?"

"Local gossip says Lee couldn't cut it ranching, made a mess out of taking his brother's place when Morgan went off to Korea. After some job tries in San Francisco, he was exiled to run the construction business his father got on a foreclosure. He's been with it ever since, through three wives and a bankruptcy. They say he's not too bright, but they don't say it to his face."

"Would Frank or Billy know Elizabeth Martin or J. James?"

"Investment counsellors? Bookies, would be more likely for them." She finished her wine, stood up. "Find him, Dan, please. He's important to me, dammit."

We listened to her car drive away. Out on the Channel the islands seemed close enough to touch in the evening sun.

"You still want me to go on with it?"

Kay was silent in the darkening room, the sound of the freeway outside, and, beyond it, the sea.

"Do Frank and Billy need help?"

"Probably."

"Then you don't have a choice, do you?"

Later, we went out to the Nugget for hamburgers.

7

Twenty-five years ago no one walked in downtown Santa Barbara after dark. Cabrillo Boulevard and State Street were deserted, everything happened behind closed doors. A city of private parties for the rich and reclusive, the middle class and middle-aged. Now, each night State Street was a party in itself and ten times more on Friday and Saturday.

The Me Generation, the Fun Era. The young and the almost-young and the would-be-young and the too-young cruised in a mass up and down State, and off into the side and parallel streets. The streets themselves, as soon as the sun went down, became a parade of barely moving cars—stereos blaring; arms, legs, feet and heads out windows and sun roofs to wave and shout.

No one "drove" on State Street after dark. It wasn't a street, it was a party on wheels in a sea of red brake lights and dazzling headlights, preening and meeting, joining and parting, matching and mating and moving on into the clubs and discos and bars. Jazz at The Arlington Court, rock and reggae at Oscar's, progressive rock at Zelo. Everything at Joseppi's, and local bands at Rocky Galenti's and The Seabird Bar.

The Seabird is a large motel between the freeway and the sea, a block from the harbor and the Marina and Stearns Wharf with its shops. The entire northside of a cross street, the motel was built in four two-story sections, with the office, restaurant and bar in the center. An alley ran behind it.

Frank Owen's room key wasn't in his box.

"Can I leave a message?"

"Paper and pen over there."

I wrote that Dan Fortune wanted to talk to him, added my home number, gave it to the night clerk who yawned as he put it into the box. He was tired after an hour on duty. It wasn't an exciting job. As far as I knew, Frank Owen didn't know my name, the note might make him curious enough to call. At least it would convince the bored night clerk I was going away.

Frank's room was at the far end of the motel past the bar and restaurant. A West Coast motel lock doesn't offer too much resistance. Inside I turned on the light. It was safer, and I wanted Frank Owen to find me.

A backpack and a battered leather suitcase lay on the floor. The suitcase had cost a great deal of money a long time ago. It was open and packed with the neatly rolled necessities of a man who expects to be on the road for some time. The suitcase of a man who travelled alone and knew the value of order. The pants in the closet were mostly denim and corduroy jeans, the shirts were blue workshirts, the books were good modern novels from many countries, the underwear and the bathing suit were bikini. The shoes were hiking boots, there were no pajamas.

The adult toys were in the backpack: two bottles of single malt Scotch whisky; two lids of marijuana with a mini-pipe and cigarette papers; and a bag of white powder with no paraphernalia except a box of plastic straws. Big C, happy dust, snow powder, the champagne of drugs, the educated man's high. A well-oiled flycasting reel wrapped in plastic was zipped into a side pocket. A Walkman radio-cassette player with earphones.

The letters were in an inside pocket. I quickly rifled through them. From small colleges asking Frank Owen if he wanted to return this semester. From universities suggesting Frank Owen send a resume. From old army buddies. From women wondering where Frank was and when he was coming back. From women who didn't care where Frank Owen was. All to an address in San Francisco.

At the bottom of the backpack a box of rifle cartridges.

The hunting rifle was in the back of the closet. In a case with a telescopic sight. It had been recently cleaned.

The knock and the opening of the room door came at the same time. "Frank Owen?"

He was a short, compact, studious looking man, like a solid bantamweight fighter with the face of an accountant. Hornrimmed glasses and the shoulders of a middleweight in a dark brown suit. Neutral eyes behind the glasses. A flat, Midwestern voice with an edge of educated Eastern seaboard as if he'd gone to Yale or been in Washington too long.

"Who wants to know?" I said. It wasn't exactly a lie.

He closed the door, gave me a sincere if not warm smile. There was something of the actor about him. In everything he did, from the smile to the easy walk and the flat eyes and the muscles under the neat brown suit.

"Let's say I'm a friend of Billy's."

Everyone talks like a spy novel at the end of the twentieth century. Maybe it says something about us.

I can play the game. "So, what's old Billy up to?"

"Come on, Frank, we both want to find Billy." He sat down in the only easy chair in the room. "They didn't tell me about the arm. How'd you lose it?"

He didn't care about my arm, or how I'd lost it. He was simply surprised no one had told him. I sensed he didn't care much about anything except the importance of his job. It was a trait of the men of the Federal Bureau Of Investigation.

"Boating accident when I was a kid," I said. "How do you know I'm looking for Billy?"

"We've been making the same moves in a different order. Where is he, Frank?"

"You get to Hector Jantarro before or after I did?"

"After, cops everywhere. What's Billy doing? I'm trying to help."

"Who was Jantarro? I mean, really?"

"You think Billy killed Jantarro, Frank? That why he's hiding out?"

I played the outraged brother. "No, he didn't kill Jantarro, and I haven't heard your name yet."

Concentration is important for an investigator. It's important for most people in most jobs. Neither of us was aware of the outside door opening until he spoke.

"You haven't told him your name, either."

The FBI man, if that's what he was, had left the door ajar. The newcomer had pushed it open while we fenced with each other. He looked at both of us. Suspicious, curious, and indifferent all at once.

"It's Fortune, right? That note?"

He was the man Dianne Owen had described, a few years and miles older. Over six feet, good shoulders in a short sheepskin jacket that had set him, or someone, back a good four hundred dollars some years ago. An everyday jacket, the suede darkened at every crease and wrinkle, the collar properly sweat and grease stained. He wore it open over a decorated denim shirt. Hatless and clean shaven, faded boot jeans over western boots. Dark blond hair that touched his shirt collar, and a strong face tanned and creased enough by sun and wind to show his forty-six years, yet lean and youthful enough that no one would ever say he was forty-six.

"Dan Fortune. Your ex-wife asked me to look for you."

"Which one?"

It was a line he'd used a lot. A certain pride in it.

"Dianne. She's worried about you."

"Not really." He walked all the way into the motel room with that nice, easy walk you have to have in cowboy boots. "She just thinks she's got a right to worry. Why pretend to be me?"

"This guy assumed I was you, I didn't correct him yet, right, Mr.—"

He was gone. While Frank Owen and I talked, the other intruder had slipped out unseen. He'd probably had a lot of practice in getting out of places unnoticed.

"Did you know him?" I asked Owen.

"Never saw him before."

"Why would the FBI be looking for your brother?"

"Is that what he was?"

"That's my guess. Everyone's looking for Billy. Why?"

"How do I know?"

"I think you know. I think you found Jantarro's body before anyone else. I think it was you who shot at me so I wouldn't find you up at Jantarro's cabin."

"I don't give a shit what you think," Frank Owen said.

This time he closed the door behind him.

8

Singles, couples, and groups from Cabrillo Boulevard and lower State headed for the music and dancing of The Seabird Bar. No car had started after Frank Owen walked out, and a dusty red Porsche not there before stood in front of the unit. I joined the stream into the bar and the crowd and the music.

He was at the far end with a beer. The single malt Scotch was for special occasions, or for himself alone in whatever room he happened to be in, wherever he happened to be.

"You were looking for Billy before they found Jantarro, before you went to Nina, probably before you even came to town."

He waved to the bartender. "What are you? Her boyfriend, client, buddy, employee?"

"Friend of a friend," I said.

I got a Beck's. Frank Owen was drinking from the tap.

"What made Dianne think you could help?"

"I'm a private investigator."

We both drank for a time, listened to the local rock band. They were an all-female band called The Bushwhackers, and they were good. Even I could hear that they were playing all their own music, and the technique and imagination of the lead guitar was highly original. They were good to listen to, and had the dance floor packed with those who preferred moving to thinking.

"What kind of trouble is Billy in?"

"I don't know Billy is in any trouble."

"Why are you looking for him?"

"He's my brother."

He had the grace to smile when he said it.

"Hector Jantarro's dead," I said.

"Jantarro had an accident."

"So why scare me away with a rifle?"

"I didn't know who you were, didn't feel like talking."

He pointed to an empty table for two in a dark corner so far from the bandstand and dance floor the young and not-so-young out to pick up and party had no use for it. He took the seat facing the door, said, "They can't let you be alone, can they?"

"If you want to be alone, why get married?"

"I asked myself that every time." He drank and shook his head. "It's like a fever. She's special, different. You want her, you don't want to share her, you forget what happens."

"What happens?"

"The special goes." He watched three overage swingers in floppy *dernier cri* pleated and pegged pants straight out of the *International Male* catalog sit down at another table. "The same comes back. What's important, what isn't."

"Don't we change too?"

"We don't find a cave and pull it in." The three on the town at the next table were drinking the oversized margaritas with colored swords stuck into lime slices The Seabird featured. "We don't tell someone to get lost, then send a watchdog to find out what the hell he's doing."

"What are you doing?"

He shook his head, picked up my bottle and his mug and shouldered through the crowd to the bar. I listened to the latest-trend outfits next to us.

"Look at the redhead."

"Too much ass."

"Thunder thighs."

"No way, Jose."

One wore a Hard Rock Cafe—New York T-shirt under a purple down vest. The second showed his individuality with old World War II division patches sewn all over his black-and-yellow vest. The third wore a brown cowboy hat with a heavily rolled brim. But they were like triplets, did everything only to impress each other. A hydra with three heads.

"That lead singer got to have round heels."

"You believe that noise the guitar's makin'?"

"Sure as shit ain't music."

"You name it, I'll kill it."

Frank Owen returned with a full mug and a Beck's. The trio stared at his boots, jeans and shoulders. They stared at my missing arm. They dropped their voices, snickered, but not loud enough for Owen or me to hear. Frank watched the band and the dancers, sucked at his beer. The three stooges turned their collective wisdom to the state of the nation and the world.

"You read that John Dillinger book?"

"That FBI asshole never've taken him in a fair fight."

"Those old bank robbers were great, you know?"

"Sure don't have guys like that now. The crooks all got big law-yers, go crying about their civil rights."

"Can you hear one of those old-time sheriffs like Bat Masterson or Wyatt Earp reading the Clantons their rights?"

"Stood up and faced off and the best guy won."

"How about that Gary Gilmore?"

"He was tough."

"'Okay,' he says, 'let's do it!' Bang!"

They enjoyed agreeing with each other so much, they forgot all about the women walking around them. Frank Owen seemed to watch them, listen to them.

I said, "Somebody should tell them the Earps used shotguns. That it was a fight between the pimp-gamblers and robber-rustlers over who was going to collect the taxes and control the town."

Frank Owen swirled his beer. "Maybe its not real in fact, but it's real in essence. The way it was to live then, a real part of all of us. My Dad always said you can't understand animals until you hunt them. The balance of nature and what it really means. What a man is. Our essence. We're hunters, and if we don't feel that we'll never know ourselves."

"Is that what Billy is doing? Hunting?"

He shook his head at me. "I don't know about Billy, but you sure as hell are. You're a hunter, Fortune."

"No, I'm a searcher. There's a difference."

The Bushwhackers were in a harddriving piece the crowd seemed to know. The bass led the enthusiasm like a cheerleader behind the lead singer, while the guitar played a Frip-influenced line that set the afficionados screaming and dancing.

Frank Owen said, "Billy never had a father, never really had a brother. He didn't have anyone to teach him about the woods and the rivers and the mountains. He joined the Marines, but there wasn't any war. No one had taught him duty and discipline, so without a war he couldn't make it."

"The Marines kicked him out?"

"In peacetime they don't do things that simple. He ran with a fast gang, drank, brawled, went AWOL. A bad apple. Discharged for the good of the service. He drifted around doing odd jobs, carpentry, anything for a day and a buck, and met Nina. He was never good with women who know more than he does, women who can do things. Nina was a high school dropout in a family of dirt-poor fundamentalist farmers who happened to end up out here. She liked him, believed his hot shot stories, got pregnant, so Billy married her. I helped out, they got a camper and went right on moving around doing nothing. He got bored, who wouldn't?"

"And went down to Central America as a guard or a gunrunner, smuggler or mercenary?"

"As near as I can tell, the guard story is a cover. His old Marine buddies signed him to get supplies down there for private interests. He tried to join the Contras, doesn't speak enough Spanish. He maybe did some drug smuggling, maybe worked with the CIA. I never was sure what was real and what was phony."

"When'd he come back here?"

"Eighty-four, eighty-five. Knocked around again. Then he hooked on with Canton Construction as a night guard, moved up to a real job as one of Canton's top people. Getting it together."

That wasn't how Billy Owen's job at Canton Construction had been described by Nina or Lee Canton. Billy glamorized himself even for his big brother.

"How did Jantarro come to work for Canton?"

"Billy ran into him somewhere along the line. He showed up in Santa Barbara, Billy got him the job."

"Some people say he wasn't Mexican."

"Does it make a difference?"

"It could explain the FBI in your room."

"How?"

"If he was from down in El Salvador or Nicaragua. Honduras or Panama. One side or the other."

He stood, picked up his mug, and vanished into the crowd. The band was taking a break. They talked to their fans, relaxed and out-going, yet there was something private about them too. A sense that some part of their music was only for them. That's true of all real artists. In a sense we're eavesdropping when we read or look or listen or watch.

Frank Owen set a Beck's in front of me, sat down with his mug in both hands. "You go back to Dianne and tell her I don't need a watchdog or a nursemaid. Tell her to pay you, and to get the hell off my back."

"The rugged individualist," I said.

He looked at the mug in his hands. Looked at the crowded bar. Looked at me. "You know, Fortune, I don't need you. I don't know about rugged, but I'm one individual trying to live in this world we've got today. I fought in a war politicians got me into and then lost for me. I came home to a country where people want to turn everything into a fast buck or put it in a museum and I don't like either way. I live in a world I don't figure has much future the way it's going. All I've got is me, and maybe Billy, and I really don't need you."

"What do you need?" I said. "Or want?"

"I don't *need* a damn thing, Fortune. I *want* you out of my hair. I want to go out, get behind the wheel and drive. Nowhere I have to go, no one I have to answer to, nothing I have to do. Fast and loose and fancy free. Sleep all day and drink all night. Find Billy or forget Billy. But whatever the hell I do it'll be on my own, so fuck off!" His voice rose, his fists clenched, he leaned toward me. "Now!"

"Don't be a jerk."

"You think because you've got one arm I won't fight you?"

"You wouldn't like my way of fighting."

"What the shit does that mean?"

"It means no rules, no sporting chances. Only a damn fool puts the fight above what he fights for."

If he would see that as challenge, confession, or threat, I never found out. A waitress called out, "Frank Owen? Frank Owen, room fifteen?"

"That's me."

"Telephone. Take it at the bar."

I drank my Beck's. He was too civilized to start a fight in a bar unless he was falling-down-drunk, and I still had to know why he was worried about Billy.

It was five minutes before I realized he wasn't coming back.

"The good-looking cowboy?" the waitress said. "Hell, honey, he left right after he got that call."

9

A fog had drifted in from the sea, settled raw and wet on the parking lot. The neon signs and the street lamps diffused through the drifting white. A halo around every light.

The headlights of a car came slowly along the block and turned into the parking lot. Lights on high beam that entered at the far entrance and turned ponderously to sweep the rows of parked cars in front of the rooms, and then straight along past where I stood in front of the bar-restaurant.

I thought of old World War II prisoner-of-war movies, the searchlights probing the foggy barbed wire of the *Staatslager*. The inexorable shafts come closer to the escaping heroes. Sweep past, then suddenly back as the headlights turned into the space between the blocks of two-story units and the bar-restaurant.

It was a battered pickup truck. It cruised silently like a bird of prey in the fog night, a yellow-eyed panther that stalked its victim. As the lights sliced back toward the alley behind the motel, I knew who the victim was, the prey.

I ran through the fog. At the far end of the dark space between the bar building and the two-story units, Frank Owen leaned against the back wall of the alley. He smoked under the solitary alley light.

"Owen!"

He glanced around, searched for the voice that called him.

The pickup's motor roared and its tires screeched.

"Owen!"

He heard the pickup and saw me behind it at the same time. Cigarette frozen in his mouth, his wide eyes reflected the glare of the headlights coming at him.

The rest happened in seconds.

Floorboarded, the pickup burned rubber like a drag racer. Owen jumped left and fell. The truck swerved toward him. Owen crawled, stumbled up, ran along the alley. The pickup screamed brakes to turn after him, slammed and scraped the wall showering sparks, and careened out of sight from where I ran after it.

The shattering, tearing, rending, horrendous crash of metal and glass and stone filled the night and the fog. A violent, reverberating crash—and with it, a split second before it, the echo of an almost unheard hopeless scream of despair.

I stopped running.

Pieces of metal fell and clattered around the corner of the bar building.

Then there was only silence. I walked around into the alley.

The building extended back, and the alley ended in a loading dock ten yards in. Shattered against the concrete and steel of the dock, the pickup was telescoped with its back broken and its rear in the air. Steaming, pungent with the stink of gasoline.

I looked for Frank Owen.

"Fortune."

He was in the shadow flat up to the building. His hands were against the dim wall as if nailed there. Or as if holding onto the wall to keep from falling. His eyes were fixed on the wreck of the pickup that had tried to kill him. White eyes, luminous in the stray light from the single lamppost back at the entrance to this end of the alley.

"You okay?"

"Oil?" His voice was as rigid as his body and the wall, ready to crack if touched.

"What?"

"There." A nod toward the smashed truck.

Thick liquid dripped dark from where the engine was crushed into the cab. A pool had formed under the ripped door. Only then did I think of the driver. Our brain is numbed by violent action, raises its own defense. A force field that shields, concentrates a kind of tunnel vision of the mind.

It wasn't oil. The buckled door came off at my touch, fell into the pool of blood. There was no way of knowing what he had looked like. His face had been crushed by the windshield, his throat cut so wide and deep his faceless head hung back over his shoulders. The steering wheel had left him no chest. The post impaled him to the seat. His legs were gone.

We have to be an insane species, or a terrified one. I didn't know which the driver had been, and all that gave an indication was a bloody black 4X beaver Stetson on his faceless head, legless skintight jeans with a silver conch belt, and what looked like the remnants of a black and silver western shirt.

I returned to Frank Owen where he still stood flattened against the building wall. "He's dead. Not even a face. How'd he get you out here?"

"The call in the bar. It was Billy. He was in trouble. Meet him under the alley lamp in five minutes." A long, deep breath. "No face?"

Sirens, close now on Cabrillo Boulevard, filled the silence between us. Gawkers crowded under the single lamp back between the buildings.

"Black Stetson," I said. "Jeans, conch belt, expensive from the look of it, black and silver cowboy shirt. Probably boots. His legs are gone."

He shuddered, came away from the wall. "Jesus, he tried to kill me."

"Does Billy dress like that?"

"I know a hundred dress like that."

"You better look."

I wasn't sure he'd make it, but he did. He stepped over the pool of blood, looked into the cab.

"No."

He went back to hold to the wall. The sirens growled into the motel lot out front.

"Tell them the truth," I said. "All of it you can."

From the slow, menacing approach of the patrolmen from the first two black-and-whites it was going to be a long night.

"Step back please."

They looked into the cab. They were both young.

"Christ," one of them said.

The other licked his lips. "Guess we can pass on the rescue team. How'd he crash so bad way back here?"

"Shortcut? Didn't know the alley deadended?"

"Must have been doing sixty," the one who couldn't stop looking at the body said. "Stoned."

Frank Owen said, "He was trying to kill me."

Each turned with his hand on the butt of his holstered pistol. The one fascinated by dead bodies was the senior.

"You witnessed the accident, sir?"

"May we have your name and address, sir?"

Frank Owen gave his name and address.

"You're a guest in this motel, sir?"

"Yes," Frank nodded. "Fortune and I were in the bar. I got this phone call—"

"Who's Fortune?" the senior said.

"I am." I gave my name and address, nothing more. I'd wait for the detectives. They were happier with my address. I was local, a citizen.

"He said he was my brother," Frank said. "I'm looking—"

"You'll get a chance to tell your story later, sir. Now, if you and Mr. Fortune will please just step over there."

More black-and-whites, two CHP cars, and the patrol sergeant arrived. They dispersed the crowd, taped off the scene, and we waited. There was no question of reviving the driver, so we were spared a "load and go" fiasco. The major crimes detectives, the coroner's deputy, and two CSI men showed up together. The CSI people started taking photographs, combed the pickup for physical evidence. The deputy sheriff took charge of the body.

The detective sergeant came over to us. His name was Gus Chavalas, I'd met him when I was getting my license. Short and swarthy, he was Greek, but most people assumed he was Latino, and he didn't correct them. It gave him an edge in the *barrio*.

"Sergeant Chavalas. Which one of you's Owen?"

Frank said he was. The sergeant got out his notebook.

"What's the name of the dead guy?"

"I don't know," Frank said.

Chavalas looked up. "You told Officer Bush the guy tried to kill you, run you down."

"He did. But I don't know why."

"A guy you don't know tries to run you down and you don't know why? Maybe you better explain that some more."

"I'm in town looking for my brother Billy," Frank Owen said. "Fortune and I were talking in the bar. I got a phone call. He said he was Billy, told me to meet him under the light in the alley in five minutes. I had a cigarette, waited. I heard Fortune yelling my name and saw the pickup start at me. I jumped, managed to get back in here. He turned after me on two wheels, I don't think he saw the dock until he slammed into it."

He looked at the truck and the mangled body the coroner's deputy was removing. Chavalas looked at me.

"What's your part in this?"

I told him my part in it.

Now he recognized me. "You just got a license, right? You know the driver or why he wanted to run Owen down?"

"I didn't know the driver, but I'd say he didn't want Frank looking for his brother."

"I guess that's one possibility," Chavalas said. "We better go into headquarters and get some statements."

He let me drive in on my own, but took Frank Owen with him. I had a hunch I wouldn't see Frank for a while. I sat alone in a corridor for hours before Chavalas came and took me up to one of the two bugged and padded holding rooms on the top floor. We sat facing each other, and he had me go through it all again.

"Jantarro? You mean the guy that fell over his own cliff up on Camino Cielo? Worked for Lee Canton?"

"That's right."

"You think this Owen or his brother or the guy in the pickup or all of them had something to do with Jantarro's death?"

The more you tell, the more they wonder what you're holding back. We're a paranoid species always afraid of being lied to, cheated, taken advantage of. The answer is to tell only what they can find out on their own, let them draw the conclusions.

"So Jantarro was a loner," Chavalas summed up when I'd finished, "didn't drink all that much, and maybe wasn't Mexican. Billy Owen tells fancy stories about his past. Other people are after him besides his brother. Maybe the FBI. That it?"

"His wife doesn't seem to care where he is or why."

"But his brother Frank does, and Frank's ex-wife is worried, and some total stranger tries to kill Frank Owen."

"That's how it reads."

"Not much help, except maybe the FBI if they'll talk to us."

"You can check on Jantarro, look for Billy Owen."

"Jantarro's dead and everyone's after Billy Owen."

"There's the pickup driver."

I sat alone in the locked room for two more hours. Frank Owen was probably in the second holding room. They would be comparing our stories, which was another reason for telling only the bare facts. It gave me time to think. The key seemed to be Hector Jantarro, and the simplest answer that Billy Owen had killed him and run. Occam's Razor says the simplest answer is the right one. But that depends on knowing all the variables. The FBI and the others could be in it because of Jantarro only, but the pickup driver didn't fit, brought in an unknown.

"His name was Murch Calhoun. In town only a month or so." Chavalas had come in, sat behind me. "Oklahoma driver's license, had a room on Haley, no regular job. Turned up at the wall near the unemployment office for day work sometimes, has a good set of car-penter's tools in the room."

"What did the Oklahoma police say?"

"Left Tulsa maybe two months ago, good riddance. A record of drunks, fights, assaults, thefts. All kinds of petty crime."

"Before that? The service? Central America?"

"As far as they know he never left Oklahoma before."

"The truck?"

"Stolen an hour before," Chavalas watched me. I waited. He came out with it. "Had a big wad of cash in his pocket."

"How big?"

"Not that big. An even thousand, all twenties. A cheap hired hand. We'll check bank accounts on the wives, Lee Canton, Billy Owen and Jantarro himself. You never know."

I shook my head. "Probably from bank machines, more than one. No way to spot the withdrawal."

"We'll dig into who he knew in town." He stood up. "You can go home. Do I have to say keep in touch?"

He wouldn't find a connection between Calhoun and anyone who knew Frank or Billy Owen. Not without knowing where to look.

Frank Owen wasn't downstairs, the night desk officer said they were still talking to Owen. It was past three A.M., I stood on the out-side steps taking deep breaths in the cool night. The air was clear and clean, the stars sharp over the small city. Flowers and trees moved on the wind.

I thought of New York, the thick air of grime, the unseen stars, the concrete and glass that reflected only more concrete. The weight of crowded people heavier than concrete. No one could want to live in a massive city, yet the poor swarmed to them all over the world. From Brazil to Zambia, Mexico City to Shanghai, Tashkent to Timbuctu. To find work, food, a vague hope for the future. Only the rich could live with the clean air and the trees. It said something about us, about our future. Neither capitalist nor socialist. A human problem. Like the lemmings.

When I reached Summerland the house was dark. Kay was asleep in our big bed. I undressed, slipped under the covers. She stirred, wiped her eyes sleepily.

"What happened?"

I told her. "Someone wants Frank out of the way or dead."

"Someone who knows he's looking for Billy."

"Dianne knows."

"Dianne wants him back," she said. "Billy is in the way."

"No, Frank's in the way. He's a cowboy without a frontier, a hunter with nothing to hunt."

She has fine hips and firm, tight buttocks. When I pulled her close I knew she wasn't really ready, too full of sleep. But she didn't resist. Opened for me. This time would be for me.

It's good to have someone to think about you, care about you. Even if that means you have to care about them.

10

No one answered Frank Owen's door at the Seabird Motel, the dusty red Porsche was still in front. I got coffee and a danish from the coffee shop, sat in the warm morning in front of Owen's room with my face turned up to the sun like Lazarus risen from the grave. They told me I'd miss the seasons, but the sun felt like therapy after five hours sleep. I could have soaked sun all day if a black-and-white hadn't dropped Frank Owen at the curb.

He looked even more tired than I felt. Neither of us was that young anymore. Inside, he went straight to the bathroom, turned on the shower. I sat on the john while he stripped.

"What did you tell them?"

"That I'm looking for Billy and haven't a clue where he is."

"And Jantarro?"

"I don't know anything about Jantarro."

"Did you tell them how you knew Billy was missing before you got to town?"

Naked, he reached into the shower to test the water. He was nicely built. Flat belly, strong legs, a big chest without much hair. In good shape, but it was health club shape. Diet and exercise, not a physical life and hard work.

"I didn't know he was missing before I got here."

He stepped into the shower to wash off the hours of weary questions.

"What did you know?"

"Suitcase. The zippered pocket."

Steam rose in clouds from the shower. I closed the door and found the letter in the suitcase. Postmarked Santa Barbara April 20, the day after Jantarro died: *Brother Frank, Old Billy is in a bind again, could use advice and the brotherly helping hand. Make it quick, keep it quiet, bring money. Thanks, Billy.*

I quickly searched the suitcase. Under the clothes were two boxes of 9-mm cartridges and a compact SIG-Sauer P-230 automatic in a small belt holster.

Owen came out drying his hair.

"You got the letter in San Francisco?"

"Flew down, went straight to the house. Nina hadn't seen him for days. He must have gone right after he wrote the letter, and that meant he was missing."

"Maybe he decided he didn't need you."

"He'd have left a message. Unless he went in a big hurry and had no time, or was afraid a message'd be read."

"You think something changed and he had to run?"

"Or someone took him."

Dry, he climbed into the bed, lit a cigarette.

"What makes you think anyone took him?"

"That phone call last night." He smoked. "I told the police the guy said he was Billy, asked me to meet him. They didn't ask me how come I was fooled so easily, walked right out there no questions asked."

"Why did you?"

"Because the voice used the words Billy would have. He did his Russian spy imitation—'Meet under lamp in alley, comrade. Come alone, da? Tell no vun, bring Amerikanski cigarette'."

"Someone who knew Billy pretty well."

"Or someone who has him."

"Or Billy himself."

He crushed the cigarette in an ashtray. "Get the fuck out of here, Fortune."

"You can't be sure, Frank."

"I'm sure." He lay down with his back to me.

"If he killed Jantarro? If they were in something together that went wrong and Billy killed Jantarro?"

He pulled the covers up to his neck. "He didn't."

"He writes you saying he's in trouble, needs help, but he disappears. Something was so important, or scared him so much, he couldn't wait. What if Jantarro was more than he seemed? If he had friends who want to find Billy? What if Billy was scared you'd lead them to him, sent Calhoun to stop you looking?"

"He's my brother!"

"How much that means might depend on how scared he was, or how much was involved."

He turned to look at me. "You're a cynical bastard."

"With that pickup," I said, "there's more in this than a flaky brother off on a spree. Jantarro's the key. Who and what he was, and how he died. It could all be a coverup after an accident, but Billy not waiting for you looks bad. We better find out what did happen to Jantarro, and who he really was."

"You find out, Fortune."

"What are you going to do?"

"Right now, I'm going to get some sleep. After that is my business."

"Everyone can use help, Frank."

He lay silent with his face to the wall. Billy Owen wasn't the only one who lived in an unreal world.

The people in a neighborhood bar at ten in the morning are old men, alcoholics and the unemployed. Men who have nothing to do and can't sleep. Alcoholics who've lost the ability to do anything. The rare woman is usually all three, the bar still a men's club. Especially in the *barrio*.

In The Xochitl there was one brown old man and four silent unemployed. They had no interest in me. Morning drinkers are too far down to be hostile to anyone. Even the morning bartender didn't seem to care that I was anglo.

"Bello? Too early, you know?"

"You know where I can find him now?"

"He eats over La Paloma. They got great *huevos jalapeños*. Bello, he likes *huevos jalapeños*. Got real hot eggs, right?"

My small Spanish is Puerto Rican Spanglish, and the joke was Mexican, but I got the idea.

La Paloma was on Haley Street. The pungent odor of chiles doesn't do a lot for my anglo stomach at ten A.M., but the patrons seemed to be enjoying it. A waitress pointed to a corner table when I asked for Aguado Bello.

He was a stocky man with the hooded eyes, mustache, and broad Indian face of the stereotypical Mexican *bandito*. His clothes didn't fit the cliche: a pearl gray suit, pale blue shirt, gray tie, shined black half-boots, diamond rings on both hands. He ate slowly, neatly, absorbed in a thick book.

"Mr. Bello?"

He looked up, his black eyes vague, still thinking about what he was reading. It was a novel: *Terra Nostra* by Carlos Fuentes. The book was in Spanish, but he spoke English without an accent.

"Do something for you?"

"Can I talk to you about Hector Jantarro."

He closed the book. "Sure. Take a seat." He eyed my arm and then my face. "Out-of-town cop?"

For the great majority of the blue and white collar middle class the police are remote, in another world. For the poor, the outlaws and the minorities, they are as close as family, part of everyday life, known on sight.

"Private. Looking for Billy Owen."

"The *gringo guerrillero*?"

"He really fought in Central America?"

"Hector got to know him down there doing something. You think he blew Hector down?"

"You don't believe it was an accident?"

He ate some eggs. "I was a cop too. I think the odds say if a guy like Hector dies hard it's no accident."

"What kind of guy was Hector?"

Bello ate the eggs and hot peppers in their lethal looking sauce, seemed to think about how much more he should say.

"He was a cop like me. Got kicked out too."

"In Mexico?"

"Somewhere else. He talked about doing a job, doing what he had to, getting screwed. He didn't talk about where."

I realized he wanted justice for Hector Jantarro. A personal matter. He wanted to help me, and if he knew where Jantarro was from, he'd have told me.

"Did you get screwed?"

Bello asked the waitress for another cup, poured coffee for both of us. "Do I look like I'm still a cop in Mexico?"

"Maybe you're undercover. You speak English like a *gringo*."

He laughed. "Grew up in Juarez/El Paso. Went to school on both sides, family all over Texas. Original Tex-Mex, *Nortena*."

"What was Jantarro doing up here?"

He drank coffee, looked at me the way I expect he'd looked at a lot of prisoners down in Mexico. There isn't much a cop in Mexico can do to get screwed, unless he does it too often, too hard, and in public. I should have been in trouble with such a direct question, but he wanted me to do what he didn't seem to think the police would. He drank more coffee.

"What's your name?"

"Dan Fortune."

"Fortune? English?"

"Polish. It was Fortunowski, my father changed it."

"Mexico's a funny country, Fortune. We got a constitution one part says we're socialists, another makes private property like God. Our ruling party calls itself revolutionary, but it's run by a rich middle class that'll do anything to protect itself. Our artists are Marxist in a country where the working class got no power. Together we're radicals, alone we're capitalists."

He poured more coffee. He was telling me about Hector Jantarro in his own way.

"You know the word, *chingar*, Fortune?"

"Anything to do with *chingada*?"

He nodded. "*Chingada*'s the ripped open, raped. *Chingon*'s the macho. *Chingar*'s power, violence, strength. In Mexico everything's *chingar*. There's only two ways to go—you can *chingar* other guys, or they *chingar* you. You screw or get screwed. You rip open, or get ripped."

"It's a male society, I—"

"No, not like we mean up here. It's power, violence. Look, up here a macho guy hates queers, right? All queers. Not down there. It's okay to be homosexual if you're *chingar*, the aggressor. If you're the passive queer, you're shit, worse than zero. That's the way it is in everything. Only being strong counts. A guy in any kind of power position who don't use his power against the weak and for himself is despised, sneered at, a *chingada*. He ain't just a jerk, he's not even a man."

He sipped his coffee more slowly, his black eyes seeing his near and yet so foreign country. "The general and the bandit are the same guy. It just depends on what's going on, what year it is. The President of the Republic, the governor of the province, the police chief, got to be millionaires before they retire. A detective lieutenant owns a couple of buildings. A guerrilla leader better have a nice nest egg in a Cayman bank. Or they ain't real men."

Hector Jantarro was a man who would have had to be manly, dominant, use whatever power he had for himself. That was what Bello had told me. He'd also told me how he'd gotten the gray suit, the elegant boots, and the diamond rings, and, indirectly, what both he and Jantarro were doing up here.

"Jantarro was sort of in exile?"

Bello nodded, looked past me at some distance I couldn't see. "Maybe a month ago we went down to L. A. for a night on the town, like we always done twice a month. Only this time it wasn't like always."

11

Hector Jantarro arrives at Bello's beachfront condo wearing his gray silk suit with the pale gray shirt, yellow tie and shined black shoes as usual, driving the rented Cadillac. It is the night they go to Los Angeles. Twice a month, as always. He parks in the rear, as always, does not take off his wide-brimmed gray hat and dark glasses until he is in the apartment.

"A disguise, no," he has explained to Bello, "but I do not want those fools I work with to recognize me and ask questions. Or my nervous benefactors to become weak in the knees that I must have a night of civilization out of this graveyard."

The usual twice a month trip to L.A. But after Hector's arrival, nothing else will be as usual this night.

First, there is the woman.

Since they met over breakfast at La Paloma, found they had much in common and became friends, Jantarro has driven to L.A. twice a month in the rented Caddy where Bello has arranged an evening of cooperative Latin ladies and night spots and eventually a hotel. The ripe ladies like Jantarro. He takes charge, spends well, has good if provincial, even foreign, manners, holds his liquor, and is lively and enjoys a good time.

This night Jantarro has a woman beside him in the front seat of the Cadillac. But not a woman, a girl. No more than sixteen. It does not fit the plans Bello has made. One of the Los Angeles women will be angry, and they will not be allowed into the night spots or the usual hotel.

"She'll get over it," Jantarro says. "And we do much that is different tonight, okay?"

Her name is Gloria Castro. Jantarro is obviously anxious to impress her, show that he is much more than a common laborer for an anglo boss, is a Latin gentleman of taste and refinement and connections. He parades her through Bello's condo, pointing out its size and elegance, but most importantly that it is in a choice beachfront location and out of the *barrio*. Jantarro's great friend Aguado Bello does not live in the *barrio* like a common beaner.

He draws the girl's attention to the ultramodern furniture Bello has had sent up from Mexico City, the expensive tequila Bello imports specially, the elegant hors d'oeuvres Bello has brought in from the best Mexican restaurant in town. To all the wealth and position his good friend Bello has had the *huevos* to bring with him in his exile.

Gloria responds well, but is not as awed as Jantarro clearly wants. She is too young, too shy, too inexperienced, but most of all she is too American. She may not have what Bello has, but it is all commonplace in the homes of her acquaintances, the houses she has probably cleaned, and Gloria herself is the next thing that is different this night.

Young, shy and inexperienced, she is also small, slim, and intelligent. The ladies Bello has provided have been older Latinas, if not ladies of the evening then close to it. Heavy-breasted, full, in short, skimpy dresses, usually red or green or yellow. Gloria wears a simple white dress with a wide skirt but a shade tight over her breasts because it was bought some years ago for grade school graduation.

The Angeleno ladies have not graduated from any school, speak poor English and only slightly better Spanish. Gloria, like Bello himself, is bilingual, but she is a high school girl, has been educated entirely in the States, speaks better English than Spanish, and better English than Bello. This seems to be important to Jantarro, and he insists that tonight they will all speak English.

This, too, is not as always, and neither are the drinks. Normally, man to man, they have two glasses of the good tequila, neat as befits its quality, with the customary salt and lime. Jantarro is careful to never drink too much when he is driving to Los Angeles. This night Jantarro asks for margaritas for Gloria, has four neat tequilas himself.

"You drive tonight, Bello. Tonight I will pay attention to my lady."

On the drive to Los Angeles, Jantarro and Gloria ride in the back seat, his hand on her thigh, but the dress not pulled up to reveal her underpants as with the Angeleno ladies, and he does not openly fondle her breasts. He simply rests his hand heavily on her bare thigh and talks to Bello as he drives. This is as always. The two men talk, the woman sits silent with her touched body, and Bello notices in the rearview mirror that Gloria makes no objection, is as accustomed to it as the Angeleno ladies.

Not as always are theater tickets to The Dorothy Chandler Pavilion of The Music Center to see the latest hit musical from Broadway with a cast of famous names and all in English. Bello's lady in red, still angry over her friend being stood up, is bored by the show, annoyed by the English she finds hard to understand, and uncomfortable in the sedate and largely anglo audience. It is even worse in the expensive French restaurant Jantarro insists on, where the people are all anglo and some even stare at them.

Bello is not enjoying himself, but he can't take the woman's side against Jantarro in public. Jantarro is arrogant and expansive, takes charge as if he has been in such a restaurant many times before. Gloria is dazzled by the elegant restaurant, all the well-dressed anglos, is more than a little intimidated to be there, even afraid, and so is finally impressed by Jantarro.

"In the city of my country there are many such fine French restaurants for the rich tourists and we who can afford them," Jantarro tells Gloria.

Jantarro has talked little of his past even to Bello. Only that he had also been a policeman in another country, that he had been "screwed by the communist pricks and their liberal ass-kissers," and that he is hidden in Santa Barbara under an assumed name by his *benefactors*—a word he uses with cynical irony, implying that the *benefits* are more for them than him.

"They give me money besides what I am paid on the miserable job they had Billy get me, but I could make a thousand times that if I changed sides at home, only I am not that kind of *cabron*."

But now, this night, Jantarro becomes expansive to the shy American Latina.

"In my country I had my own table at the best restaurant in the city. Held always for me. No one else could sit there unless I would send him with my special permission."

Gloria says, "My father told me about the *hidalgos* like that he worked for when he was a boy in Mexico. He didn't like them, said they were bad for ordinary people like his family."

"Your father is a weakling!" Jantarro says. "You think I was born a rich man with my own table in the restaurant? I was born in the dirt of the slums. My father was as weak as your father, my mother good for nothing except to tell her beads on her knees in front of the golden statue of the Virgin. I left them there in the slums with their weakness and their piety. Six of my sisters and brothers died, but I did not die. I learned how to fight and win and got out."

Bello listens as Jantarro tells of his days in the military, his police work, his triumphs and rewards in the country he has not named but Gloria seems to know if Bello does not. What Bello does know, suddenly, is what Jantarro is doing this night, what it is that Jantarro needs.

The girl is from *here*. She is not an anglo, but she is an American. She looks, acts, speaks like one of them. She belongs here. Jantarro has reached that moment of exile when he has lost the sense that he is a man. He has no respect, no power, and, even to himself, no identity. Among these aliens there are no automatic references by which they know him. In his country he had merely to step onto the street and everyone knew who and what he was. His status, his importance, his power, his superiority. He, and they, knew all the signals, from his police uniform, to the pistol carried openly under his civilian clothes, to the civilian clothes themselves. The expression on his face, his walk, the words he used for each person at each time. The size of his tips, where he lived, the car he drove. The people he was seen with in public. His women.

Here, exiled and in hiding, he does not know the signals, they do not know him. He is a common laborer from Mexico—a greaser from beanerland. But he is not a Mexican, and is invisible to the anglos, and there is no ground for him to belong on. The girl is a bridge. A Latina but American. To have her, to gain her respect, to impress her, intimidate her, make her afraid of his power, is to restore his power. To make him whole again, if only for a time and in his own eyes.

This night, then, has been to conquer Gloria Castro, to own her. To dazzle her, intimidate her, make her have admiration and a small fear of the power of Hector Jantarro no matter how weak and nothing he appears to be now. It has been to make her mean more to him than a woman he has bought, and so make him mean more to himself. It has been to restore a sense of his lost power.

So when they finally leave the restaurant, Bello goes with his lush Latina in red to the usual small hotel, but Jantarro and Gloria do not. Instead, they go to an expensive anglo motel where Jantarro has had Gloria make a reservation by phone from Santa Barbara and no questions are asked and Jantarro can feel he has power in her world. He is now a man in her world.

But while they are all still in the anglo restaurant where Jantarro has insisted on having after-dinner brandy of the kind he always had back in the capital of his country, and the ladies have gone to freshen up, shy Gloria leading the lush Latina who feels the eyes on her, Bello learns the last of what is not as always this night.

"You like this American child, Hector?"

"She reminds me of the young girls of my country, of the many young girls I had only to reach out for."

"Then you're lucky, *amigo*."

"Perhaps I will be luckier. Perhaps I will take this young girl home to my country with me."

"We all dream."

"Perhaps soon it will be more than a dream."

"You have said big trouble waits for you at home."

"Money calms many troubles."

"For big troubles there must be big money."

Jantarro smiles. "Much is possible to a man who keeps himself ready, who knows how to use what he can do. And when I return, what better way than with an American girl? A very young American senorita who speaks such good English and Spanish, has been to school, yet is an innocent."

The ladies return then, and Bello watches Jantarro walk ahead of them with the slim, shy, yet intelligent young girl on his arm. Jantarro is right. To return to his country, wherever it is down there, with money and this American child on his arm, would be a signal of triumph and power, a real *gran chingon*.

12

I said, "He said nothing about when, or how he'd get the money?"

"No."

Bello didn't say that he thought someone had killed Jantarro for the money or because of it, or that he felt a kinship with Jantarro that made him want the killer caught. It wouldn't have been *chingar.*

"Anyone who could tell me more, Bello?"

"Gloria Castro. I talked to her, but she doesn't like me."

He wrote out the address on a napkin.

"Mexicans aren't all that different from us, Bello."

He looked up. "Yes we are, Fortune. We're hot, not cold. Violent, not ruthless. When we steal, we feel guilty. If we kill, we suffer. We share the world with other people. No matter how savage we get, the enemy is a human being. You're enemies aren't really human. It makes it easier."

He couldn't return to Mexico, or even Texas, but he could mourn for a man he'd hardly known. Maybe we are different.

The ceiling was so low I had to bend my knees as well as my head to stand inside the rickety door. Before noon on a sunny day a single naked bulb hung on a bare electric cord, and I saw the two women seated side by side on a sagging bed.

The address was a rundown Victorian on Bath Street. Castro didn't show on the mailboxes, but a crudely lettered card read: *Raul Castro—In Back.* There was a tiny trailer without wheels in back, a windowless lean-to built against the rear of the house, and a five-foot high door into what looked like the crawlspace under the house.

Castro was written on another card tacked beside the low door. The voice that answered my knock was young.

"Who is it? I mean, come in."

They watched a television set with its back to me. The older woman could have been anywhere from fifty to a hundred in a voluminous brown peasant dress and yellow-striped shawl that hid everything except her impassive face and her skinny bare ankles stuck into men's *huaraches*. The fullness of her stoic face made me think she wasn't much over forty. The younger was no more than sixteen, dressed in the skirt, blouse, socks and tennis shoes of any American teenager.

The girl got up. "You want me or my mother?"

"You if you're Gloria."

She was so small she could walk upright in the low space. The room had a dirt floor, electrical wires and pipes overhead, two beds, two bureaus, a tiny refrigerator, a small window, and the single bare bulb. It was maybe fifteen feet deep and ten feet wide. There was no bath or toilet. Not even a sink.

"The two of you live here?"

"Three. My father's working."

It had to violate every provision of the city housing code. It stank of damp and sewage, there were spaces under the walls, and it was so dark the light had to be on all the time.

"How much do you pay for this?"

She became scared. "Are you from the city? It's okay, we like it fine."

"I'm not from the city, and no one could like it here."

"It's okay," she repeated, stubborn. "Who are you anyway? What do you want?"

"Dan Fortune, a private investigator. I want to talk about Hector Jantarro."

She sat on the bed at the front of the room. "Hector's dead."

"I know," I said. "I found him."

"You? What happened to him? Where—?"

"The police haven't talked to you?"

She shrugged. "I guess they don't know about me." She looked up. "How did you know?"

"Aguado Bello told me."

"I don't like him."

"Why not?"

"He was a policeman down in Mexico. Hector said communist students got arrested and beat up and some died. Bello accused the chief of ordering it. The other policemen all said he was lying, and the chief demanded that Bello face him in court. Only Bello escaped and came up here. He was afraid to face the chief, and he's got lots of money so he was crooked all along."

"Don't you think the chief has money, Gloria?"

"He's an important man, but he didn't run away like Bello."

Chingar. There wasn't any point in telling her Aguado Bello's escape and flight had been convenient for the Chief.

"How'd you meet Jantarro?"

"He works . . . I mean, he worked for the landlord, came for the rent a couple of times."

As Bello had said, she had no accent, spoke like any other Santa Barbara high school girl.

"One thing led to another," I said.

"He liked to go to nice places. Go down to L.A."

Nice places Canton Construction and the barflies around Milpas didn't know about. No wonder the police hadn't found Gloria Castro. And she wasn't like any other Santa Barbara high school girl, had never had a chance to be.

"You know where he came from, Gloria?"

"Guatemala. He was a soldier and a policeman, was kicked out when they got a new government."

I didn't remember a new government in Guatemala in five or six years.

"You're sure it was Guatemala?"

"He told me, and he got mail from there."

"How do you know that?"

"I saw the letters up in his cabin."

"You went to the cabin? Ever see anyone else there?"

"No."

"Did he get mail from anywhere else?"

"Florida a lot."

"Why Florida?"

"He'd been training other soldiers there before he came here."

"What soldiers?"

"I don't know. From Guatemala, I guess. You know, like the other side?"

High school and college kids in an America going into the Nineties didn't have much interest in geography or the troubles of a larger world. Diamond Jim Brady would be right at home.

"He talked about training soldiers in Florida?"

"All the time. He was always mad about it. About whatever made him leave Florida. Him and a friend at Canton he met back there. They talked about it when they got drunk."

"Billy Owen?"

She nodded. "Yeh, that's him. Him and Bello were the only two of Hector's friends I ever met."

"He ever say where he was in Florida? Where he met Owen?"

"Somewhere around Walton Beach. Fort Walton Beach, that was it. Eglin or Hurlburt or like that. He said they had swamps and beaches and jungles just like where the soldiers would fight."

Eglin Air Force Base reservation is about 700 square miles of swamps and jungle five miles west of Fort Walton Beach. It's a lot like northern Nicaragua, and was where the Contra guerrillas trained back in 1985, '86 and '87. Hurlburt Field is a Military Airlift Command base, home of the 2nd Air Division with a special wing tailored for covert warfare with MC-130 transports, AC-130H Spectre gunships, and HH-53 Pave Low helicopters.

"He never said who the soldiers were he trained?"

"No."

"Anything about drugs?"

"I guess. Hector was mad about how the government handles drugs. He said the big-shot users get a slap on the wrist and rehabilitation in Hawaii, the cops and judges get paid off, the sellers get rich, and we start a war with bombers, and gunships, and tanks to wipe out the poor farmers that grow the stuff." She thought about it, smiled. "Then he'd laugh, say he shouldn't get mad, the way the U.S. handled it kept the price high."

"He should have told Washington that."

"I don't think he liked the people in Washington much."

"Maybe because he worked with them?"

"I guess. He used to get letters from there too."

"How about visitors? Men in suits who don't smile much."

She looked at me as if I were psychic. "Only one most of the time."

"Most of the time only one?"

"All the time before he . . . died. But a couple of days ago two of them came around. Real serious and polite. They asked a lot of questions like you."

"What kind of questions?"

"What Hector told me. Who I saw with him. Like that. I couldn't tell them anything. I don't know anything about what happened to Hector."

"Because the cops never came to tell you or ask questions."

"They never did."

The well-dressed men asking questions about Jantarro hadn't confided in the local police. With the rest she and Bello had told me, I had a pretty good idea who they were.

Footsteps came around the house. The mother turned off the TV, shuffled past us and out the low door without a word. She was so short she didn't have to bend to go out.

The man who came in did.

"Who the hell are you?"

Canton Construction's foreman, Kenneth McElder, held what looked like a plumber's tool kit, but it wasn't plumbing he had in mind, and he wasn't happy to see me. Gloria Castro looked at the dirt floor.

"Dan Fortune. We met in your office yesterday."

"The private cop don't know how many he killed in the war." He shook his head in disbelief.

They're not just Mexicans, the *chingons*. McElder would urinate aggressively. Dismount to advance on the urinal with a slow, swaggering step. Legs set solidly apart, his weapon drawn slowly, deliberately, eyes unsmiling, lips tight.

"And you're the guy who'd remember every drop of blood," I said. "Take the gold teeth, collect the scalps, notch the gun."

I had only one arm, and McElder would bully anyone weaker or lower, but Gloria Castro was a witness. And I was a kind of cop, could be more dangerous than I looked. He settled for words.

"What the fuck you want here? This is Mr. Canton's place."

"You mean he admits it?"

"If they don't live here, Fortune, where do they live with what they pay?"

That wasn't the point, of course, but neither he nor Lee Canton were going to see it. Economically, and that was all they cared about, they were probably right.

"Did Canton know about Hector Jantarro and Miss Castro?"

"Hell, no. I run this end of the business."

"So you knew about them?"

"I knew he had a *chiquita*. He got her in here."

"But you didn't tell the police?"

"They never asked me about her."

"Anything else about Jantarro or Billy Owen you didn't tell the police?"

"What else would I know?"

"Where Owen's gone and why? Some scheme they had going."

He wasn't amused. "You watch your fucking mouth, you hear? Those two was dumb enough to try anything, probably did and then had a fight over it. But I don't know a damn thing about them, you remember that." He turned to Gloria Castro. "I'll be up fixing the sink like you want. Be back about twenty minutes."

He didn't even nod to me as he ducked through the low door and I heard his heavy tread go up some rickety outside steps.

"That were your bathroom is? Upstairs?"

"It's not that bad."

"Only when it rains," I said. "Why, Gloria? What are you, sixteen? In high school? Is it that bad for your parents?"

"My father has no job, gets day work. My mother never worked. They don't speak English. They've been here over twenty years but don't have papers. I want to finish high school, go to college."

"How much do you pay here?"

"It was three hundred, Hector helped a lot. Now its a hundred and fifty."

The place should be condemned. But the city knew they had to live somewhere, and Jantarro's money, McElder's hundred-and-fifty-dollar reduction, put meat on their table twice a week. They were in America, the girl was getting an education. What she did for it the mother expected and the father didn't want to know about.

13

At the sheriff's office they had me cool my heels, then sent word out that the Jantarro accident investigation was disposed of and closed, *sayonara*.

The way to a Washington law firm is through the White House or Capitol Hill, and most investigators are ex-cops. The second oldest cliche on earth—it's not what you know but who you know. It says most of what's wrong with us, capitalist or socialist. In New York I had my contacts, out here there was Lieutenant Holley in Santa Maria and Detective Sergeant Chavalas at SBPD. Chavalas was closer. He also had an open case in the death of the pickup driver, Murch Calhoun, who'd tried to run Frank Owen down, and could use help. That's the oldest cliche.

"No one's even claimed Calhoun's body."

"What about people he knew in town?"

"We've located four drifters who shaped up at the wall with him, a semi-hooker he saw off and on, and two almost reputable builders he'd done day jobs for. The only one who told us anything we didn't get from the Oklahoma police was the amateur lady of the evening. A couple of times when he was with her he got calls in the morning, she thinks from the same guy, and had to leave right away. And about four days ago they were in a bar on lower State when the bartender told him someone wanted to see him out back and he was gone maybe fifteen minutes."

"She didn't see who it was?"

"No."

"What about the caller? The voice. What he said to her."

"Short and hard. 'Murch Calhoun there?' and 'Get him.' "

"Both times?"

"Exactly the same according to her. No accent."

"The Hector Jantarro case is closed?"

Chavalas leaned back. "Physical evidence, investigation, and autopsy all say the same: accidental death while intoxicated. No evidence of anyone else helping him over that cliff, no motive they can find, no witnesses. If anyone was partying with him, they were illegals and long gone. Body already released and shipped home."

"The body's gone? Who claimed it?"

"The family. Took it back to Mexico."

It was too fast, too final, and too far.

"What if someone told you Jantarro didn't come from Mexico, wasn't even a Mexican at all?"

"I'd say someone was lying."

"Can you look at the sheriff's file on the case?"

Chavalas thought about it. "I've got a possible connected case still open. What do I look for?"

"Who claimed the body. His identification, and theirs."

The Jalisco Cafe was all but empty in the early afternoon. The same bartender mopped the bar before a solitary old man, and Sergio played his perennial pinball machine. The bartender remembered me.

"Find Billy?"

"Not yet. That Jay guy been in today?"

"Sergio? You see Jay yet today?"

Sergio made a soft shot at the pinball machine. "Gone."

"Already?" The bartender was surprised. "How come I don't see him?"

In the back, Sergio guided the ball carefully through the hazards. "Gone out o' town."

"Hey, I remember," the bartender said. "Those same guys was in talking to him. Then he says he was gonna take a trip, maybe go down to Baja. Lucky bastard."

"What same men?"

"Couple o' guys was in before you talked to Jay."

"What kind of guys?"

"Anglos like you. Younger, better threads. I mean, suits, ties, the works."

I had a hunch that Hector Jantarro's "family" had arranged the trip for Jay at about the same time they claimed the body to take "home." I wondered if Jay would find his home in Baja too?

In the fenced rear yard of Billy Owen's rented cottage, the pony, Taffy, grazed on a lush patch of alfalfa. The two small children played in a dusty corner of the yard, the drone of a television came from inside the cottage.

Nina Owen sat on one of two straight chairs in the living room, watched the TV. There was a worn out rug, a floral couch, a plastic leather armchair, a wood and rope armchair, and some small tables. The TV was color.

"Anything from Billy?"

A young woman clapped her hands in triumph on the TV. Some morning game show.

"No."

"You know a man named Murch Calhoun?"

The commercial came on. She turned off the set.

"I don't know. I never heard of him."

"Young, drives a truck too fast. A journeyman carpenter, no steady job, shapes up at the wall sometimes. He lives in a room on Haley, drinks, gets into brawls."

"Sounds like all of Billy's friends."

"This one's from Oklahoma, in town a month or so."

"An Okie?" She almost smiled. "I'd remember anyone from Oklahoma. I was born back there. We had a farm out in the panhandle. I was just real little, I liked it. My Daddy he remembered everybody leavin' in the Dust Bowl. His folks hung on, but the land never did really get no better."

Perched on the straight chair in a skimpy flowered dress, white socks, and running shoes, a cheap plastic purple barette in her dark blonde hair, she could have been the child she talked about. A child with a sudden need to talk. To herself and a world where she'd never found a place of her own.

"There was a lot of us, we had so much fun. Playin' down by the river, not that it ever had water 'cept in winter. But my momma had too many kids. I guess she never did feel real well. That's why when we come out here she never did nothing, not even cook."

An anger came into her voice. Anger for a time when she had been happy but now knew she shouldn't have been. Anger for then and for now.

"She never wanted to leave the farm, but my daddy said it was worn out an' he was goin' to California like his daddy should of and get his share of the good times. I think it was more the church momma didn't want to go away from than the farm. She never did find a church she liked down in L.A., people really believed in the Lord. That's why she started drinkin' worse. I guess daddy liked it better, workin' in a garage. He always was good with machines, but momma just didn't have nothin' to do with us kids most grown."

She was bringing herself up to date, telling herself who she was beyond Billy Owen. Calling up all her ghosts, and burying her dead to prepare to face change. Before you can change you must establish a base of your own, become yourself.

"We all left after momma died. That's when I married Billy. I was real dumb, fell right over for his line of crap. Back in Oklahoma I didn't get much schoolin', didn't know how to do nothin' I could get a job. Billy married me 'cause momma taught me never let a man have more'n a couple o' tastes without we got married. He never changed an' he ain't never goin' to."

She swung slowly from side to side on the straight chair, like a girl sitting on a porch swing in Oklahoma.

"What about those other people who came asking about him? Have any of them been back?"

"No."

"Where could he have met someone like Murch Calhoun without you knowing it?"

"I guess any bar in town."

"Somewhere he'd get to know him better?"

"Maybe with that prisoner construction team."

"Prisoner construction team?"

"Billy got picked up drunk an' speeding. Judge saw he was a carpenter, gave him community work. Mr. Canton didn't like Billy to do it, talked to the D. A. and got him off. But Billy liked the guys, used to go around nights and Saturdays."

"How do I find the project?"

"I guess the cops or someone'd know."

She still rocked on the straight chair like a teenage girl with nothing to do on a Saturday night.

The cars parked in front of the Canton Construction office spoke for themselves. Four cheap compacts dull from age, a white Jaguar XJS, and a burly Bronco. It was an hour before Lee Canton came out and drove off in the XJS. Kenneth McElder wasn't far behind. The Bronco went away in a cloud of dust.

A red Corvette with a longhorn steer for a hood ornament and the license plate "SAM II" beat me into the yard, screeched to a halt. A small, blond young man in jeans, Hard Rock Cafe—London T-shirt, and worn Western boots climbed out and trotted into the office. He didn't look at me as I parked beside the Corvette. I don't think he even noticed I was there.

Inside, the boy bantered with the only young woman in the office. I pushed through the gate in the visitor's fence and smiled at the older woman who sat at the desk next to McElder's. She should be the senior in charge when he was out. She looked up with the same cold expression McElder did. The second in command always tends to imitate the boss.

"I'm tracing a man named Murch Calhoun," I told her. "He's a day carpenter, I wondered if he ever worked for you?"

"Mrs. Ojeda handles personnel records. First desk to the left over there."

Mrs. Ojeda, a motherly Latino lady, said she'd look up the payroll records for the last two months. She suggested I wait outside the fence. The blond kid with the real boots and phony car had left the young woman when told to by the lady in charge. He sat on McElder's desk and gave the older woman a hard time.

"Hey, you gotta be nice to me, Maggie. I'll tell Uncle Lee you been hitting on old Kenny."

"You better get off Mr. McElder's desk."

"Now here I am just trying to cheer up the workers, bring a little light and good times into Uncle Lee's sweatshop."

The women all smiled, except the second in command.

"I bring sunshine, Maggie. Cheer the slaves, protect my inheritance."

"We've been told not to talk to you, or Morgan, or your father, or your grandfather."

The boy's smile grew tighter, and his pale blue eyes were like those of a prince told what he didn't want to hear. He didn't seem like a bad kid. The worn boots said he worked hard on some ranch. But not an ordinary ranch kid either. There was the Corvette outside, the eyes, the way his feet swung angrily as he looked at the lady in charge. A prince the king made work, and work hard, but a prince.

"Hey, okay. I'll just go wait for Uncle Lee in his office."

If the lady in charge had been going to say anything, she didn't have too. A growl and a heavy step said that Kenneth McElder was back.

"You'll wait where you're supposed to wait."

"Hey, Kenny, how's the boy?" The brash youth grinned, but his eyes were thin. "I'll be out of your way in Uncle Lee's office. He always says I should wait in there."

"He didn't tell me."

Young Sam Canton's obvious next line never came. He wasn't quite old enough. He wasn't sure his uncle would back him, knew he probably wouldn't. He wasn't sure McElder wouldn't throw him out physically, knew he probably would. He wasn't sure he could stop McElder, wasn't ready to lose, so couldn't fight. I watched all this struggle behind the pale blue eyes. All Sam Canton II could do was retreat. He looked at his watch.

"Hell, I ain't got the time now anyway. I'll tell Uncle Lee to fill you in on where the family waits for him, Kenny."

It was a lame try. Even the young woman looked away.

"You do that," McElder said.

He held the railing gate open. The boy had no choice except to walk out past the burly man with everyone watching. The only one who made a sound was the pit bull. It growled.

McElder turned to me. "What do you want this time?"

I told him.

"Calhoun?" He walked to the motherly Latina who was looking Calhoun up for me. "You find him, Carmela?"

"No, Mr. McElder. He isn't on any payroll the last three months. Maybe he was one of those day workers you all sometimes hire and pay in cash."

"It should show. We put in vouchers for the cash."

"Unless someone got careless and forgot. It happens."

I said, "Who can hire day workers like that?"

"The boss, me, any crew foreman, and Billy Owen." He pushed through the gate in the railing, herded the pit bull under his desk, sat down. "Calhoun mixed up with Billy?"

"He could have been."

He heard the past tense. "Not anymore?"

"Calhoun's dead."

He listened to the story, even seemed to think about it. That wasn't what I would have expected from a man like McElder. Neither was cooperation.

"Tell you what, I'll ask around, okay? The crew foremen and work gangs too."

"I appreciate it."

He heard the surprise in my voice.

"I don't like my people in trouble. You got a number?"

I gave him the Summerland phone number.

Outside, Lee Canton's white Jaguar XJS pulled in before I reached my car. A red Mercedes 450SL came behind it, the top down and a windblown blonde behind the wheel. When she got out, she was taller than Canton. In a short white skirt, backless white halter, white high-heeled sandals, and a tan like saddle leather, she looked ready for almost anything: to step out of the skirt and plunge into the pool; to kick off the high heels and join a 12-meter crew; grab a tennis racket and hit a few.

"Fortune, isn't it?" Lee Canton said. "Have you found Billy Owen?"

"Not yet. The name Murch Calhoun mean anything to you, Mr. Canton? Maybe a day worker on one of your jobs?"

"Murch?" the woman said. "Good God, is that really a name?"

She gave me a nice smile. Warm and dazzling. Up close she wasn't as young or as sporty as she'd seemed at a distance, and the smile was all business. She wasn't ready for play, she was working. Or, to be accurate, play and work were the same thing for her. Play and work among the rich.

"Not a thing," Canton said. "I don't know most of the day workers. Talk to Ken McElder."

"I already have."

"Then that's about it."

The woman said, "You're an investigator, Mr. Fortune?"

Whatever she did, she'd be good at it. Not many people remember a name on a single mention.

"He's a private detective," Canton said. "He's not interested in our fund, Elizabeth."

She gave me the dazzle again. "He's an American, isn't he? He likes to make money and knows a good investment when he sees one. Am I right, Mr. Fortune?"

"Why not?" I said. "You have a card?"

She dug into her white bag, handed me an elegant, engraved, oversized card: *Elizabeth Henze Martin, Investment;* and in the bottom right corner, *J. James & Co., Suite 12, Montecito Village.*

"If he buys in, he's mine," Canton said.

"I spoke first, Leland." She had great teeth and a long, lean face. "But we'll talk. Nice to meet you, Mr. Fortune."

They walked on into Canton's office. She'd used my name three times in three sentences. Buttering me, and fixing it in her memory at the same time. No wasted motion.

15

Around the corner from Canton Construction the sheriff's car was parked in front of a mom-and-pop Latino grocery. Lieutenant Holley sat behind the wheel eating a hero sandwich. I bought two Coors, joined him.

"I just ran into your Elizabeth Martin."

"Doing what?"

"Going into Lee Canton's office with him. Trying to sell me some fund."

"Did you buy?"

"Too rich for me. Is she business or pleasure for Canton?"

"He's a married man. But she is damn good looking."

"Knows it and uses it," I said. "Whatever else she does, pool to party, sailing to screwing, she's always selling."

Holley laughed. "You haven't been out here long. That's standard in Montecito. Whatever they do, they do it twenty-four hours a day. Their work and their life are the same thing. That's how they got rich. Stocks, bonds, real estate, export-import, auto agencies, construction, jewels, you name it. Wherever they go, whatever and whenever, they're buying, selling or making deals. The rest is downtime."

It wasn't a bad description of all the rich and powerful. Carnegie, Rockefeller, the DuPonts hadn't left their work in the office, and even those who inherit their millions protect their advantages twenty-four hours a day. It's only the poor who separate work and play, have nothing to protect.

"I hear the Hector Jantarro case is closed."

"An accident, his family came from Mexico for the body."

"Did you see the file?"

He nodded. "You'd made me curious. Autopsy showed death from massive cerebral trauma caused by that large rock at crime scene one. Coroner says he's sure the rock fell on Jantarro. No prints, no physical evidence of anyone else, enough alcohol in him when he died to have drowned him. It looks like the rock was just knocked loose and hit him."

"Yeah," I said.

"You're thinking about this Billy Owen? Bring some proof and we'll listen. Until then, we don't even have a crime."

"How did you identify the family?"

"They had documents, including his birth certificate. Now get out of here, I'm working."

Around the corner I parked again where I could watch him through the yards and cyclone fences. After ten minutes, a car came from the direction of Canton Construction, and he went after it at a tailing distance. It wasn't the white XJS, it was the 450SL convertible with Elizabeth Henze Martin driving.

I never tail a police car. They're not amused. I drove back to Canton's office. McElder seemed to have forgotten his moment of cooperativeness. The pit bull growled.

"You're getting to be a pain."

"Sorry, I'm new here. Where's Montecito Village?"

He leaned back, beefy arms up and hands behind his head. "She wouldn't let you smell her, Fortune. Jags and Rolls Royces for that stuff, not Tempos."

And not Ford Broncos. He'd made a move on Elizabeth Henze Martin himself. Or thought about it. Lee Canton was the boss, but McElder wouldn't hesitate to move in against him man to man and worry about his job later.

"I can dream," I said.

"It's out on East Valley Road at San Ysidro Road. Jensen's Chevron."

"How about those prisoners Billy Owen worked with? You know where I can find them?"

He was all instant mood. Reacted to whatever touched him, automatic and as changeable as a chameleon. Each instant unconnected to the last or the next.

"That fucking freeloader outfit? You're mixed with them, Fortune, you can get the fuck out of here. The boss don't like that deal, or our little brown sister that runs it."

"Owen could have met Murch Calhoun with them."

He thought about it, and the hostility metamorphosed into a new reaction.

"Sounds like something one of those creeps'd do. I don't know where the hell they are, but the boss does." He punched an interoffice telephone button. "Boss, where're those prisoner scabs this week? No, Fortune wants to know. Yeh, he's back."

Lee Canton came out of his private office shrugging into a blue blazer over his white ducks. "What do you want with Prison Projects?"

"I thought Billy could have met Murch Calhoun there."

"It's possible, I suppose. I told Owen not to hang out with them. They're working for an old lady deadbeat. I hope one of them doesn't rape and kill her. Not that I'd cry a lot. I can take you, but then I've got some business to take care of."

In the white Jaguar we drove out of the yard, went north to Haley, and over to Garden Street. In a car a man is relaxed, and I could pick up my Tempo anytime.

"What if I told you Jantarro wasn't Mexican, and it could be the CIA had him stashed here?"

"I wouldn't be surprised. He was one lousy worker."

"Any idea where he'd get money to take home?"

"They all gamble, deal dope. Like I said before, they save up their cash and head back below the border sooner or later."

We were on Garden Street headed north. Santa Barbara is an even smaller city than it seems, and on Garden you go fast from the *semi-barrio* to the middle class to the affluent and gentrified Upper

East. Almost everything is neat and clean and green, the differences are in size and elegance and power.

"How do you know about this Prison Project?"

"I'm on the Construction Industries Council, the Landlord's Rights Committee, and the Taxpayers Association. We fight all do-gooders who use tax money for handouts, try to fix rents." He grinned, and winked at me. "Besides, the Latina lawyer who runs the thing was a squeeze of mine a while back. She took it more seriously than I did, you know how women are, so I had to break it off. But we still talk to each other, even out of court."

"You don't approve of the project?"

"Coddling criminals? Robbing taxpayers for dubious social experiments? Taking jobs from honest workers? Not to mention substandard work and putting dangerous people on the streets. You bet I don't approve."

Santa Barbara's Upper East is big old frame Victorians, red-tiled Spanish Colonials, Mediterranean villas, stone and stucco mansions, sprawling one-story ranches of the more recent rich on plots sold off to maintain the Victorians, and quirky hideaways built over long years by rich eccentrics. Some of the Victorians are unchanged and as elegant as the dowagers that live in them, others are renovated and repainted in pastels and contrasting trim as precise and detailed as bone china. A few smaller houses have survived the real estate boom and upscale mobility to stand in shabby gentility among their imposing neighbors.

"Here they are," Lee Canton said.

He stopped before one of the rundown older houses in need of paint and repair. Three men were on the roof laying tarpaper for new shingles. Another, wearing a carpenter's tool belt, was replacing rotted siding all around the lower exterior walls, and a fifth was digging dirt away where it had built up to touch the wood and cause the rot and termite damage.

Two women stepped out of the house onto a screened rear porch. One was an elderly lady, frail and stooped in bright blue silk lounging pajamas. The other was small and dark, her black hair pulled back and tied at the nape of her neck with an orange ribbon jaunty against her pale brown skin. Full lips, vaguely Indian cheekbones and eyes, and a firmly curved body in a tailored beige suit. The older woman remained on the porch, but the Latina came down the back steps and across the ragged lawn. Canton got out of the Jag with me.

"Still taking work away from honest men, Connie?"

"Who else would visit his slums in a white Jaguar, Lee?"

Canton introduced me. "This is Dan Fortune, Connie. He's a private cop with questions for your pampered poodles. Fortune, meet Connie Ochoa, legal eagle and bleeding *corazon*."

The small woman sighed. "Lee is so fluent in Spanish, Mr. Fortune. It makes it so much easier to collect the rent from his tenants, even communicate with his laborers."

"If they want to communicate, they better learn English. If my tenants don't like where they live, they can move."

"You're all *corazon*, Lee."

"I don't subsidize criminals and deadbeats," Canton said. "When your cons get this dump fixed up it'll be worth twice as much and the public pays for it."

Connie Ochoa nodded to me, "Are you working for Lee, Mr. Fortune?"

"Looking for one of his employees."

"Then let me tell you what Lee's really against," she gave Canton a cool courtroom smile. "It's not that we're repairing one house. Mrs. Roberts can't afford the work herself, her church is paying for the materials, no one is losing business."

"What I'm against is the principle. Free convict labor robs legitimate contractors. Let some charity pay for the job."

"I never heard you object to convict labor on the roads. Clearing creeks, chopping brush. What saves you money."

Canton made a sound, but he said nothing.

"No," Connie Ochoa said, "what annoys Lee is that our work might mean more living space in Santa Barbara. Mrs. Roberts rents rooms, many of the elderly we help do. Without rentable space they'd have to sell their houses. A new owner probably wouldn't rent, and Mrs. Roberts would become a tenant herself."

Canton shook his head. "Believe that, Fortune, you believe anything. I have to go. Don't let her con you all the way."

The Jaguar pulled away with too much burned rubber. Connie Ochoa had made Canton a lot angrier than he wanted her, or me, to think. She looked after him almost sadly. She had more regrets for their past than he seemed to.

"Funny how things turn out," she said. "I used to think he was special. You're a detective, Mr. Fortune, what do you think of our project?"

"I don't know your project."

"There's not a lot to know, really. We bring nonviolent prisoners from minimum security prisons to do community work for mostly elderly homeowners who can't afford needed repairs. We believe there are better ways to punish nonviolent offenders than locking them up in overcrowded prisons. They live with local families and they have to work hard."

"Almost anything has to be better than our prison system."

"You know our prison system well, Mr. Fortune?"

"I know it dehumanizes almost everyone it doesn't kill."

"Over eighty percent who get out are back in under four years. Only the Soviet Union and South Africa have higher rates of incarceration. This is one way to take those who can still be changed and break the cycle. Would you like to talk to them?"

"That's why I'm here."

The five men had stopped working, were seated on the ground opening paper bags. Lunch time. She sat down with them. Aging one-armed detectives aren't fit for sitting cross-legged. I leaned on a tree.

"Mr. Fortune is a detective. He wants to talk to you, and I'd like you to tell him how you feel about the project," she said to the men.

The young one with the carpenter's belt said, "Beats sittin' on your ass two, three years."

"Inside, we just numbers."

An older one said, "They get to see they don't have to be afraid of us. They learn we're people."

Two of them said nothing, just ate and watched me.

"Inside there ain't nothin' to do," the first said.

"We're in the world," the older one said. "What did you want to talk to us about?"

"Any of you ever work with a man named Murch Calhoun?"

The silence was unanimous. Shakes and shrugs.

"How about Billy Owen?"

Connie Ochoa said, "Owen was here for a time. Lee got him taken away. Is Billy the man you're looking for?"

"He seems to have vanished. He could be in trouble."

"Billy?" the young carpenter said. "Hell, he's probably on a bike headin' north or south."

The older man said, "Owen was restless. He was fascinated by us because we were real convicts."

"Did he ever mention a Murch Calhoun?"

The same silence and head shakes. Connie Ochoa walked me to the street.

"Billy Owen can be pathetic, Mr. Fortune, but he isn't a bad person. He worked hard here, seemed to enjoy it. If only he wasn't so desperate to play a role that isn't him."

"A lot of people play roles," I said.

"Yes." She looked to where Canton had disappeared as if she could see his image in the air. "Lee didn't start as a wheeler-dealer, a slumlord, but it was inevitable."

"I've seen one of his rentals."

"Which one?"

"The Castros on Bath Street."

She shook her head in a mixture of anger and disgust. "I'm not against private enterprise, but the control landlords have over tenants in most places amounts to feudalism. Tenants aren't angels, but many times what they do is out of sheer frustration and helplessness against the total disregard of their rights by owners. I'm representing a case now where an owner evicted twelve households under the plea of renovation. The so-called renovations were purely cosmetic, and the new tenants will pay eight hundred to a thousand dollars for units the old tenants rented at four hundred to six hundred." She stood there in the warm sun, gestured helplessly. "And it's not even outrages like that, it's the attitude that doesn't really grant the poor and weak any rights, and certainly no power." She turned to face me. "Did Lee tell you about us?"

"He mentioned you'd been close once."

She smiled. "I doubt he put it that politely, but, yes, we were close once. He was married to his second wife at the time. They were breaking up. He was confused, making a last stand against his family. Fifteen years ago I was just out of law school, starting in local practice."

16

The car that cuts you off is always a Mercedes. Or a pickup truck. The shiny car that turns from a side road and forces you to slam on your brakes as it drives on oblivious is a Mercedes or Jaguar or Rolls Royce. Or a pickup truck with a lone male at the wheel. It is a Mercedes that parks in no-parking zones, drives the wrong way against the arrows in a parking lot.

She is at the window table facing the lawn and Channel Drive in the alcove of the cocktail lounge of The Biltmore. It is winter, the islands are clear far out over the water. There are a lot of Mercedes and Jaguars and even a few Rolls Royces on Channel Drive and in the hotel parking lot.

She drinks a Corona. Lee thinks it amusing that a woman as young as she drinks beer. He calls her his cheap date, kisses her when he says it, squeezes her hand. He is late. She knew he would be. She parked out on Channel Drive to avoid the young Latino attendants who stare at her, crossed the elegant hotel lobby alone. She is always aware of the faint reaction, the heads that turn, the half step of the bell captain before he notices her clothes, the briefcase. Less than the reaction of the lawyers, the judge, the court attendants, her first day in court. Less than each time she rises before a new judge or courtroom. Much is relative. The not-too-important. The really important isn't relative. There are absolutes.

Lee is always late. She is sure it is a matter of status. Status and importance. The man who must wait loses face. With women it doesn't really matter, but habit is hard to break. He will have a reason, an explanation, as he kisses her and sits and looks immediately for the waitress. A late hitch in a deal. A meeting with an official—state, county, city—for some vital aid to get into or out of something. A call from his lawyer.

She orders another beer. She doesn't really expect him to care that much, knows by now what she is to him and what she can never be, but she wants to have her say and needs to relax. The Anglo cocktail waitress radiates more hostility than lobby or courtroom. Probably thinks she is a hooker plying her trade in the waitress's domain. Again, there is progress. Thirty years ago the waitress would have been sure a young Latina drinking alone in The Biltmore was a hooker and ordered her out. Fifty years ago she wouldn't have been allowed in the front door of The Biltmore. A hundred years ago the only relation she could have had with the Cantons was to wash their clothes. Or, of course, the one she has with Lee.

She is twenty-five years old, newly admitted to the bar and the list of *abogados* at La Casa, when she meets Tomas Lopez Villareal, a sixteen-year-old from Mexico. In the country a year. Illegal. He speaks no English, his Spanish isn't that good.

"The man he does not pay me. I work ten months, he pay me three-hundred-and-fifty dollar. Even the Lord's Day I work. All day while the sun it is up. I ask that he will pay me, he say he tell *La Migra*."

The farm is on the vast Double C Ranch north of Los Alamos. Lopez has a dirty one-page letter in Spanish signed by Morgan Canton that agrees to pay $2.50 an hour. His actual pay has been nine cents an hour. He lives in an 8-foot-by-8-foot shed with a stove but no heat or running water. He is sometimes given a sack of beans and a package of tortillas. They check his story, take pictures, contact California Rural Legal Assistance. Together, they plan a lawsuit for back pay of $7175, plus $200,000 punitive and other damages arising from intentionally inflicted emotional distress and violations of California labor codes. Unless the Cantons will make full restitution out of court. She gets the case, CRLA makes an appointment for her to meet Morgan Canton.

She drives out in the new Honda Civic her father gave her when she passed the bar exam. The turnoff is hard to find, marked simply with a small intertwined pair of "Cs" and the name: Canton. The road is narrow, but blacktopped. A half mile into the brown hills she passes under a rustic arch with the Double C brand displayed much more proudly. A dirt track gouged by horses now runs beside the blacktop, like two centuries joined. It goes on and on for miles. At the first view of the sea she has to stop, get out to look at the sweep of brown oats and dusty green oaks and shining ocean out to the distant islands.

"Hey! Hey!"

He is a teenager on a big brown horse with a silver-trimmed saddle. He wears the jeans, denim shirt, Western boots, wide-brimmed straw hat she has seen on all the farm boys in the state, but this boy has a fancy leather vest, spurs, and a real horse.

"You made a wrong turn five miles back, Miss. This is a private ranch."

"You work here?"

"I own the place." The boy smiles from the big horse. "I will. Me and Sam. My Dad and Granddad own it now. We been here over a hundred years. Built the whole place from scratch."

He isn't boasting, he is proud of what his name has built.

"Which one is Morgan?" she asks.

"That's me and my Dad. If you come to see Dad, he's up at the house. Another five miles."

It sits down among the brown hills, sheltered, yet with a wide view of the sea and the islands. A real California ranch house. Parts of it true adobe, all of it whitewashed and dark-beamed and red-tile roofed. Corrals and barns and stables and fences. A large garage. Many horses and two Mercedes are visible. The boy has reached the house across country ahead of her, and a solid man of fifty-odd in the same jeans and denim shirt and leather vest and boots, but with a gray Stetson instead of the straw, stands with him on the veranda.

"Mr. Morgan Canton?"

"Do I know you, Miss?"

"Connie Ochoa. I have an appointment."

Morgan Canton has wind-and-sun-creased eyes, a leathery face that is genuinely confused. He knows he isn't a man who forgets appointments, but—?

"Rural Legal Assistance called you. I'm an attorney."

The boy says, "Uh–oh."

His father looks at him, and the boy misunderstands.

"Hey, how could I know? I mean she's . . . I mean—"

"Do something, Morg," Morgan Canton says, and says to her, "I told your man it'd be easier to talk to our lawyers in town."

"We thought if we spoke to you directly, we might settle the matter without any legal trouble or expense."

"What matter?"

She tells him Tomas Lopez Villareal's story, the investigation, the planned lawsuit.

"Hey," the boy cries. It is his expression for everything. "The *cholo*'s a liar! We don't do stuff like that."

She and Morgan Canton both ignore the boy.

"If there is some mistake, Mr. Canton, a misunderstanding, I'm sure we can agree on proper restitution for Lopez."

"I'll look into it."

"Time is of the essence, Mr. Morgan. We'll have to file the suit if we don't hear from you soon."

"We'll look into it, Counsellor."

She drives the narrow ranch road back. The boy trails her on his horse, angry at the insult to the Cantons. A Mercedes appears behind her. It catches up and honks. She stops. A man gets out, strides up to her window. He is a younger, thinner version of Morgan Canton. Perhaps forty.

"I'm Lee Canton. I was in the house. Want to talk?"

"I'm sure your brother—"

"Won't talk to me. I'm the black sheep, don't even live here. Maybe I can help. It's Attorney Ochoa, right?"

"Connie," she says. He acts more like an older Morgan The Third than a younger Morgan The Second.

"Lee. Let's go over to Mattei's Tavern."

It's been a long day, she is tense, and a drink sounds good. She follows Lee Canton's Mercedes to the old stagecoach station. They take a corner table in the empty afternoon bar where he seems well known. He has bourbon. She orders a Corona.

"You don't have to order beer," he says. "It's on me."

"I drink beer."

"Really? I never knew a young woman who drank beer. Is it something Mexican? I mean, a custom?"

She laughs. At last. "What did you want to talk about, Lee?"

"You mean besides getting your address and phone number?"

"Besides that."

"I didn't hear all of what you and Morg were saying."

She summarizes the charges of Tomas Lopez Villareal, and the lawsuit. Lee sips at his bourbon. His eyes are bright as if he is enjoying it all.

"You have pictures of the shed, the farm?"

"And the boy's pay records. Scraps of paper and money order receipts, but they look honest and we can't find any other cash."

"What did Morg have to say?"

"That he'd look into it."

He is, she realizes, excited. She senses that he is a soft man compared to his brother. That is why she thought of him as more like his young nephew. He is the different Canton. Perhaps weaker, less sure of himself, less confident, but more human.

"He'll look into what my old man wants him to do, that's what he'll look into. That's why I got out years ago."

"You don't get along with your father?"

"The second son, right?" He waves for another round. "Morg does everything Sam's way, I do everything wrong. Standard Psych 101. When I tried to be a rancher, sit tall in the saddle, I blew it. He gave me a rundown construction company he'd been stuck with. Told me if

I could run it it was mine. I still run it, and a lot more. We can't all be ramrod night herders."

She'd had enough Psych 101 herself to know his father means more to him than he pretends. It makes him even more human. Her mother isn't really happy with a female lawyer. A Latin woman must not make men feel less.

"How old is he, your father?"

"Seventy-five this year. Born in the last century. Don't let that fool you. If he fights, he won't be easy to beat. I'll do what I can, Morg at least listens to me sometimes."

"What can he do? We have the boy's statement, the contract, the photos."

He twirls his glass. "Last year Morg caught young Morgan snorting C. He grabbed the kid's supplier, beat the shit out of him, and hauled him to the sheriff's office in Santa Maria. The bleeding hearts demanded the DA charge Morg with vigilanteism, kidnapping, assault. The twenty-year-old pusher sued for $150,000 damages." He drinks. "Morg paid a fine for disorderly conduct. The kid pusher was arrested, took a plea to possession and a suspended sentence, settled out of court, and moved away."

"I see."

"One lawsuit Sam doesn't fight could lead to fifty more. He can make it hard to win, hard on you, and hard on that boy."

"But you'd help us fight him?"

"For you, I'll fight dragons."

They both laugh, have a third round. She agrees to see him again. He is married, but separated from his second wife. They talk about the Lopez case. One thing leads to another. He has never had a Latina, finds her exotic, exciting. She likes that, likes being with a man she can talk to about what she never can with the Latin men she knows in Santa Barbara. She likes the crossing of so many barriers, the differences in them, that he so obviously finds her fascinating as a woman.

It turns out that a foreman on the Canton Ranch is the one cheating Tomas Lopez and other illegal field laborers. The Cantons say they will fire him, offer to give the boy his back pay but nothing more. The lawsuit is filed. The Canton lawyers counterfile for various delays, motions, exceptions, dismissals and denials. The case drags on. She sees a lot of Lee Canton. He is nice, but can't do much to help against his father and brother. It is a long summer.

In late fall, Morgan Canton calls and summons her to the ranch to discuss the case.

"My father wants to see you."

The office in the old ranch house is relatively small. Full of leather, old wood, books, ledgers, photographs as old as the wood, paintings of cowboys. Cluttered and comfortable. For a time she thinks that to see her is exactly what Sam Canton wants and nothing more. After his initial greeting, "Sit down," he sits in his desk chair and swivels slowly from side to side as if he were on a walking horse, and studies her.

He is smaller than both his sons, but thick and solid like Morgan. Darker skinned. His face is broader, almost Indian, his mustache thick and dark, his hair iron gray. His hands are small, and his skin is not wrinkled but soft like pale glove leather. He looks many years younger than seventy-five, except for his eyes. They are light brown flecked with green, and there is a hundred years of owning the land behind them.

"You're Mexican."

"No," she says, "I'm American."

He swivels. She notices the chair makes no sound. It is well oiled. Sam Canton takes care of details.

"My mother was Mexican. She was proud of it. Fine people, the Mexicans. Good friends, tough enemies. My mother was proud of her people."

"Were her people proud of her, Mr. Canton?"

He continues to swivel, as if he has spent so much of his life on a horse he can't think or talk without being in motion.

"She had her family, Miss Ochoa. Descended on both sides from the soldiers that came with Portola, three *comandantes* of the Royal Presidio, one governor of Alta California. Her father owned ten times this ranch. It took my father five years to get the old Don to let him marry my mother, another five to get this land as dowry. The old Don didn't give anything away easily."

"But your father got the land."

"He got the land."

"And all the people on it, and around it, and hired by it? The Mexican people who weren't part of your mother's family."

The slow swivelling has a soothing, lulling effect in the small office.

"He got the land, and I got it, and Morgan will get it, and young Morgan and young Sam after that."

"Not Lee?"

For the briefest of seconds she sees a flicker in his eyes, amusement, and realizes he knows all about her and Lee.

"Lee doesn't count."

"Because he doesn't do what you want? Does everyone have to do what you want, Mr. Canton? Lee, the Lopez boy, the sheriff, the California Rural Legal Assistance, Casa De La Raza, me?"

Even as she says it she knows that she is missing the point. That what Sam Canton himself wants is not important. It is something else, and he isn't thinking about what she has said.

"You're a woman. A Mexican woman. A good-looking woman. I'm an old man, but I can appreciate that. I'll always admire a good-looking woman. I'll always appreciate a really pretty *chicana* like you."

She feels her anger, and at the same instant realizes that he is making her say what she is going to say. He is making the meeting go where he wants it to go.

"I'm a lawyer, Mr. Canton. I'm here as a lawyer."

"That's what's giving me some trouble, Miss Ochoa. I'm not sure how to deal with it. It's a big change. I don't know if it's a good change. It comes from different values, different ideas. I think it's going to destroy the country as I know it, as it has to be for a man like me." He is making a speech—one he has led her into so he can tell her something he wants her to know. "I told you about my mother and her ancestors. Ancestors and descendents, Miss Ochoa. Family. Everyone has a place. My mother's father got the land, my father developed it. The women had the children to continue it, protect it. A man builds, a woman continues. A man builds for himself and his family. The strong survive and pass it on."

The silence of the small office, study, whatever it is, is total. No sound of the moving chair. Not even a distant dog.

"The ranch is what counts," she says. "Your family is the world."

"Then you'll understand when I talk to you as a lawyer and only a lawyer. When I tell you we'll fight your lawsuit as long and as hard as necessary. We will give no cooperation. The foreman is gone, the incident is closed. It was our problem, we have solved it. We will not let you, or your organization, or the state of California, or anyone or anything decide what this ranch should do."

She walks out into the sun and brown hills and wide view of the sea and gets into her car and drives back to Santa Barbara. No one follows her this time. At the Casa she learns that Tomas Lopez Villareal has returned to Mexico.

"Fifty thousand dollars," her boss says. "He can support his mother and sisters for twenty years in Oaxaca. They saved a bundle, but that wasn't what counted."

"No," she says.

The Casa and Rural Legal Assistance drop the lawsuit.

In the empty cocktail lounge she wonders if she went on seeing Lee to get back at the old man, the way Lee took up with her in the first place as a defiance of Sam Canton?

She won't be unfair. Lee genuinely likes her as a woman, if not the kind of woman he is used to, and there is the titillation of sex with a lawyer, the hint of taboo with a Latina. There is the divorce, and he is a man who has to have a woman.

(He married his first wife in San Francisco on a last foray at living and working outside Santa Barbara. The job lasted one year, the apartment two, the wife three. He is not a man who can live alone. The job and the apartment didn't send him home, but the wife did. No one knows where she disappeared to, she never wrote. He speaks of it now as a clean break, mentions her name, Janet, fondly, and implies that the end was a mutual blessing.

Two years later, installed at the construction company, he married the daughter of a local tycoon. This marriage was stormy from the start. Extravagance, infidelities, bankruptcies, no children. It lasted fifteen years, neither husband nor wife ready to give up the advantages and privileges of being a Canton and a Waite for the hazards of single life, or a new, perhaps lesser, attachment. So it lasted until just before she, Connie Ochoa, *abogado*, arrived on the scene.)

His Mercedes turns in for the valet parking. She waits for him to reach the table, kiss her, wave for the waitress.

"God, what a day."

"Business or personal?"

He orders his bourbon and her Corona. He hears the tone of her question that isn't a question. But, as usual, he hears it only through his preconceptions.

"Hey, we're in a bad mood."

"Finish your drink, Lee."

That is the ritual. The first drink is taken deep and long, the reward of a busy day.

"Ahhhh."

The bourbon is gone—before the ice can kill it. The joke is part of the country club bar scene when the bosses gather for one or two before they go home to their wives. This time he doesn't say it. He senses she has something on her mind, only motions for another drink.

"A young man came to my office last week." She shakes her head to the waitress. Three beers are enough. "Single, been in town for ten years. He's got a good job, wants to buy a home, hasn't enough cash for a down payment. He heard about the 'affordable' home program, found he qualified."

"Lucky him."

"He went to the county, they sent him to a condo developer. The developer says the 'affordable' units will be given out by lottery. Two weeks later he hears the units are all sold, calls county and developer. The county says the units can't be sold, they must approve any sale. The developer says the lottery will be soon. Another two weeks, same story. The young man goes to the development. People are being shown units, he asks a saleswoman about the 'affordables.' She is curt, they are all sold. Now he's really mad, goes back to county and developer. All is well, he will be contacted." She twirls her empty bottle. "One more week. He calls the developer. The units are sold. It's over. The end. So he comes to me."

"What can you do? Developers don't have to hold a lottery."

"I can find out what happened to those 'affordables' all you developers have to build for the young and the old, the poor and the disadvantaged, to get city approval for any development."

He laughs.

"All five units were given to 'friends' of the developer before a nail was driven. All of them qualified, but none of them had shown interest in owning a condo before. I mean, I know most of them too, don't I? Since you're the developer."

He smiles, drinks. "It's all legal, Con. Nothing says how I have to sell the 'affordables' as long as the people qualify. The kid won't be so gullible next time. Hey, you want to help him? Give me his name, I'll see what I can do."

"That's not the point, Lee."

"Then what the hell is the point?"

"That you and your 'friends' will sell those 'affordables' at full market price and split the profits. That the young and the old, the poor and the disadvantaged are robbed again."

He calls for another bourbon.

"What's this all about, Con?"

She looks toward the waitress. "The waitress doesn't like me. She's right. A waitress needs lords and ladies to give her big tips, to be hoodwinked and lived off. People like me will ruin her world."

"Am I supposed to understand that?"

"Your father would, but never mind. The deal with the affordables is just the tip of the iceberg, Lee. There's the Rolls Royce, the solar heating, the—"

"Hey, honey!" He grins at her, drinks the bourbon too fast. "The Rolls was all mixed up in the divorce. Okay, I shouldn't have tried to get money out of the insurance company, but the judge was going to give Pauline the car. When I had McElder hide it, everyone thought it had been stolen. I needed cash, I wasn't thinking straight. The judge believed me. I paid it all back."

"The solar heating, the earthquake repairs, the land deal?"

"There's nothing illegal about the solar heating. We sold those units in good faith, passed on what the manufacturers told us they'd do. It wasn't our fault the buyers didn't get the savings they expected, and we really thought their houses would increase in value. I'm not alone in that suit, there's thirty-five contractors and sixteen lenders, and they haven't ruled against us yet."

"Is it legal to tell mobile home owners a new state law requires stricter earthquake safety standards when there isn't any such law? Then hustle them into repairs they can't afford, get down payments bigger than the law says you can?"

"I only invested, Con. I didn't know what they were doing."

"You knew what you were doing when you faked that letter saying Fed-Mart wanted to buy land you were selling, got an inflated apprais-al of the value. You'd have been charged if it hadn't fallen through and the buyer didn't want to look stupid."

He holds his drink, leans back. "What is all this, Connie?"

She glances around the elegant lounge. "Did you ever notice that when a car cuts you off it's always a Mercedes or a pickup?"

"You've lost me."

Now she wishes she had another beer, watches the waitress. "When the adventurers, the farm boys, the debtors got off the boat in America they immediately adopted the attitudes of the nobility. That's from a history book, but it's true and it hasn't changed. All that mattered was their interest, their advantage, their power. Freedom meant to exploit, rob, cheat even kill to get for themselves and keep it. They still think the same, Lee, in more modern terms, and so do you."

He is silent for a time. "You're telling me we're through?"

"You're exactly like your father, Lee. The flip side of the record. You father's principles without principles." A weak Sam Canton. Denial not confrontation. Cunning not strength. Coyote not eagle, but both predators. "Everything you do is to show your father he was wrong about you, but it won't work. Tricks and schemes don't impress Sam Canton. Strength does. Strength and power, and you don't have either and never will."

"Thank you, Miss Ochoa. Thank you very much."

"I can never be a serious woman for you, Lee. You're the marrying type, and you could never marry me. That would be defying your world, the country club, the powers that be."

It has taken her months to realize all she has said, but on his face she sees that he has understood in an instant. They are wrong for each other. She wants out. He is off the hook.

"What are you going to do, Con?"

His fatherly tone almost makes her laugh. She hails the waitress, orders another Corona and a bourbon for him. It's all right now.

"Put it on my check." She takes a tiny clipping from her bag. "Let me read you something, Lee. Dateline, Santa Ana: 'A homeless woman has given the city $20 for her two-year use of public restrooms at Santiago Park. The note, signed Jane Lee, simply said, *I am a homeless person and have used Santiago Park for two years.*' I'm going to work for people like that, Lee."

She feels totally relaxed. His smile is almost real.

"A newborn militant, Con?"

"A fighter for a new world."

"Government control? Socialism? You'll kill the country. My Dad, much as I'm *not* like him, is what made this country."

"You're right. Sam Canton *is* what made this country." She drinks. "I think what most people want, Lee, is a varying number of needs and services, then to be left reasonably alone. Beyond that, I'd rather have a society where the rich are the criminals, not the poor. Where the arrogant are ignored, not the humble. Where the thoughtful and fair and brotherly are admired, not the pushy and powerful and rapacious."

"Well," he finishes his bourbon, looks at his watch, "I guess that leaves me out." He seems about to reach out and take her hand, stops. "What do I say? It's been good? I'm sorry it came out like this? I am sorry. Can we stay friends?"

"I'll ask you that after we tangle a few times in court."

It isn't the answer he expected, and he will never know what to do with what he doesn't understand. He stands, drops money on the table.

"Have another beer, Con." He shakes his head. "Beer! That should have told me from the start we'd never make it."

He bends quickly, kisses her cheek.

She says, "Does your father drive a Mercedes or a pickup truck? No, don't tell me. He drives both, right?"

He smiles in total incomprehension before he walks from the lounge. Alone, she leans back in the chair, looks out at the wide lawn and Channel Drive and the sea and the islands beyond. She doesn't even notice the waitress when her beer comes.

17

Montecito Village is a fire station, two gas stations, and three shopping centers between downtown Santa Barbara and our new home in Summerland, a mile in from the freeway. J. James & Co. was in the larger of the centers, a U-shaped complex of shops and offices built around a square of grass with a fountain.

I walked up the outside stairs to the second level, Connie Ochoa's parting words still in my head.

"Remember the foreman who cheated Tomas Lopez, Mr. Fortune? The one Sam Canton fired fifteen years ago? His name was Kenneth McElder. He went to work for Lee a year or so later."

The door to Number 12 was open in the warm April afternoon. Inside, a single large room looked more like the living room of some Montecito mansion than an office. Except that it was far too small. What it really looked like was a semi-pro New York brothel, the room where the johns waited for the ladies to make a little polite conversation before going upstairs to work. There was a couch, a love seat, arm chairs, and coffee tables, all in some French period that had thin legs and not much upholstery.

There was also a well-stocked bar, and two desks of the same period. Both small, delicate, with a leather writing surface and a single drawer in the center. The larger of the two was clean and empty. Nothing on it except a gold fountain pen, a leather memo pad, and a telephone. The smaller desk was almost as neat, but it wasn't empty. Elizabeth Henze Martin sat talking low on her telephone, making notes. She waved to me to sit down.

"Well," she said when she hung up. "Don't tell me I made a sale that easily? Absolutely blue chip, a very high return."

"A white chip is about my speed."

"Poker? Is that what they call hardboiled repartee, Mr. Fortune? I hate last names. Are you Mike, or Lew, or Sam?"

"Dan," I said.

"I also hate diminutives. I shall call you Daniel. You may call me anything you care to except Lizzie."

She still wore the all white short skirt, halter and heels. And her tan. Long and lean from face to ankle, she looked all business from the other side of the elegant desk. She changed her manner to fit not so much her surroundings as the moment, what was called for. She knew I wasn't there for investment, so I was getting a mild satiric workover. She had a sense of humor.

"How about Beth?" I said.

"*Touché*. I'm no 'Little Woman' am I? Then you're not all grim gristle. The mean streets personified."

"Real men don't move to Santa Barbara."

"Then the next step is investments, right? A good fund."

"I never play another man's game."

"You don't believe in The American Dream?"

"That depends on which American Dream."

"There's more than one?"

"Afraid so."

She watched me with the small smile of someone trying to figure out a new opponent. She was in her early forties, and had probably never looked better. A bouncy girl through high school and college who had taken time to find who she was and what she could be. Now she was in her element.

"You *are* a little grim, Daniel. You don't want to believe in Horatio Alger, do you? Personal success, wealth, happiness."

"You ever notice that Horatio never really made it on his own? Always had a lot of help and luck, got his big break from someone else's trouble?"

I wasn't saying what she wanted to hear, and her sense of humor was fading. She hadn't time for conversation that didn't go her way, but she was too much the saleswoman to show it.

"Well, if I can't sell you our fund, what can I sell you?"

"How about Lee Canton? What you know about him?"

I told her about Billy Owen and the death of Hector Jantarro and the attempt on Frank Owen's life. About the FBI man, and the others hovering around Billy Owen and Jantarro.

"What could any of that have to do with Leland?"

"They both worked for him. Maybe they were doing something in one of his enterprises behind his back."

"I suppose it's possible, but I know nothing about his work beyond our fund except that he's a solid, intelligent businessman and community leader, which is why we wanted him with us."

"What does he do in your fund?"

"He's invested, and acts as a representative."

"I thought you repped the fund up here."

She smiled that dazzling smile. "Yes and no, Daniel. I'm J. James & Company, but the fund is too large for one person to rep in an area as rich as this and still give everyone an opportunity."

"What exactly is the fund, Elizabeth?"

"The fund is the greatest opportunity to come along in decades. The fund will take your money and turn it into—" She stopped. "My God, Daniel, I'm giving you the pitch."

She laughed aloud. The beautiful tan, the bright eyes, and the lean face animated. She radiated a physical sexuality she should not have been wasting on me. Single women in her world save it for the rich, the elite, Give a few samples and a lot of decorative companionship until marriage. But there was something different about her. An independence that wanted to win on her own, make her own rules, run the game.

"Okay, the fund is a mutual that trades in the foreign currency exchange market. We get up to forty percent return, never less than thirty percent. Obviously, the more investors we have, the more we can use to trade large blocks, and the more money we all make. So we offer a small override to any investor who goes and sells more shares to other investors."

"Is that what Lee Canton is doing?"

"Leland has many friends in town. He's invested himself, has done very well I might add, and is offering his friends the opportunity to do the same."

"The Canton name can't hurt."

"It doesn't."

"You get a cut on what the investors sell to their friends?"

"Of course. We do have overhead, expenses, our profit."

"Nice deal."

"The deal, Daniel, is high-risk investments which Mr. James has an uncanny ability to make successfully, as his record shows. For that we get paid."

She was getting short, would get rid of me the moment anyone arrived or the phone rang. Lieutenant Holley was watching her for a reason. The fund was high risk, but she admitted that. They must be paying, or clients would be howling. The rich don't have much patience.

"Who belongs to that other desk?"

"Mr. James. He works in the Los Angeles office during the week, but he lives up here and comes in on weekends."

Then the telephone did ring. She faked a nice farewell smile, and there was no invitation from her eyes or anything else to come back or meet again.

I drove the easy back route along Cabrillo Boulevard to the Seabird Motel to avoid the evening rush hour.

The dusty red Porsche wasn't parked at unit fifteen.

In the office I wrote a note telling Frank Owen to call the Summerland house.

"He's checked out, sir."

"When?"

"About noon, I think."

"Any note for me? Dan Fortune?"

"No sir."

I took the freeway back to Montecito.

18

Dianne Owen had a small house at the end of San Ysidro Road where it becomes Eucalyptus Lane. Most of the ground floor was garage, and the railroad passed directly behind. Beyond the railroad were the elite houses on Miramar Beach. There was a full view of the sea and the islands from the upstairs living room.

She answered my ring from a call box, "Come up, Dan."

The dining room, kitchen, and study took up the ground floor. Photographs of Dianne and Frank Owen covered one wall of the study through the open door, with shots of her stage roles, business posters and awards on the other walls. In the upstairs living room, with the view and the Danish modern furniture, two men, one on the couch, the other at the street window, watched me come up. Dianne sat on the edge of a teak chair.

"They're from the FBI, Dan," she said.

"For the State Department," the one on the couch said. "A favor, Dan, right? Nothing official."

He was large and overweight, with an imperial beard and a slouch hat. The other was smaller, slimmer, and silent at the window. They both wore suits and ties, neither smiled.

"They know where Billy is," Dianne said.

"Where is he?"

The window one said, "You don't need to know, Fortune."

"The fewer who know, the better," Beard said. "But since State feels you, Miss Owen, and his brother are endangering him, we're authorized to tell you this much—he's working top secret for State, they want you to stop looking right now."

"You two have I.D., of course."

"Of course," Beard said, showed me his badgeholder and paper-work. It looked authentic. I'd expected it would.

"How do we check with State about Billy Owen?"

The one at the window said, "You don't."

"You'll have to take our word, Dan," Beard said.

"If we don't?"

Window turned to look. "You a radical, or just a comic?"

"Okay, Walt," Beard said. "For the good of the country, Dan. I mean, we have our job, right?"

"So do I. What do you know about Hector Jantarro."

"Who?" Window said.

"Look, Dan," Beard said. He'd started to shift around on the couch. It's hard for a man of his bulk to get comfortable on Danish modern. "Your job was working for Miss Owen there, right? Now it's finished, right?"

"Dianne? Am I still working for you?"

All this time she hadn't moved an inch where she sat staring at them and at me. She'd never been this close to real federal muscle before. Now she blinked, startled, and then nodded.

"I guess so, Dan. I mean, whatever you think."

"Jantarro," I said to Beard. "And don't say 'who?' I've talked to enough people to know you two have been making the rounds of any-one who knew Billy Owen or Jantarro."

Window said, "Look, asshole, if we have to we can—!"

"Shut up, Walt." Beard had rank, but I was glad this wasn't Central America where rank can't always hold the mindless back. "We heard about Jantarro, Dan. The man was a drunk who had an accident. A coincidence, that's all."

Window said, "People have accidents all the time, Fortune."

Beard looked like he wished Window would disappear. Superpatriots don't usually have much imagination.

"It was just a coincidence Billy knew Jantarro, got him the job at Canton?"

"That's all," Beard said.

"A wetback from Mexico who fell over his own cliff? No part of Owen's new job for State. The one that's so vital to the nation we have to stop looking for Billy."

"No." Even Beard was sounding embarassed.

"Hey, Fortune. Jantarro never worked with Owen," Window cleared it all up. "Just a bum and hanger-on."

"Hey," I said. "That clears it all up. We stop looking for Billy, forget Jantarro, and go home. That it?"

"Not quite," Beard said.

Dianne said, "They don't know where Frank is. He's checked out of the Seabird."

Her voice told me she knew more about Frank Owen's whereabouts. He wouldn't be in the house, they would have looked.

"You know where he is, Dan?" Beard asked.

"I talked to him at the Seabird this morning. That's it."

Beard heaved himself up. "Okay, Dan, Miss Owen. If you see him or he calls, have him call us at this number." He gave her a blank card with a phone number on it. "We appreciate your help."

He smiled at us as he went down the stairs. Walt the Window gave us the long hard look. He would have been funny, except he had a gun under the neat suit, was as lethal as a jumpy sixteen-year-old guerrilla in Beirut.

I waited until I heard their car go. "Where is he, Dianne?"

"Gone." She shivered where she sat on the narrow chair. "My God, they frighten me. The neat suits, the polite manners, but they never smile, look at you like you're a cockroach. They listen, but you never know what they hear."

"They should scare you. In this case they're also lying."

"About Billy?"

"About themselves. I already met one FBI man. It doesn't figure there'd be two FBI teams on this small a case not aware of each other." I told her about the man at the Seabird Motel.

"Then who are they?"

"My guess is CIA. I think Billy and Jantarro both worked with the Company in Florida and in Central America."

"Billy *is* on some top secret job?"

"Maybe," I said. "Where is Frank, Dianne?"

"I don't know." She stood up. She was wearing a stylish purple jump suit with a wide white belt. It didn't suit her. She searched the pockets for a cigarette, lit it, walked to the picture window overlooking the railroad and the beach houses and the sea beyond. "He was here today."

"What did he say?"

"He was angry at me for hiring you, told me to pay you off." She left the window and the sea, sat on the couch where the big fake FBI man had been. "He stayed all afternoon. Just the two of us, making love, it was always good." She ran her hands down the legs of the purple jump suit. "I'm different, but I'm not different enough. I have a career. At first men are attracted to that. To my knowing what I want and doing it, succeeding at it, taking care of myself. Then, if I stay independent, keep moving ahead in what I do, they feel threatened because I'm doing better than they are. I know who I am, what I can do, more than they do, and they can't hack that."

I said. "The only way most men ever get to feel important and superior is by believing that being male makes us superior."

Out at sea the oil rigs looked like a flotilla of aircraft carriers sailing into battle. She seemed to watch them, maybe seeing all those male sailors who would always think they were superior to any woman.

"Then there's the other side. I show vulnerability, a need for security and dependability, and they freak out. They have to run before we turn them into *castrati* with fat hips and high voices. That was Frank's favorite phrase when we'd fight over my asking him to stay with me when he wanted to roam or climb a mountain, or when I asked him to take me with him. 'You want a goddamn soprano,' he'd yell, 'a *castrato!* '"

She waved the cigarette in the air. "Then he comes around, we're together in bed, and, *voila*, it's fine. It's great. The way it was in the beginning. Why does it start so well and end so wrong? Because we both lie? Men want it to be always a one night stand? Women hide whatever else they need as a person?"

"Maybe as good an answer as any," I said.

She stubbed the cigarette in a heavy blue ceramic ashtray on the coffee table, stood and walked the room.

"When I was a girl it was made very clear by my parents, school, movies, books, that a boy's dreams would be about his vision of himself, what he was going to do and be. A girl would dream of a home and family of her own. A boy is supposed to dream of adventure. A girl is supposed to dream of a man."

"You don't think boys dream of girls?"

"They dream of having a girl, of fucking. Even if a man does dream of a wife and family, it's only as a part of his life, and the less important part, and he's done his full share in the family by working. When a woman gets married, that's it, *finis*. Even a career doesn't really change that. For a man it's barely a stop on the way to real goals."

"Isn't it better now?"

"For the majority of us there's still no middle ground. You're independent with an identity of your own, or you love and marry. One or the other." She left the window, sat again on the teak chair. "Frank married me because I was 'different.' What he meant by different was that I had a a life of my own, I was like a man. When I turned out to be a woman too, that's when it fell apart."

She searched the jump suit for another cigarette, waved the match. "Frank, his friends, Billy, their idea of leisure time was a kind of orgy without sex. Fun was cruising and boozing, stoning and snorting, raising a 'ruckus' as one of the more rednecked put it when an owner or a neighbor told them to quiet down. Their girlfriends, wives, dates—there never seemed to be much difference—either took care of everything outside the guy's work, or had two-bit clerical or menial jobs. They drank and snorted too, took up aerobics because they were alone so much, seemed to have babies to fill the void left by their men."

Her eyes were unbelieving. "Those women had all gone from one lousy relationship to another. But what got me was none of them could make a life of her own, only through a man. That's when I knew I had to end it before I became like them."

"Yet when Frank comes around, you want him."

"When he comes around I want him. The way he could be. As he really is if he could break out of himself, break the cycle of the past, break from Billy and his ghosts."

"Did you tell him that?"

"Not in so many words, but he knows."

We both let that hang in the room. She was right. Frank Owen knew she was there for him, and knew what he had to do.

"Where's he gone, Dianne?"

"He had a call from Billy. That's all he'd tell me. From somewhere out of town. Billy is okay, wanted to see Frank."

"Nothing about why he ran off?"

"Frank didn't tell me anything. Just that Billy was okay, and I had to call you off. He said you only made things worse. You're a professional detective, you'd scare Billy and anyone he was involved with. He said a man tried to kill him, he thinks it was because he was with you."

"Are you going to call me off?"

"What else can I do? Frank's gone. If Billy is really working for the government—?"

"The CIA is involved, but they wouldn't do anything as crude as that truck trying to kill Frank. Someone else. Mercenaries, drugs, Jantarro, or trouble we don't even know about. Maybe now, maybe from the past."

She put out her cigarette. "I don't know where he's gone. What could you do now, anyway?"

I stood up. "I'll send you a bill."

"I'm sorry, Dan."

On my way out I passed the wall of photographs in the study of their wedding and life together.

Kay and I went to work to fix up the back bedroom in our Summerland *hacienda* for my office—framed certificates, photos with New York and national brass, testimonials. Everyone has to impress the clients.

We went to the beach, made love, talked about the foul New York weather. To keep my mind from reaching back to the city I'd lived in all my life. There is adjustment in everything new and different. In the end, it was the city that reached out for me.

Dianne Owen called three weeks later. Frank had found Billy, and lost him.

"Where?"

"In New York, Dan. He wants help."

NEW YORK

19

The first lights of evening came on in Rockaway as the great jet shuddered and settled over Jamaica Bay. The long breakwater of Breezy Point curved out to the open Atlantic. As a boy, before my father vanished, we'd fished down there. From the two piers at Breezy Point for fluke, off the breakwater for striped bass, out in rowboats in the riptides of the bay. We'd caught a lot of fish before he caught the guy with my mother and they kicked him off the police force and his only answer was to run.

I'd hated him and loved him and understood him, and loved my mother and hated her and only now was beginning to understand her. It's not easy to be the wife of a tough cop whose duty is his life, and her answer was the only one her society had taught her. Rockaway and the Jacob Riis Bridge below, and Billy Owen, brought it all back. The woman who had stayed with me, and the man who had run for the far hills.

The taxi took me around Brooklyn and through the Battery Tunnel to the hotel where Frank Owen had found Billy and lost him and now waited for me. A warm May night in the city that would always be my closest thing to home. That says a lot about the end of the twentieth century. Less than two hundred years from a planet of villages where few people moved ten miles from their birthplace, to a world of the rootless and global. I felt the streets and towering walls, the mass of unknown lives, the lure of success. It's a narrow success. The city a creation of man so we can feel important, huddled and safe even when afraid of ourselves. A paradox of fear and safety, the city. A paradox solved by suburbs, gates, patrols, and barriers.

It was a small hotel in The Village, The Tudor Arms. From the immaculate lobby, the clerk called up.

"Third floor to the right. Room 32."

The four-person elevator still had a telescoping metal grid inner door, creaked its way up. An old but elegant hotel, small and discreet, unknown to tourists, a secret kept jealously by the lucky few who returned time after time. I'd stashed a defense witness here once. Captain Pearce hadn't even considered checking it out. No noises reached the bright green and gilt corridor, my feet made no sound on the dark green carpeting. The door of Room 32 opened before I could knock.

"How could Billy afford this—"

Frank Owen sat in a high-backed chair in the center of the large, dim room, a single light behind him. He faced me but said nothing. He couldn't. He was tied to the chair, hands behind him, feet together, upright, his eyes closed, blood all over his face and bare chest.

"He's alive."

The voice came from behind the door. Whoever it was had opened it the way an anxious Frank Owen would have. And he held a large revolver pointed in my-general direction. "Probably a strong sedative after they worked him over. He's breathing okay."

It was the bantamweight with the shoulders of a middleweight and the face of an accountant who'd pretended to be an old friend of Billy Owen's at the Seabird Motel. This time his eyes were less neutral behind his hornrimmed glasses, and his voice had some color. He even moved with more honesty, the big revolver announcing pretty clearly who he really was. "You better sit down, Fortune."

"He needs a doctor."

"He'll keep, we have to talk. You figured out who I am?"

"What you are," I said. "Not who."

"Alan Cox." He showed me the badge and papers. "I work out of the Washington office. Go on, sit down. I'll make it fast."

I sat in a large brocade armchair in front of the old-fashioned high windows and heavy green-and-gold drapes someone had taken the precaution of drawing tight to make the room virtually sound proof.

"What's your interest in Billy Owen?"

He shook his head. "First I ask the questions."

On the edge of the king-sized bed facing me, he was a different man—quiet, serious, efficient. The actor was gone. Instead, I had a cop who didn't like what he was seeing. That's how it looked, anyway.

"What were Owen and Jantarro working on?"

"Were they working on something?" I said.

"That's what I'm asking you."

In the center of the room, Frank Owen moved in the chair, groaned in pain. Cox blinked but didn't look at Owen. His voice didn't change.

"Come on, Fortune, I'm on your side."

"Then you know more than I do."

He thought about that. "Tell me what you do know."

If he knew as much about me as he seemed to, he probably knew most of what I could tell him. What I needed was to find out what I didn't know, and honesty might lull him into telling me something.

Frank Owen's groans of pain were sharper as the drug wore off. I told him all that had happened in Santa Barbara since I'd seen him in Frank's room at the Seabird.

"Mexico?" he said. "Jantarro was going to Mexico with money?"

"That's what I've been told."

"Money from what?"

"I guess that's the big question."

The FBI's interest in two apparent nobodies had to mean they were somebodies. Unless it was Cox's private interest. Drugs corrupt all the way, top to bottom. Not drugs, the money. The unimaginable profits that turn a pauper into a king in weeks. A temptation so powerful a navy admiral had said there was no way the navy, army or marines could stop the traffic as long as the market for it was so strong. No one was immune, from rich to poor, general to guerrilla. It takes money to run revolutions as well as armies.

Frank Owen jerked against his ropes in the high chair as if coming out of a nightmare. He screamed with some sharp pain. His eyelids fluttered, tried to open and stay closed at the same time. Cox showed no expression, but there was anger in his eyes.

"That's how I found him," he said. "Someone else was here too. Not the people who did that, someone else."

"How do you know?"

The anger on his face seemed to deepen. "I've seen a lot of beatings, Fortune. It takes time for blood to darken, wounds to stop flowing, drugs to take effect. When I left the elevator, I saw the stairs door close. I ran and checked. Someone was going down. Fast. When I got here the door was open and he was unconscious, his blood was dry. And, believe me, this wasn't the work of one person."

"Someone else could have gone down before you got here."

"No. The people who did this wouldn't have been scared off. They'd have wanted to talk to anyone who came here." Another sharp cry, a blind thrashing against the constricting ropes. Frank's eyes were just opening. "This was questioning, Fortune. A mild little beating, not a real workover to teach him a lesson, warn his friends. They'd have been glad to 'talk' to me also. No, whoever ran out just before I got here was someone else. Any ideas?"

Anyone looking for Billy Owen, from Dianne Owen to the Santa Barbara Police. But I didn't say that. I said, "How do I know there was anyone? Maybe you did the 'questioning' with some friends, waited for anyone who might come. Feeding me a cock-and-bull yarn all the way."

Cox stood. "I guess you don't." He reached into his jacket pocket, took out the SIG-Sauer P-230 I'd seen in Frank Owen's suitcase at the Seabird Motel. "It was under the chair, didn't do him much good. You better get him to a hospital."

The big revolver stayed on me as he backed to the door and out. An FBI man wouldn't use a pistol on me—if he was acting as an FBI man. I gave him a full minute, then checked the corridor. It was empty. I called the desk, told them to get the paramedics and the police.

20

"Stay in California, okay?" Lieutenant Marx said. "Christ, we haven't had blood spilled at The Tudor Arms since Boss Tweed."

"The criminals are getting classier," I said. "Or a better class of people are going into crime."

We were outside the emergency room at St. Vincent's Hospital. They were still working on Frank Owen. The first report had been broken ribs, cuts, bruises, heavy sedation. They were looking now for internal injuries.

"Both," Marx said. "You think this Billy Owen killed that guy in California, is hiding out?"

"He's missing. I don't know why. I'm still not sure what the hell's true about Billy, or Frank, or any of them. The FBI and CIA are in it, but doing what? It could be as simple as this Hector Jantarro was a refugee being watched by the FBI and CIA, he had an accident, they want to be sure, and Billy Owen has nothing to do with it."

"So why'd he do a rabbit?"

"Maybe his wife's right, he's just off on a spree. It's his history. Wild oats and fancy free."

"Everyone else is making a mistake?"

"Everyone else is just being careful."

"Including that redneck who tried to run Frank Owen down?"

The doctor came out, gave us the final report. Frank Owen had four cracked ribs, a broken nose, one finger broken and three with torn ligaments, bruises and abrasions, cigarette burns on his arms. No internal injuries, nothing serious. He would be in the hospital two to three days, we could talk to him when his sedation wore off, probably tomorrow.

"What are you going to do, Dan?"

"Look for Billy Owen."

"We'll put the word out on him, try the FBI. They talk to us sometimes. The CIA doesn't operate inside the States, right? With them we'll get *nada*."

I went back to The Tudor Arms, found that the room was paid up for another three days, unpacked my bag, got on the telephone. It had been six months, and turnover is rapid in the underbelly of any city, but my sources of information who weren't dead, in jail, or on the run somewhere else, would look for Billy Owen. If a man is hiding, he is a stranger where he is, and sooner or later someone will notice and report him for a price. The higher the price, the sooner the report.

It was 3:00 A.M. by now. I got a beer from the pay bar in the room, called Kay. She answered at once.

"It's 3:00 A.M. there. Are you all right?"

"It's midnight there. What are you doing up?"

"Waiting for you to call, you bastard."

"I'm fine," I said. "I'm glad you waited up."

"I'm glad you're fine."

"I miss you. The city's not the same."

"Good. How's Frank?"

I told her that Frank Owen wasn't fine, but was okay, asked her to call Dianne, Nina, and everyone else in the case to make sure they were in town. After that we chatted, I finished my beer, then let her go so we could both get some sleep.

I slept past noon, went down to look at my old building. It was still a burned-out shell, but a sign was up announcing the imminent erection of a luxury high-rise in resurgent Chelsea. If I did decide to come back, there would be no place for me in the building. I did the rounds of the Chelsea and Village saloons. By late afternoon I had a sidewalk seat at The White Horse Tavern, watched the career girls coming home. The surge of life that is five o'clock in a great city. It's something you don't have in the peace and open spaces outside the city, and I missed it, but you have distance and air and a vast sky and I was already missing that. Sometimes I think we're too adaptable.

At St. Vincent's, Frank Owen was awake and more or less alert. His nose was cut and swollen, his left hand was bandaged and splinted, he had bruises all over his neck and chest. Yellow instead of brown, the weather creases on his rugged face looked more like wrinkles. His long dark blond hair was stringy. In the hospital gown he looked smaller, showed every one of his forty-six years.

"You okay?"

"So I'm told."

He made a face. I could tell it hurt him just to talk.

"Who were they?"

"Thanks."

"Thanks?"

"For assuming there had to be more than one."

"I had an expert opinion." I told him about the FBI man, Cox. "Was he one of them? The boss, maybe?"

"They were on me so fast I never really saw them." He shifted in the bed to get comfortable, winced, took shallow breaths. "Two of them. One big, one not so big. Funny, it was the smaller guy who did the hitting. They wanted to know where Billy had gone."

"Where Billy 'had gone'? Not where he was, where he 'had gone'?"

"That's what they said."

"Did the big one have a beard? An imperial, maybe?"

"He could have had. I tried to explain who I was, but they didn't believe me."

"They believed you. They just wanted to make sure."

"I passed out fast. I'm not as tough as I thought I was."

"Few people are."

"They used the cigarettes to wake me up."

He shivered in the bed, instantly caught his breath and let out a small grunt.

"You feel up to talking about it from the beginning?"

He nodded, grimaced in pain. "Billy called a buddy in Santa Barbara, got where I was, called me. He said he was fine, but wanted to talk, so I flew east."

21

Frank finds Billy installed at the Tudor Arms, wants to know why Billy didn't wait for him in Santa Barbara, what the hell he's up to, how he can afford such a hotel?

"Top-secret, big brother," Billy laughs. "Hush-hush and all that. Don't ask, right?"

Frank sits in the elegant room with its well-stocked bar refrigerator. Billy perches cross-legged on the big, extra-high, extra-soft king-sized brass bed, grins like a kid with a gallon of stolen ice cream to share.

"What did you want to talk to me about, Billy?"

"Hey, relax and enjoy. It's fat city. Everything paid, expense account, anything old Billy and his big brother want."

Frank looks at Billy rocking back and forth on the bed like a puppet, his grin almost rigid.

"You were in a bind in Santa Barbara, needed money. What happened?"

"Sorry about that, Frankie. That's why I called you to come talk. I knew you'd be worried. I kind of panicked on that one, but it all came out roses. I'm having a ball, want to share it with my favorite brother. The Big Apple! Girls!"

"What came out roses, Billy? Make sense or I'm on the next flight out. You're so uptight I can hear your asshole squeak."

"Okay, okay."

Billy is off the bed, gets a beer for each of them from the bar refrigerator, sprawls in one of the gilt-and-brocade green chairs like an infantryman in a captured mansion.

"I owed a guy some bucks in Santa Barbara, you know me. Nothing big, but I was broke, so sent that letter to you. But—"

"What guy, Billy? What kind of bucks?"

"I was in a poker game, lost a couple of hundred, didn't want Nina to know. Then, shazzam, this big top-secret job turned up after I wrote you. I paid the guy, came east, and forgot to call you off."

"What job? Why didn't you tell Nina? You just walked out on your boss? Can you give it to me straight, for God's sake?"

Billy laughs, more relaxed now that he's talking. "You know I go for drama, Frankie. A born ham. Okay, I can't tell you much, and I couldn't tell Nina or Mr. Canton, because it's a job for my old company, understand?"

Frank studies his brother. "You're saying you're working for the CIA?"

"The government anyway. It was supposed to take two weeks at most, everyone would say old Billy was just off on a spree somewhere, right? Hell, Nina doesn't give a damn if I'm gone, and maybe I wouldn't even need that rotten job at Canton any more. I mean, maybe I was on my way to the big stuff this time."

In the elegant hotel room, drinking a bottle of beer with his brother sprawled in a brocade chair, Frank doesn't know what to believe. There is an aura of unreality, of some desperate illusion or delusion. Yet, Billy is in a hotel he could never afford on his own. He is in New York. He has money. What he has told Frank fits the facts, has its own logic.

"What about Jantarro?"

"Hector?" Billy looks at Frank. "What about Hector?"

Frank tells Billy about Jantarro. "He disappeared the same time you did. They found him dead a week later."

"Oh, Christ!" Billy sits up in the elegant chair, holds his beer between his knees, head down. "Poor Hector. They're sure it was an accident, Frank?"

"The police seem to be," Frank says. "You didn't know about it, Billy? It looks like you were still in town when he died. He was your friend. You both worked in Central America, right? In Florida? Maybe you were working on something up here?"

"I got him the job at Canton, Frank. We had some beers, that's all. What a rotten accident. Did they bury him and all?"

"His family came and took the body back to Mexico."

"Poor old Hector. He never made it much." Then he shrugs, smiles that rigid smile. "I guess we all got to go. No sense missing out on the fun. You ready to howl, big brother?"

"That's it? Jantarro fell over the cliff, and you got a hush-hush CIA job? That's the whole thing?"

"What else? Hey, come on, we got some balling to do."

Frank says, "You know a guy named Murch Calhoun, Billy?"

"Murch? Christ, no. Calhoun? Sounds like a cracker."

"He was an Okie."

"Was?"

Frank tells about the pickup attack on him. He thinks Billy goes pale, but all Billy says is, "Hey, he must have been some crazy I met around the bars. Some nut on a speed trip."

"He imitated you. Had you down good."

"Hell, I crawled a lot of bars in S.B., right? I pulled that Russki act a lot of places."

"But why would he attack me?"

"How do I know? You think I know why every crazy in Santa Barbara goes over the edge? Christ, you want to have some fun or not?"

Frank feels cold deep inside where he doesn't really want to look, knows something is very wrong, but Billy will say nothing more. They go out cruising the bars and coffee shops and clubs of The Village and Chelsea and NoHo. It is a strange night on the town. Billy is manic. They move rapidly from bar to club to cafe, hopping in and out of taxis, running along dark streets with Billy whooping like an Indian as he drinks more and more. They talk to women, but Billy makes no real attempt to be serious, no offer to settle on one or the other, take them to the hotel room, and after the last bar they go home alone and Billy falls asleep instantly with his clothes still on while Frank watches him uneasily as he undresses.

This goes on for a week. They spend all day in the hotel room doing lines, drinking beer, blowing pot. They have their meals sent up, watch television, and then go on Billy's aimless cruising at night. Billy never stops talking, mostly about the past, his and theirs. His view of their shared past seems to be in a kind of fun house mirror, through a flawed lens. Frank recognizes most of the facts, but it is all distorted, blown up, twisted. He wonders if the stories of Billy's private past are as twisted and distorted.

"Once we was running guns to the Contras and our pilot was so stoned we landed ten miles short in Honduras and the Honduran troops thought we were a Sandinista invasion . . . We blew away a whole Sandinista company on one merc raid I was with . . . Down in Florida I got to know the big drug kings. Hell, some of them were the same guys commanded the mercs, supplied the Contras . . . Hector and me used to fly whole planeloads of guns from Florida to Costa Rica, stop on the way at an airbase in El Salvador . . . I been all over those countries. We got almost as many Yanks down there as we got Cubans, old Somoza guardsmen, and Colombian drug dealers in Florida."

Talk and eat and snort. Drink and eat and talk.

"This job," Frank says on the seventh day they are lying around the hotel room, "when the hell do you work at it?"

"It's on hold right now. I got here ready to go, then something blew up somewhere. You know how that is, hurry up and wait, right? It ought to get off the ground any day. Hey, we're having fun, right? A ball and all free."

But Frank is getting tired and bored. He is also worried. He tries to get Billy to go out in the day. Billy tells him to go out alone. He does, but then Billy becomes depressed, and won't even go out at night. Frank finds Billy on the phone a lot. As time goes on, they go out to the smaller bars and restaurants, walk only in the back streets. Billy begins to disappear at odd times during the day, and when Frank asks him where he goes, he says it is the start of the job. But days pass and Billy still sleeps in the room. At night he never takes the first taxi that passes.

"What the hell is it, Billy?"

"The job, big brother. I never said it didn't make me nervous."

They are in the Lion's Pub near Sheridan Square, over two weeks after Frank arrived in New York. Billy has been quiet all day, they have let two taxis pass.

"I'm always nervous, Frankie." He smiles that rigid smile again. "It's funny, I wanted to be in battle. I used to envy you, and then you'd say how lousy it all was, and I figured you didn't have any guts. I wanted to test myself, prove I was brave. I wanted to be a hero, a real man. Only I never found out. I went down there to fight, but I don't speak Spanish, and I'd never been in combat, and I wasn't really trained, so all they let me do was ride along and help load and unload. I had a gun, but I never did fire it except at targets, beer cans, empty huts. I spent most of my time in Florida."

"What about now?"

"Now? Oh, the job. It's not real dangerous."

And Billy changes the subject, calls for a new round. It's the last time they talk. Next morning, Billy is gone. With all his things. Without a word.

22

"I called Dianne. I mean, something was wrong. I didn't believe the government job. Billy was scared, really scared, and I was in over my head. New York is your town, you could find him again. So I called, then circled the bars we'd cruised hoping I'd spot him, and then those two were waiting when I got back."

"Waiting? They were in the room?"

He nodded, let out that involuntary grunt of pain, almost fainted. The talking had worn him down, his drained face was ten years older than forty-six.

The nurse came in and threw me out. I walked to The Tudor Arms through the quiet Village streets in the city heat that comes out of all the brick and stone and concrete. No trees blew here on an ocean breeze. I walked in a strange limbo between the familiar and the oddly new, and thought about the two men who had beaten and questioned Frank Owen. They had to be the two in Dianne Owen's house who had wanted us to stop looking for Billy Owen. The two phony FBI men.

At the hotel I walked up the fire stairs in case they were waiting for me too. They were.

The one named Walt leaned against the corridor wall this time. He watched the elevator. The thick carpeting was soundless, he didn't sense me until I was halfway from the stairway door. He turned in a crouch, hand moving to his side. I held my old cannon straight out and steady on his chest.

"With one arm," I said, "I had to practice a hell of a lot."

He had mastered an expressionless sneer of intimidation. It goes with the job. But his hand stopped moving toward his belt.

"You won't shoot, Fortune."

"No, but you can't be sure, right? Get that gun out and I might have to."

The big one with the beard appeared in the room doorway.

"Put it down, Mr. Fortune. We're here to talk."

"You talked to Frank Owen," I said. "I'll keep the gun out."

A third man stood behind Beard. Alan Cox of the FBI again.

"It's okay, Fortune, I'm here too."

"Why don't I find that totally reassuring?"

Cox laughed. "With these two stormtroopers, I understand. But believe it or not, you and I really are on the same side."

The scenario suddenly clicked. They *were* CIA, and it was FBI vs. CIA. I dropped my cannon back into my jacket pocket. I'd been wrong before, but you have to trust your judgment. Inside the room the bearded CIA man took the high-backed chair. I sat on the bed with my back to the wall so I could see them all. Cox flopped in an armchair. The one named Walt leaned against the door. I had a vision of his whole life—leaning against walls and doors looking menacing. Sort of like a trained Doberman.

"The big fellow there with the elegant imperial is Mr. Bruce McIver," Cox said. "Our watchdog is Walter Enz. Heavy Langley artillery for one third-rate self-styled mercenary."

"How did you know we were waiting?" the bearded McIver said.

"Frank Owen told me."

Walter Enz said, "Shit. He never got a good look at us."

"You were in this room waiting for him," I said. "You didn't ask him where Billy was, but where Billy had gone. You knew Billy had been holed up here, you had a key. Who else could you be? You still have a key, you know what I'm doing, and if you didn't find Billy you'd be around. I just played it by ear."

"That's smart," McIver said. "We could use you."

"You wouldn't like what I think," I said. "And I don't like what you do."

"You don't like your country, Fortune?" Walt at the door said. He had muscles in his voice, was ready to beat the shit out of anyone who didn't love the country.

I said, "Ambrose Bierce wrote that a patriot is someone who forever defends the part against the whole. Einstein said that nationalism is an infantile disease, the measles of mankind. I forget who said patriotism was the last refuge of a scoundrel. I don't like patriotism that thinks the whole world and everyone in it exists for its country's benefit, that subverts, kills and destroys other peoples to protect its interests, that beats up its own people like Frank Owen because the country has to be saved. Is that enough, or do you want me to go on?"

Walt the Door looked about ready to ask me to step outside. McIver just looked at me.

"Billy Owen called us, said Jantarro was dead, someone was after him. He was scared to death," McIver said. "We got him out of Santa Barbara, stashed him here. A couple of days ago he called us again, said he was afraid his brother had led them to him, wanted to be moved. Before we reached him he ran on his own. We couldn't be sure the brother wasn't a danger, we didn't know what the brother knew or what he was up to. We had to know if he could help us find Billy before someone else did."

"So you worked him over," I said. "Sure, what else do the secret police do? The mission first. The good of the nation. It makes no difference if the victim is a Cuban, a Chilean, or an American if they're in your way."

"Not our way, buddy," Walt said. "The country's way."

I turned on him. "Who the hell decides what that is? You? One guy in the White House basement? Some ex-general with private money? The President's personal opinions?"

"All right," McIver said. "We're not here to hold a debate. You don't like the CIA, Fortune. We probably don't think a whole lot of your views. But we do want to find Billy Owen and who's after him and why."

"Why?" I said. "From everything I've seen or heard, Billy Owen never did more than heave boxes of ammunition, fly around Central America in cargo planes, hang around gawking at narco-politicians, and shoot his mouth off about his adventures."

Cox said, "It's not exactly Owen, Fortune."

"No," I said. "It's Hector Jantarro. They had him hidden in Santa Barbara, even from the FBI, right? A phony name, a phony identity, and a phony job Billy Owen got for him. Someone want to tell me who he was, or do I guess on my own?"

They looked like the Politburo meeting on a nervous subject as they each waited for the other to talk first. Cox the FBI man was the most relaxed, just grinned and waited. Walt at the door looked at McIver. The senior CIA man realized he couldn't let Walt give the CIA version.

"Hernan Javier," McIver said, "an officer in the Salvador police. He worked with us against the Marxists out to destabilize the government down there, was one of the first to blow the whistle on Cuban and Nicaraguan infiltration. He believed in a free El Salvador, fought the Marxists hard. When the compromise government of Duarte was put in, the damn liberals forced Hernan out, tried to put him in jail. He was too good to lose, knew too much about the Reds in Salvador and Nicaragua. We got him to Florida, put him on our payroll, and he went on working for us. But rebel and Sandinista agents almost got to him a couple of times. We take care of our friends, hid him in Santa Barbara."

"But someone got to him anyway?"

"That's what we're working on, Fortune."

"Hernan Javier," Cox said. "George Washington and Joan of Arc rolled into one."

"Fuck off, Cox," Walt said from his door.

McIver said, "You have odd opinions for an FBI man, Cox."

"In the Justice Department we don't have opinions," Cox said. "But on Javier we're working with State. You want to hear State's version, Fortune? The real reason they hid him out?" He leaned forward in the chair. "He wasn't even from El Salvador. A guardsman kicked out of Nicaragua before Somoza. We think he already worked for CIA in Nicaragua, they got him the Salvador police job. He found a home with the Salvadoran right wing, served the landowners, the generals and himself. When Duarte took over, Javier was indicted for being a leader of death squads, for extortion and corruption. CIA got him out, maybe because he knew as much about them as he did about the rebels. He was still under indictment, State and Justice both wanted him sent back. We went after him. They kept a jump ahead of us, then hid him out, and I didn't locate him until he was dead."

The bearded McIver was up. "What the hell were you looking for? He worked for us. Who cares what else he did? He was useful. What side is State on? You probably got him killed."

"He was a corrupt, murderous son-of-a-bitch, McIver!"

"That's a matter of opinion, Cox!"

"No, it's a matter of principles, laws, sanity!"

"Shit," Walt said.

They glared at each other in a Mexican standoff of opinions.

I said, "So who killed him? Us, them, CIA or FBI? Is anyone telling it straight? Did Billy kill him? Maybe they were both really on some CIA job and it's all a coverup."

"Billy Owen was never more for us than a gofer," McIver said. "We had nothing going down with him or Javier."

"Come on, McIver," Cox said. "A man like Javier doesn't get killed over nothing. A man like Javier doesn't just hang around doing nothing. He's always got some angle, some scheme."

"The police are satisfied it was an accident, Cox."

I said, "The police will do what you want. For the good of the country. Isn't that what you told them? It's your case, top secret, international intrigue, not a local matter. They even let you grab the body, send a talkative mouth on vacation."

"They have absolutely no evidence it was anything but an accident," McIver said, "and neither do we. All we asked was their cooperation in keeping Javier's true identity secret."

"If you're sure it was just an accident, why hide Billy Owen?" I said.

Cox made a sound that was half laugh, half snort. McIver glared with eyes that would file Cox under uncooperative and unreliable for future CIA reference.

Walt said, "There's sure, and *sure*. We don't take chances."

"You always doubt, Fortune," McIver said. "In anything and everything. We can't afford a margin for error."

"Meaning you don't really know any more than the police," I said. "You could have told me that from the start and saved a lot of time. You said Billy Owen called you. Can you tell me when, from where, and exactly what he said?"

Walt said, "Why the fuck should we?"

"Because Frank Owen's your best bet to find Billy, and he isn't going to be cooperative after you put him in the hospital. Not even for the good of the country."

Walt came away from the door, "You know, Fortune—"

"Shut up, Walt," McIver said. "He called us from Santa Barbara. It was a Wednesday. Fifteen hundred hours Washington time. We went out, put him on a plane to New York, had him holed up in the Tudor Arms, and looked around out in Santa Barbara."

That would be the day he had mailed the letter to Frank.

"What did he say? You talked to him yourself?"

McIver nodded. "He was scared. He told us he'd found Javier dead at the bottom of that cliff. Only he called him Jantarro, he never did know Hernan's real name. He was sure it was enemy agents, and he was being watched too. We told him to sit tight, we'd be there in hours, and we were. Walt brought him to New York, I stayed in California to look around."

"You didn't report Jantarro's death to the police?"

"He was in deep cover, top secret. We had to know who'd gotten to him before we could reveal anything."

"Translation," Cox said. "Javier dead was no use to them, and a hell of an embarrassment if the whole shabby story got out. CIA was harboring a corrupt killer, in violation of U.S., not to mention international, law. They'd gotten him killed, brought their dirty war into the States where they have no mandate. A sweet mess, especially with the Bureau and State on the other side. Can you see the headlines? 'CIA Protects Murderer From FBI. Who Is In Charge In Washington? Dirty War Invades U.S.' "

Walt the Door refolded his arms.

McIver said, "Finished, Cox?"

"I haven't even started on this one, McIver."

They were at an impasse, law against necessity.

McIver talked to me. "As far as our people could tell without an autopsy, the fall killed Hernan. He wasn't in any operation, there was no sign of an operation against him."

"Just you and Cox screwing around," Walt said.

"We'd about decided Billy had made it all up when he called us and vanished. We still think he's playing soldier-of-fortune, but we've got to find him again and make certain."

Walt at his door was already certain. "He's a drunk cokehead never did a fucking thing."

"Unless he killed Javier himself," Cox suggested, "is conning everyone into thinking someone's after him."

"Hell, he never knew who Javier really was," Walt said.

Cox said, "He had to know Javier was *somebody*, and if he did kill him, you'd have to hush the whole thing up, right? Move the body out of the country, pay witnesses to get lost."

"Believe what you want, Cox," McIver said. "Right now, what we need is Billy Owen. Maybe—"

From the bed I listened and watched. None of them really cared how Hernan Javier, or Hector Jantarro, had died or why. He was of no importance now. Not to the CIA or the FBI. People and events were real only as far as they helped or hurt their goals. No good or bad, right or wrong, only what helped or hindered their job. Talleyrand, a French statesman of the late eighteenth century, said it when someone told him an action had been wrong—*It was worse than wrong, it was a mistake.*

I said, "Did Billy make up the pickup that tried to kill Frank Owen?"

"Pickup?" McIver turned from Cox to look hard at me.

"What pickup?" Walt came away from the door.

I told them what pickup.

"Murch Calhoun?" McIver looked at Walt. Walt shook his head. McIver turned back to me. "Describe him, Fortune."

I described the dead driver. They did their eye-to-eye act.

"We better check it out," McIver said.

Walt opened the door. McIver stopped to look back, toss a card at me.

"You don't like us, and that's fine. But if you find Billy Owen, that's where you call us."

"Sure," I said.

"We're not playing, Fortune."

"I didn't think you were," I said.

They left the door open. Cox picked up the card for me. McIver's name, a phony company, and a New York telephone number.

"Sometimes," the FBI man said, "I think they'll be the end of us."

"Do we believe them? About Jantarro and Owen?"

"I couldn't find evidence of an operation in Santa Barbara," Cox said. "or anything Owen was doing except construction work."

"Did they know the pickup driver? Calhoun?"

"I'd say no. But I wouldn't put it past them. They'd do anything and everything they felt necessary, Fortune. Anywhere, to anyone, at any time." Cox took out a cigarette, offered me one. I shook my head. "Hernan Javier was more than a corrupt policeman. He was bodyguard to a politico charged by the U.S. government with stealing two million of U.S. aid money. The politician was a pal of Duarte's son, so the CIA got Javier to take the rap, then got him out of the country. That's why they didn't want State to blow the whistle. If they'd save someone who swiped two million U.S. dollars, they'd do anything."

He stood up, walked to the door. "Watch your back all the way."

23

The first call came while the windows and the walls outside were still gray.

"Fortune? Got your Billy. NoHo flop. Young, mustache, through from California. Marine jacket. Skinny blond."

"How long's he been there?"

"Two weeks plus."

"Too long."

The second call was another false alarm. A fugitive young male drinking alone for three days in an upper Westside bar. He had tattoos. The third was Kay. It came with the sun up and hot, and me on my way out for late breakfast or early lunch.

"Morning low clouds. I can't see the beach."

"I miss it and you."

"I'm here." She sounded in the room with me and distant at the same time. "You've got somewhere to come back to."

"I'm sorry I'm not there now."

"I'm glad. You want your report before we get maudlin?"

"I'd rather get maudlin, but go ahead."

Dianne Owen's office said she was in Los Angeles, at home her machine answered. Nina Owen had no telephone, when Kay went to the cottage Taffy was there but no one else. At Canton she hadn't been able to talk to Lee Canton or McElder. Both were always out, never returned her calls. The office wouldn't give home phone numbers, neither was in the phone book. Elizabeth Martin was in town, but she'd hire someone anyway. There was no way I was going to learn anything about the FBI, CIA, or police.

"I'll have to see what Frank can turn up to find Billy."

"Stay away from old flames."

"At my age they've all moved to Florida." We hung up.

The doctors insisted on keeping Frank Owen two more days, and I had nothing to do but wait for phone calls, and wander the city in a twilight zone between familiarity and distance that was like having dinner with an ex-wife. It was my city, always would be, but there was a sense of standing outside, seeing from a different angle.

Maybe that was why there were no more calls, false or otherwise. Nothing is shorter than the memory of a dark street nightrunner. If you're not here, they can't use you. If they can't use you, they don't owe you. If they don't owe you, you don't exist. Influence has the fastest rate of decay on earth, ends the instant you leave the office or cross the border. Out of sight is out of everything.

The second morning Frank Owen was up and waiting for the clothes I brought. Jeans, safari shirt, red *funiyoshi*-style briefs, white socks, all matching what the CIA had bloodied and the hospital wasn't going to wash. We all have our uniforms.

His finger was in a splint-cast. His cuts were stitched, his bruises purple, his nose swollen.

"CIA," I said. "They're sorry. But if you try to sue they'll deny they ever met you and prove you're a Sandinista agent too."

On our way to the hotel in the taxi, I gave him an account of my talk with Cox, McIver and Walt. He held the plastic sack of bloodied clothes and looked out the cab window.

"Billy didn't kill Jantarro, whoever the hell he was."

"You don't know that. No one does except Billy."

"Or the real killer. If there even was one."

At the hotel, the laundry service took his clothes while he called everyone who knew Billy whose number he had. There were a lot of them, Billy had rambled as much as Frank. After four hours he came up blank, left messages and the hotel number in case anyone thought of someone or somewhere else Billy might go for help or hiding.

Then we both waited for calls.

We had beer sent up, Frank cleaned the blood off his belt holster himself. I gave him his pistol back.

"How long have you carried that thing?"

"I've had it since the army. I don't usually carry it."

"Warn me when you do so I can get out of the way."

We drank the beer. Smoked.

"What's he doing, Fortune? What's really going on?"

"The CIA says he's playing the international mercenary. The FBI isn't sure. Jantarro/Javier was real, but is Billy? Is it a game he's made up—consciously, unconsciously or some of both—from the accidental death of a drunk lying low and involved in nothing, or was Javier/Jantarro in some kind of intrigue that got him killed and there really is someone out there after Billy?"

The acrid odor of his marijuana permeated the room.

"If it was an accident, Billy is crazy," Frank said. "If it was murder, Billy could be next."

"Not crazy," I said. "Living a fantasy, playing a role. We all do it. A psychotic lives in a world of one. The rest of us live in a more or less real world of others. A matter of degree. In our 'real' world we repress in the name of freedom, lie in the name of truth, make war in the name of peace. Everyone believes what they want to believe."

On the bed he smoked with his eyes closed. His ankles were crossed lazily in the cowboy boots, but there was a rigidity to his lean body on the elegant bed. One hand under his head, boots on, like a soldier in a captured palace resting between battles.

"Why, Fortune?"

I drank my beer. Outside the sun was hot in the afternoon city where millions of people moved in a chaos of noise. But the room was air-conditioned, and behind the closed windows the noise was distant.

"Maybe an imitation of you," I said. "The soldiering, the rambling, the marrying, the leaving and moving on. Everything except the war. That's what he's looking for. You've known this all along. You're afraid he's found his war."

He held the thin joint between his thumb and first finger. "I never glamorized, Fortune. I didn't see much action, and I told him that. Spent most of my time in Nam on staff in Saigon. I did my job, and I did it well. I didn't love it, but I did it. We're always going to have wars, always going to fight each other and kill each other. So a man learns to do the best he can without being too damned gung-ho about it, or too damned shocked and holier-than-thou. That's what I told Billy when I got back, but when you're eighteen it's not what you want to hear."

"And Billy never stopped being eighteen."

The roach burned his fingertips. He barely noticed, dragged deeply to get the last taste. "I got an education. It took a while, but I got it. If you want to do what you want to do when you want to do it, you have to pay your own way. Billy never did learn that. He never had a father, never grew up. I'd thought he was maybe getting it together. I hoped, I guess."

"Now?"

He finally crushed the last shred of the joint between his fingers, dropped it to the floor beside the bed. "Maybe he'll never grow up, or maybe he's grown up too fast."

I got another beer, sat back down on the ornate brocade chair in the fine old hotel room with the afternoon sun already behind the buildings outside the windows. The shadows come soon to New York.

"Is that what counts, Frank? Do what you want, when you want? Do as you damn well please?"

"That's where it starts." He got off the bed, took the plastic bag of cocaine, a thin square sheet of plastic, and a short straw from his backpack. He looked at me. I shook my head. He sat against the headboard of the bed, poured a line of the white powder on the plastic, snorted it up slowly through the straw.

"Nightherder and nightrider?" I said. "The midnight man?"

He sat with his eyes closed. "If that's what it takes to keep out of the cage, out of the zoo."

"Women want you in a cage, an exhibit in a zoo. Is that what you told Billy when he was a kid? Or did he just watch?"

He didn't open his eyes, but held his hand out, pantomimed drinking. I got another beer for each of us. When I gave him his, he opened his eyes, looked me over.

"You sure an arm's all you lost?"

"A castrato, Frank?"

He drank. "*Castrati*, so the world could have sopranos with power and stamina. Eunuchs for Turk and Chinese emperors. Safe and tractable. Men are crude, wild, violent, you have to tame them." Drank. "Cut off our balls to make us good husbands, fathers, providers, baby-sitters. The women and the society."

Cut another line, snorted it up, lay back, eyes to the ornate ceiling. "Women don't want the right to say no, they want the opportunity. As soon as a girl realizes she can do almost anything with almost any man as long as she'll fuck him regularly she has more power than any man ever will."

Sucked on his beer bottle. "What do women want. That's the number one male chauvinist question, right? But what the hell *do* women want, Fortune? I read a quote by some woman that says it straight out: 'What I like about love is there's this guy going crazy because of me.' That's what she wants, a guy crazy because of her.' Lit a cigarette. "Even then there's a catch. You've got to want her for everything *except* her cunt. She wants you to go crazy for her even if she didn't have a cunt, if she wasn't a woman. But the reason you want her is because she *is* a woman, has a cunt."

"She wants you to want her not only for her cunt."

He smoked. "That's when it gets tough. How does she tell? How can she be sure you want her for something besides sex unless she says no and you still hang around? If she fucks every day she can never be sure you want her for anything else, so she has to say no to prove to herself you want her for herself. Shit!"

"Do you want a woman for anything except sex, Frank?"

"Shit! Shit! Shit!" He smoked, waved. "How do I know? How does she? If she wasn't a woman I wouldn't want her. It's a dumb question, she *is* a woman." He stared at his feet on the bed in the boots. "We used to talk about it, Billy and me. When he was a kid, and later too. You have to have a woman, but men are more fun to be with. Men want the same, think the same, have the same dreams."

"How are women different?"

"Men want adventure, women want safety. Men want women, women want kids."

It was dark now. I turned on a lamp. Frank went to the john. I got two more beers. He laid a line of Big C on the plastic. I went to the john. The telephones were silent.

He took half the line. "Ever see *Man and Superman*? Bernard Shaw's play? The Life Force?" Closed his eyes, let it charge. "At first it's passion, only each other. The magic when you're meeting a couple of times a week, fucking every time, waiting to meet again." His arm with the bottle as automatic as a robot arm. "The magic goes. The house comes. The kids, the security. Even if they don't think they're going to be like that, they can't help it. Maybe it's got to be that way. The Life Force against the individual." Finished the line, stared at the walls as if they moved with his boots. "War of the sexes, the species goes marching on. She has to build the cave, pull it in, hatch the eggs. He has to roam, hot for another cunt. Lots of babies. Cavemen died like flies. One *him* had to spread it around. One *her* had to protect what she had. The Life Force."

Silent telephones.

I said, "Prehistory. Obsolete."

"Tell that to our genes."

I said, "Age cannot wither nor custom stale her infinite variety. *Antony and Cleopatra*. That's love."

"Never met her, Fortune. My luck."

"Different is a two-way street."

A great silence over the room and the city.

"Different is hard. Different doesn't live long. The world is too much with us. My Dad said that a long time ago."

24

Frank is nine years old when his father meets the woman. At the end of a day's ride over and across what years later will be world famous as The Ponderosa. To and from a high lake where native cutthroat still swim.

Buck Owen is a dark man with eyes that always seem amused but never smile at the same time as his mouth. It is the sensual mouth of a man who gives in often to indulgence. A generous man, an easy touch in the saloons and casinos of Reno and Tahoe. Reno and Tahoe suit him. Mountains suit him, and whitewater rivers. Horses suit him, and fishing rods, and fine hunting rifles. Anything a man can do alone or with casual companions and strangers that does not require him to think too far ahead or lay a groundwork for future actions, make plans, set goals.

His wife does not suit him, her views of what should and should not be. Buck Owen is not a man for shoulds and should nots. Through Eastern prep schools, Princeton University, he found no calling or career worth the effort of learning the required fundamentals, resisted all attempts to convince him of theories, enlist him in causes. He quoted Thomas Hardy to the effect that since life was "a brief passage through a sorry world," the only important cause was a free man, and told his new bride that he had decided on a literary career back in Nevada, where, after all, Mark Twain and Bret Harte had both started.

At nine, Frank is confused by his parents' marriage. He listens to their fights while he lies in bed, sees his father talk with so many other women, hears his father come home in the dawn light, watches his mother angrily turn the big house into exactly what she wants it to be where there is hardly a place for his father to sit. Later, he knows that his father, alone and isolated in Princeton, far from his rods and rifles, horses and hangouts, needed a woman, and his mother happened to be the one he fell in with who, at the time, wanted him. He also guesses, much later, that his mother would have none of what his father wanted without marriage, and learns that there were certain pressures from his grandmother and his other grandfather, both who saw the marriage as useful. At the time, when he asks his father why he doesn't like his mother, all his father says is, "You'll find out, son. I'm sorry."

Children do not suit Buck Owen. At nine, Frank is an only child, and until he was seven spent little time with his father. All those first seven years he lives essentially alone with his mother in the big house where the evidence of his father has been steadily expunged despite the fact that his father does indeed live there, appears and disappears constantly if irregularly. His father is clearly there, it is only any solid evidence of his father's presence that is missing, as if his father leaves no tracks, is all shadow without substance.

Children do not suit his father, but boys do, and when Frank is into his eighth year, without actually leaving his mother and the big house built in her image, he starts to live where his father lives. Where his father lives is in the saloons, the casinos, the lodges on his own and other men's lands. In the mountains and fast streams, on horses, in other bedrooms and on other women. At seven-going-on-eight Frank does not understand all this, but he sees it. Buck Owen is not a man to hide from a boy what a boy needs to know. Frank is now a companion, and will understand each fact as he needs it.

"When the boy's ready to see, he'll see," his father says to his other companions, male and female, smiles under the eyes that don't smile but are amused. "He'll know what he needs to know when he needs it."

Frank is nine when he and his father ride back from the day in the mountains. He becomes thirsty long before they reach town. His canteen is empty because it has been hotter than expected, and, being nine, he has drunk more than he should have. His father's canteen holds wine still cold from the last stream, of no use to a nine-year-old. It is The West, the big country, so they stop at the first ranch to ask for water.

"Come in," the woman says.

She is tall and dark, rich black hair in a braid, Indian cheekbones but pale skin, eyes that are neither wary nor open. Injured eyes.

"Perhaps the little man would prefer a Coca-Cola."

"Yes, ma'am!" Frank says.

The woman leads him across a large, rustic living room of leather and old wood toward the kitchen at the rear. Buck Owen still stands in the open doorway. The woman looks back.

"The kitchen is down the hallway," she says. "The soda is in the refrigerator. Take what you like."

Frank looks at his father.

"Go ahead, son. No more than two, so make them last."

His father still stands in the entrance, but he has closed the door. He has an expression on his face Frank has never seen. Almost scared. It is an expression Frank hates. He hurries into the large ranch kitchen with its curtains and flowers, gets his Coke, sits at the long kitchen table.

Outside they talk.

"He's a good boy, Mr. Owen. Would you like a soda too?"

"Something with more substance? How do you know me?"

"Everyone knows you. I'm afraid my husband locks up the liquor when he goes on a trip."

"Don't believe all you hear. I've got a decent Chardonnay in my canteen."

"That's sounds very good. I'd hoped I could believe all I've heard about you."

She laughs then. A low laugh that sends chills up Frank's spine where he sits in the kitchen with his Coke. He hates the talk. Hates the sound of them walking farther away, the clink of glasses that, in his house, always brings a violent tirade from his mother. But hates most the silence that comes while he is finishing his second Coke alone in the kitchen.

A silence in the all-but-empty ranch house through a third and a fourth Coke. Forbidden Cokes he knows they will not care about when the woman and his father finally return smiling to the kitchen. They are holding hands. They smile at him, the woman quiet and openly, his father with only his mouth as always, under eyes that are not amused anymore.

She walks them out to their horses in the fading summer dusk, raises her hand to hold his father's for a long second before they ride off back to town and Frank's mother.

For the rest of the summer, wherever his father takes him, the woman arrives also. Sooner or later, they disappear, leave him to amuse himself one way or the other. But there are also times when his father fishes, or swims, or rides in a race, or must perform some errand he has been sent on by Frank's mother. At these times Frank and the dark woman talk.

He learns that her name is Helen. That she is part Northern Ute, and part French, and part Norwegian.

"A mongrel of the western mountains," she says with her laugh. "A tough breed, Frankie, all of us. We do what we must, apologize to nobody."

She is married to an older man who owns the large ranch they live on and must travel often on business. He leaves her alone, this old man, shut up in the house, the liquor locked up and without money. She can buy while he is gone only where they have credit and the old man is well known.

"We grew up dirt poor, Frankie. My Daddy died in the copper mines. It's hard to be poor, but there are harder things."

Frank falls in love with her, and their talks, and his father's laugh when they are all together, and hates it when he has to go back to school. All that winter his father comes home late, comes home drunk in the afternoon, passes through the big house where he leaves little trace. Only his voice and his presence when he is there, an empty space when he is away.

Everything is as it has always been, and Frank waits for next summer, and Helen, and the time to ride the mountains.

Then everything is not the same.

His father sells the horses, the saddles. The mountain lakes go unvisited. Buck Owen appears in the house, sits in a large leather chair Frank's mother buys and establishes properly in front of the fire where a proper master should sit and rest from his patriarchal labors. All that summer and into the winter Buck Owen looms large in the house. At dinner, in his office that had been empty for years. Large and yet somehow smaller before ten-year-old Frank's confused eyes.

Into winter. Silent in the massive leather chair that holds him like a large hand in front of the comfortable fire in the safe fireplace. There but gone. A ghost.

Says once, "The world, it's too much with us, son."

Sits in the house where nothing is of him all summer and into winter. Then sits from noon to sunset of an early winter day above South Gorge, smokes a cigarette, and steps off into the river two hundred feet below.

His mother closes the now-meaningless house, leaves the useless town, goes down to the city she can understand to have the now-meaningless second son of Buck Owen. The son, Frank realizes later, that came out of Buck Owen's reappearance in the house where there was nothing of him, was intended to be his mother's final seal that bound Buck Owen into the living room chair in front of the comfortable fireplace.

The meaningless son, William Jr. as a final vindictiveness, who Frank tells later, "She'd found out about Helen and the rides and the meetings. About me being with them. I guess it was that sent her over the edge. She had dates, reports, even photos, threatened to expose them both, ruin Helen. Dad'd have to leave town with me and her, and if he wouldn't she'd take me away and fix it so he'd never see me again. She'd take the money, and Helen's old man would throw her out, and they'd have nothing."

Billy is seventeen. "He shouldn't of done it, Frank. He owed me at least. He shouldn't of killed himself."

"He probably didn't even know about you. He was alone, Billy. She was going to break him like a circus bear. Turn him into something he couldn't be. He had to do it."

"I never even saw him, Frank, never knew I had a father."

"Helen told me when I was back once. Her husband had died, she was rich, but she looked older than he did. I guess she never got over Dad, even came to the funeral back then."

Helen comes with her husband. The old man is important in the town, would be expected to be at Buck Owen's funeral. Frank is there with the family lawyer, but his mother is not. She has refused to look again at the man who has committed the final betrayal. Helen stops, touches Frank's tearful boy face. Her eyes are the same as on that first day.

"Sometimes dying is the easy way," she says, and turns away to look for a long time at the dead man in the open coffin.

Many years later she meets Frank again on one of his visits to the old town and tells him what really happened.

"He did what he had to, Billy," Frank says. "He came from a tough breed. He had to live on his own terms."

The brothers sit over their beers on the sunny California street a long way from Nevada and the South Gorge where Buck Owen had done what he had to do, left that to his sons.

25

The telephone didn't ring until ten o'clock the next morning.

"Owen? Mack Everton. Listen, I talked to Lars Broberg used to instruct weapons down Florida. He don't know Billy, but he got this call from a guy in New York, Dolph Calin, right? Dolph asks Lars if he knows how to get in touch with Charley Marion, and if Marion's still flying down to Costa Rica and Honduras. Now, Lars says Marion and Dolph was both down in Florida flying guns, they both know Billy, and Dolph's all settled in stocks and big bucks and got no use for flying anywhere with a wing-and-a-prayer flyboy like Charley. When Lars asks him what he wants Marion for, Dolph says it's a favor. So I puts two and two, figure Billy got to be the one Dolph's asking for."

On the extension, I said, "You have an address for this Charley Marion?"

"Who the hell is that?"

"Another friend," Frank Owen said.

"Well . . ." His hesitation said it wasn't proper international intrigue procedure, but in reality he was a car salesman now in Tempe, Arizona, had left his international days behind. "Okay. I don't have Marion's address, but I got Dolph's."

A large corner office on the thirty-third floor with Brooklyn out one angle, the Battery and the Hudson below out the other angle. A sense of standing at the end of a flagpole over absolute nothing. I had to touch the wall with my lone arm, hold on.

"Frank! Glad to know Billy's brother after all these years. Mr. Fortune. Sit down. Sit down."

He was a large man with gray hair, a trim body, and deep stress creases from his eyes to his jawbone. The photo of an aristocratic woman in front of a large fake Tudor house under big trees stood on his desk beside a ten-line telephone. The walls were packed with photos of a young Dolph Calin in uniform, in jungles, before heavily armed helicopters. An older Dolph in unmarked fatigues with more weight, darker hair, and less stress. In front of cargo planes, in different jungles, loading boxes under palm trees, with small dark men in uniforms, next to unarmed helicopters. An M-16 slung in the early photos, a big old .45 Colt holstered in the later shots. Smiling and laughing in all photos.

"So how is old Billy?"

"We came to ask you, Dolph," Frank said. "He's in trouble. I'm trying to find him."

"I wish I could help, Frank, but—"

"We talked to Mack Everton, who'd talked to Lars Broberg," Frank said. "You called Broberg to get an address on Charley Marion. It was for Billy, wasn't it? You've seen Billy."

He glanced out his high windows and down, something like surprise on his pale face as if he had expected to see jungle, scattered little dirt villages, not the buildings of New York, the broad Hudson. Then he looked at the wall of photos.

His glance roamed among the photos. "They'll blow it down there, but we tried hard then to save it all. The civilians got in, we didn't get backed, the whole region's going to slip away." His gaze fixed on a photo of two big armed men in camouflage fatigues, a slimmer man in a work shirt and jeans between them. One of the big men was Dolph Calin. The slimmer man looked like Billy Owen, had one arm draped around the shoulders of each of the big men. "Billy never really worked for the Company, but he wanted to. The Company was on the front line, still is, always will be. It was good for me, then and now. Got me my first job on the Street. The country doesn't appreciate us, but the important people know and help." His eyes followed the years across the photos. "He called me. He wanted to get out of the country, wanted to know if Charley Marion was still flying runs down there, how he could find Charley. I keep up some contacts, got an address. I gave it to Billy, that was all."

"Give it to us," I said.

He studied his past on the wall. "Times change. Charley still flies, but it's on his own and a different cargo. You understand? I wouldn't have told Billy how to find him if he hadn't sounded desperate."

The taxi dropped us in front of a rundown tenement on Avenue B near Tompkins Square. Latinos with dark Indian faces sat on the stoops in sandals and undershirts in the hot afternoon. They watched us. The driver barely waited for a tip. This was where whole families down to the last infant died in drug wars.

The address was a storefront with the window painted over and the door barred and doublelocked. A business card was tacked over the bell: Marion Air Freight, Charles A. Marion, Pres., By Appt., (212) 888-4345. My rings brought no response. We walked along the crowded, jostling avenue among the faces that looked more like a street in Bogota than New York, until we found a pay phone, called the number on the card. There was no answer.

"What do we do now?" Frank said.

"I can try to get an address for that number, stake out the storefront, or both. I have contacts at the telephone company. I'm not jazzed over staking out in this neighborhood."

"Don't you have your gun?"

"They have more and better."

"For a detective, you scare easy."

"Always. I'll call the telephone company."

Both my contacts were on the night shift. Being lucky beats being smart. We were going to have to stakeout. All I could do was hope we wouldn't be noticed. In this neighborhood that was like hoping no one would notice a machine gun on an airliner.

At the storefront, the undershirt Latinos with their black eyes and flat, empty faces all watched us now. Once on the block, we were strangers. Twice, we were something else.

"Come on."

A narrow alley ran beside the storefront building all the way through to the next block. A back door could give us a way inside where we could wait out of sight. It wasn't something I would have tried at night in this neighborhood, but by day they would only watch, keep track of us. That was the theory anyway.

"Fortune?"

The back door was open. We stepped into a furnished room with a single dirty back window. There was a couch, armchair, table and chairs, hot plate, refrigerator, TV set, ghetto blaster, and a slept-in cot. Beer bottles stood empty on the table and floor. A door opened into a bathroom.

"Oh, Christ!"

Frank Owen looked over my shoulder. Something about the body on the floor between the shower stall and john told him who it was before I saw more than sprawled combat boots, camouflage fatigue pants, a light khaki shirt, dark blond hair. He pushed past me, dropped beside his brother.

"Frank, don't touch—!"

If he heard me he didn't care. He held his brother, turned him over, stared into the dead eyes, the frozen gray-white face, the gaping mouth.

"Billy? Jesus, Billy! Christ . . ."

Unless it is horrible with ripped off limbs, decapitations, crushed faces, most of us don't throw up or collapse in the face of death alone. Those who deal with it on a close basis—soldiers, police—may never get used to it, but become inured. The rest of us face it more or less calmly, silent and solemn. If it is someone we knew well, we face it with a sense of injury, of waste, of sadness, but we don't go to pieces.

"Oh, Christ, Billy . . . Billy . . ."

A child or a lover, then we may fall apart, but that isn't death, that's loss. Failure and despair that we have not somehow prevented it, saved our lover or child. We don't still have what was so important to us. A brother falls somewhere between, and Frank Owen had been a soldier. So he sat there on the floor beside his dead brother, shook his head with a mixture of disbelief and reproach. How could Billy have been so stupid?

"God, Billy. Shit. . . shit. . ."

For me it is the rigidity. The end of movement, the not breathing. The stiff, motionless forever of it.

"Fortune?" Frank Owen looked up at me. Couldn't I do something? Could anything be done? Was he really . . . ?

You have to deal with the moment. Maybe that's the real reason I decided to be a detective, death becomes part of the job, and that makes it easier to handle. Work is the answer.

"He's dead, Frank. A long time. Maybe a day, maybe more."

He kneeled there and stared down at the dead eyes, gaping mouth. At what had been Billy. No marks on the body, no blood. Rigor mortis was total. He'd been dead from twelve hours to two days. He had fallen half curled around the toilet, had stiffened in that contorted position. Frank still stared down at the gaping mouth, the sightless eyes.

I touched his shoulder. He stood and walked out into the room, sat in the arm chair. With my lone arm there was no way to turn the curled body face up. I had to get down and lean all over it to search for a wound. A beer bottle lay next to the dead hand, some beer still in it. There was a small pool of dried blood on the floor that had been hidden under the body, a small rip and four-inch blood stain on the khaki shirt. I found no other marks or wounds, and all the pockets were empty.

In the main room I sat in a straight chair facing Frank Owen. We said nothing for a time. I reached out to touch him, my hand on his shoulder. No one believes it. Not *your* brother. There is nothing you can say.

"The blaster," Frank said. "It's on."

Behind me a red light glowed on the portable radio-tape machine, but there was no sound. A hand-labelled home tape was in the chamber. Frank walked to the machine to read the writing on the label.

"Pink Floyd." His laugh was high, on edge. "Probably my album. He taped my records, Dianne's, anyone's."

He pressed rewind, waited, stopped the tape and punched play. The socially militant rock band blasted into the silent room. It's not my music, I'm Lincoln Center not Shea Stadium, but even I could feel the power, hear the white heat . . . .

". . . *they had a job for me, I couldn't tell anyone.*"

Footsteps across a room, the creak of a chair.

"*I mean, it's all okay. . . .*"

Frank hit stop, stared down at the silent blaster.

I stood beside him. "Billy?"

He nodded, still stared at the machine as if it were some kind of arcane instrument of magic, voodoo, resurrection.

"Had the Pink Floyd piece finished?"

He shook his head.

"Rewind it, Frank."

He didn't move. I pressed rewind, waited as long as I thought Frank had, stopped it, pressed play. The raucous Pink Floyd beat filled the room.

"He could have hit the record button," I said. "He heard someone coming, turned off the tape, then hit record. Maybe by accident, maybe on purpose."

". . . *they had a job for me, I couldn't tell anyone.*"

Footsteps somewhere, the creak of a chair.

"*I mean, it's all okay out there, right? No sweat on the operation. Clean as shit, right?*"

Billy Owen's voice full of beer. The far-off voice soft, unintelligible. Slow and measured to Billy's quick and nervous.

"*Hey, grab a beer. All I do is sit around and wait. Goddamned CIA. God, it's hot in this dump. So how'd you find me? I mean, soon as this job's finished I'm coming back. You didn't have to chase after me. Take a beer, for Christ sake.*"

The distant unintelligible voice, sound of small movement.

"It turned out a-okay, right? We got lucky. One hell of a shock for the Company. They got to run around like chickens covering it up. We come out smelling all sweet, right?"

A laugh, high and thick. *"Dumb fucking beaner. He think all we come for's to give him money and party? The dumb bastard, pulling that kind of stuff. The way they covered, he got to be more'n he told. Always figured there was somethin' about him. Too damned quiet, watched too damned much. Should of figured he'd pull some crap. They made me fix him up in town, get him a job. Jesus, have a beer. God, we got him drunk. He should of figured what was coming."*

Slurred. *"Hey, this job's my big chance. Gonna get me into the Company for sure. Back down there with the Contras. A real command, yessir. We gonna push right through to Managua and old Billy's gonna be up front all the way. My own outfit."*

"Jesus, brew goes right through you. You don't wanna drink with me, fuck you. I gotta make a trip. Take a goddamn beer."

Unsteady footsteps, door slamming. Silence. Creak of a chair. Slow steps. A door opening. *"What. . . no . . . uh–uh–uh–uh . . . uh . . ."* *Door closed. Footsteps. Door.* The tape ran on in silence until it stopped.

"Christ," Frank said. Suddenly he began to cry.

26

"You think he hit record on purpose?"

He was Detective First Grade Alex Callow from the precinct squad. We were in the precinct squad room. Billy Owen was in the morgue. It was night out in the city.

"International intrigue," I said. "Trap the bad guys."

Billy Owen had lived by fantasy, and fantasy had killed him.

"He never said a name."

"Afraid to draw attention, make the killer suspicious. He was probably in front of the machine until he went into the john, hiding it. He was scared, Callow. Maybe it was someone whose name he didn't usually use. Maybe he just forgot. Maybe the talk never got around to a name."

"Accident or on purpose, what does it add to, Fortune?"

This was Captain Pearce. The patrolmen and Callow had been first after my call. The M.E. and his people. Callow knew me, listened while his men went over the room at the rear of Charley Marion's air service office. The office itself had turned out to be a desk and some phones and nothing else. Callow listened to Frank Owen, put a man on finding Charley Marion, took us into the precinct and called Pearce. The CIA and FBI were in it, there was probably an out-of-state killer and drug smuggling by Charley Marion. It called for some brass.

"He knew him," Frank Owen said. "Someone from California. Someone who killed Jantarro. That wasn't any accident. Billy knew it, and they came and killed him."

Pearce said, "It sounds to me, Mr. Owen, that your brother did more than just know this Jantarro's death wasn't an accident. He was there. He was part of it."

"He was fooled," Frank said. "He didn't know."

"He knew he'd been conned into hiding Hernan Javier," Alan Cox, the FBI man, said.

The two CIA men said nothing. They hadn't said anything since they'd shown up at the room where Billy Owen had died. They told Callow that Dolph Calin had called them after Frank and I talked to him. Calin confirmed that, explained that since he didn't work for the Company anymore he hadn't told them about Billy's visit, only decided to call them after we showed up and he got worried for Billy.

Pearce said, "How do we know you didn't find Owen earlier. Send someone after him. You were damned busy covering Javier's death. How do we know you didn't kill Javier too?"

"Because we tell you," Walt said. He was sitting for the first time. He didn't look comfortable.

"He was hanging around your necks," Callow said. "From that tape, he was up to something. Maybe he had some operation going against the CIA and you had to shut him up."

McIver said, "The tape makes it clear Billy Owen knew he wasn't talking to a CIA man."

"Shit," Cox laughed. "If the whole thing is one of your operations, the killer could have been anyone Billy ever worked with he didn't know was CIA."

"You're an asshole, Cox," Walt said.

McIver said, "You all seem to have a distorted view of the CIA. That's too bad. We work for you, for the country."

"So do we, McIver," Pearce said. "You have to obey your own laws first, the principles you're defending."

"You have to have a country first," McIver said.

"You people don't want the country, McIver," Cox said, "you want the world."

Cox had been the last to show. His office reached him fast when Pearce called, he arrived at the squad room less than an hour after Callow brought us in. He'd told his version of what had been going on around Jantarro and Billy Owen. We sat around the squad room filling out such details as the pickup attack on Frank while we waited for the reports. They came in from the various detectives, technical teams and labs over four hours. Callow gave us the summaries.

"We turned up nothing in the room or the neighborhood. No one saw anyone back there, no reports of strangers except Fortune and Owen, and, later, the two CIA guys. No sign of the weapon. The word on the streets is zero, dead silence. If the killer had any connections, the street doesn't know it. Charley Marion came up clean on any big deal going down."

The lab teams had found a hundred different fingerprints all over the back room and the bathroom, were running them through the computer and Washington now. Only Billy's prints were on the bottles. The room had been full of dusts and dirts, nothing yet out of the ordinary. Sifting the physical traces and the fingerprints could take months. There had been no other blood, nothing that obviously shouldn't have been there.

"Earliest we could get the autopsy'd be tomorrow afternoon, probably two days, but the M.E. says we can work on twenty-four to thirty-six hours."

I said, "Plenty of time for anyone from California to be long back there."

"Plenty of time for anyone from anywhere to be anywhere else," Captain Pearce said. "It may be a smaller world for most people, Fortune, but for a cop these days the world is a great deal larger, believe me."

Callow said, "As far as the M.E. can tell without cutting, death was from a single knife wound in under the rib cage into the heart. A long, narrow, rigid blade like a commando dagger, sharp as hell. The M.E. says it had to be someone who knew what they were doing, or was damn lucky to hit it just right."

Death was part of the job of everyone in that squad room, the weapon and the body something to be talked about. Except Frank Owen. Death was still outside, and the body had been his brother. He sat pale, silent, his face drawn and angry at the same time. Only I seemed to notice. I don't have to live with the left behind as much as they do. Most policemen go through an early stage of feeling too much, then not feeling anything, and, at the end, feel it all again heavier, alone. Maybe we all do.

"Short and quick, not much blood," Callow said. "If that's any help."

"Someone lucky," I said, "or trained to use a knife."

Cox said to McIver, "Sounds like any of your people, right? The clandestine boys. OSS stuff and all that. Behind the enemy lines. Like Walt there. I'll bet he's as good with a commando dagger as he is with his fists and a cigarette."

"Better," Walt said.

McIver said, "Or anyone who took army training seriously, Cox. Like you, I'd guess. Owen there. Maybe even Fortune."

"Merchant Marine didn't even teach you to swim," I said.

It was past midnight, Pearce in his shirtsleeves, Cox and me lying on benches, everyone with too much coffee in them and not enough food, when they brought Charley Marion in. He looked as tired as we felt and a lot more annoyed. Until he saw McIver.

"Hello, Charley," the CIA man said.

"Owen told me the Company wasn't in on it, McIver. A personal bailout or I wouldn't have touched it."

He was a big man, but skinny, permanently stooped from climbing in and out of small planes, bending in cabins. Blue eyes, a deep tan and beard stubble, he wore an expensive lightweight blue pinstripe suit, a blue shirt without a tie, and running shoes.

"He's got a real nice pad up on Riverside," one of the detectives who'd brought him in said. "Six rooms, balcony, the works. He'd just come home, was getting ready to slide into the Jacuzzi. Some guys got it all."

"Who told him we wanted to talk about Owen?" Pearce said.

"I don't know, Captain."

Charley Marion dropped into a chair, stretched his skinny legs out in the pinstripes and running shoes. "Come on, Captain, I heard about it before you did, right? Maybe five minutes after your precinct guys got there."

"I didn't hear anyone tell you to sit down," Pearce said.

Marion stood. "We going to do this hard or easy, Captain? You want me to stand, I'll stand. You want me to jump rope, show me where to jump. You want me to talk, why don't we just talk?"

"Sit down, but don't push it," Pearce said. "We know what you do, Mr. Marion."

Marion sat back down, slouched. "I fly illegal narcotics, happy dust. We both know, but you have to catch me, and I don't shit where I eat. Where you work, Captain, I'm clean, and where I work I'm not going to get caught."

"Why not?" I said.

He glanced at me, studied my empty sleeve, looked back at Pearce.

"Because everyone's looking the other way. Right, McIver?"

The two CIA men said nothing. They were having a bad night.

"You work for the CIA?" Pearce said.

"Hell, no, but I used to. The Company plays narco-politics every which way, depending on what's in it for their side, and they don't want old Charley picked up, do you, McIver?"

It was Walt who finally spoke. "We're not in on this one, Charley. You're blowing it."

McIver said, "Let him talk, Walt."

"What did you do for the CIA, Mr. Marion?" Pearce asked.

Charley Marion watched McIver and Walt, glanced at the rest of us, didn't seem to see what he needed. He chewed a thumbnail.

"No secret, I told it all before in Washington."

"Tell us."

He shrugged. "Flew clothes, food, guns down to the Contras, the Salvadoran government, and our side in Honduras, Panama, anywhere.

Brought back grass and coke they needed to sell to keep going. Flew undercover for the DEA and Customs to get the dirt on who shipped the stuff, and put the Company onto them so we could use 'em."

"Jesus," Callow said, "all at the same time?"

Cox laughed, "As the man said, our CIA works all sides its wonders to perform."

"But now you fly for yourself?" Pearce said.

"Hell, Captain, no one flies drugs for himself, you know that. It's big business, and big politics. The Contras, or the Salvadorans, or Noriega. The Shining Path Maoists, Cubans, or Salvadoran rebels. Landowners and Marxists. Everyone wants money. For themselves or the Cause."

"How do we stop it?" I asked.

He looked at me again, at my missing arm, wondering who the hell I was. But since no one stopped me from asking questions, I had to have some status.

"Only one way it stops—no market. Make people not need the stuff, or legalize it and control it. Cut the profits so far down coffee and food look good."

"Where did Billy Owen fit into all this?" Pearce said.

It was smooth, slipped in nicely, but Charley Marion had all his wits and a lot of experience.

"Not with me, Captain. Ask McIver over there. We were all Company when I met Billy."

"No more, Charley," McIver smiled. "He was on his own in whatever this one was, and so are you."

"Have fun, Charley," Walt said.

Cox said, "You work for CIA, you don't need an enemy."

No one laughed. Too late, too much bad coffee.

Marion said, "Owen told Dolph Calin he had trouble, needed out of the country. Dolph called me. I met Owen at the Avenue B office, agreed to fly him to Costa Rica on a Colombian run. I wasn't leaving right away, so I stashed him in the room behind the office. We were going tomorrow."

"Where from?" Callow asked.

Marion's smile was thin. "Come on."

"You heard about Owen's murder by early afternoon," Pearce said. "Where were you tonight? Calling the trip off?"

"Let's say I was making some changes. A killing spooks people in my trade."

"You weren't interested enough in Billy Owen's murder to come and talk to us? Talk to the CIA?"

"I wasn't working on anything with him, Captain. I didn't know what trouble he was in, I didn't kill him, and I hadn't any notion who could have or why. What could I tell the police?"

"It happened in your back room apartment. You knew we'd come after you, yet you went out to meet someone tonight. I think you're going to have to tell us everything you've done the last three or four days, Mr. Marion. Everything."

Callow said, "The killer found him in your place, Marion. How did the killer do that?"

Charley Marion looked glumly at his feet stretched in front of him. It was going to be a long night, maybe more than one. With everything he'd done in Central and South America, I guessed he'd been held before, but you don't get used to it. McIver and Walt stood up, looked at their watches in unison.

"We've got our own work, Captain," McIver said. "Billy Owen is all yours. Javier is dead and out of the country, no more problem. It's pretty clear Owen was using us to hide out from something with no connection to the CIA. We had to be sure. But if we can do anything to help, you call on us right away."

"We'll do that," Pearce said. "You two seem to have a clearer picture of this than we do, so stay in town a while. Listen to that tape, maybe you'll remember something."

On his feet, Walt was feeling more himself. "We got more to do than fuck around in some two-bit—"

McIver said. "We'll be available if you want us, Captain."

"Yeah," Pearce said.

It was past 2:00 A.M., the police gave Frank Owen and me the same message, a copy of the tape, and let us go too. We picked up a cruising cab on the nearest deserted avenue. Frank made it into the back seat before he broke down and started to cry, beat his fist over and over against the seat in the dark interior.

27

We couldn't sleep. Death does that. Sudden, unexpected death. Death close. Death at the end of the search.

Death and long waiting hours and I needed a beer to take the coffee and the night out of my throat. Frank Owen laid out three lines, snorted one, called Dianne in California. Dianne would tell Nina, and fly east. I told him to tell her to call Kay and say I was okay, would call later. They talked for a long time.

When he hung up, Frank sat propped on the bed again, a beer in his hand, the two lines of cocaine laid out on the flat plastic plate on the bed table. He watched the walls of the city through the high windows of the ornate old hotel room that had been here a hundred years.

"Why do I call her, Fortune? I don't call the others except to fight about money. She's coming east. Why do I like that?"

Across the rear areaway there was light in another building, shadows that crossed the windows. He drank, looked down at the lines on the plastic.

"When he was a kid, while I was still in the army, he was always talking about heroes, patriots, fighters. He read all kinds of biographies, histories. Men like Drake, Cortez, Jeb Stuart, Wyatt Earp, Jim Bowie. Kit Carson and Davy Crockett. Not kings, generals, the famous leaders. The loners. One on one. The Alamo."

He looked at the lines of coke, playing a game, challenging himself. Testing how long he could look at the cocaine without snorting. "He talked about The Alamo all one night. A fort with pink walls from the blood of the defenders. Tough, defiant, Americans in a stand against the two-bit asshole General Antonio Lopez de Santa Anna with his seven-thousand-dollar sword, silver-loaded uniform and silver chamber pot.

"The Napoleon of the West. Almost three thousand trained soldiers against a hundred-and-eighty-nine untrained Texans to decide if Texas would be American and free, or Mexican and slave. It was just like the revolution their fathers were always talking about. Taxation without representation, religious persecution, a dictator a thousand miles away telling them how to live, *greasers* trying to push them around."

He set the beer bottle down lightly, bent to the short straw and the line of white powder. Slow and deliberate, a ritual to take away the stigma of necessity.

"Travis. Only twenty-six, he killed a man in South Carolina for messing around with his wife, ran for the frontier. Crockett who once shot forty-seven bears in a month on the frontier. A trailblazer, explorer, congressman. When he got beaten for congress he told the farmers and shopkeepers to go to hell, he was going to Texas. Bowie, Billy's favorite. Outlaw most of his life, made and lost fortunes. He liked to fight close with his knife, rode alligators, married the richest, most beautiful *señorita* in San Antone. She died of cholera, he was roaring drunk most of the time at The Alamo, had tuberculosis, was one of the last to die."

All the windows across the areaway were dark now. The city outside the closed windows as quiet as it ever got. Frank sipped at his beer, almost motionless.

"They waited for reinforcements, for Sam Houston to ride in. No one came. Travis drew a line in the dust with his sword. Any man who wanted to go could, those who'd stay and fight step over the line. Bowie had to be carried over the line in his bed. They'd buy time for Texas, make Santa Anna pay a high price. The Alamo was the key to victory. They all died, but they held Santa Anna thirteen days and made him pay with six hundred casualties."

A garbage can fell below. Some cat after food. A silent stray dog. Someone walked along the corridor outside, solitary and slow in the early morning hours. There comes a time when beer becomes tasteless, thin on a thick tongue. A sour, flat taste like time itself in a night that seems to vibrate behind your eyes.

I said, "The only difference it made was to get the U.S. mad and make Santa Anna overconfident. When volunteers stay in a hopeless situation it's usually because they're afraid to look chicken. Bowie was a sadistic drunk and brawler, a slave trader and con man. Crockett wanted power, expected to be big in the Texas government. Travis was an ambitious egomaniac who'd written his autobiography when he was twenty-three, was going to be the man who saved Texas."

What would I have done? Probably the same as those 189 free-wheelers and freebooters, glory seekers and fortune hunters. Nobody really believes he's going to die, and it's hard to be different.

"The land was Mexico, the Mexicans had freed their slaves. The Americans in Texas were slave owners, rustlers, and landgrabbers. Restless and ruthless wanderers after a pot of gold, caught up *en masse* in a noble cause that was largely the propaganda of ambitious men who wanted to make their own laws outside both the U.S. and Mexico. All men, of course. Women on the frontier just worked and had children in one-room shacks. Texas, someone said even then, was heaven for men and dogs, hell for women and oxen."

Frank Owen laughed. Sudden and macabre in the quiet, mournful late night hotel, the cocaine and beer taking effect. Shook his head as if amazed by me, hardly able to believe I was saying what I'd said, his head almost loose on his neck, his bottle all but empty in his hand. "You're something else, you know? Tear it down, throw it out, all a bunch of lies. But it's not lies, Fortune, it's the way people feel, what they hang onto inside, what's underneath the facts."

"What they want to be real," I said. "What someone else wants them to believe."

"No one told Billy what to want. No one tells me. If he went to shit' he did it on his own."

He stared down at the last line on the plastic plate. His tolerance for the drug was obviously good, but he was reaching that stage where much more would push him over the edge into the safety of unreality, where Billy would turn into a maudlin memory. Not where his death would no longer be real, but where it wouldn't hurt as much.

"His whole life was a fantasy, Frank. Listen to him."

I put the copy of the tape the police had given us into his Walkman on the bedtable, punched play. Billy's lost voice spoke randomly from beyond the grave. A hollow, empty sound in the silent room with the dark city outside. A disjointed voice as I hit fast forward and play, fast forward and play.

The high, thick laugh of a man more than half-drunk, and yet somehow cold sober. "Dumb fucking beaner. He think all we come for's to give him money and party? The dumb bastard, pulling that kind of stuff. . . More'n he told . . . Should of figured he'd pull some crap. . . Jesus, have a beer. . . He should of figured what was com-ing . . . Hey, this job's my big chance . . . A real command, yessir. We gonna push right through to Managua . . . Jesus, the brew goes right through you. You don't wanna drink with me, fuck you . . ." A door slamming. Slow steps . . . .

"Stop it! Stop the fucking thing!"

He slid off the bed, crossed to the bar and pulled another beer out of the refrigerator. He held onto the refrigerator, looked for how to open the bottle. He was seconds from smashing the neck to get at the beer.

"Frank."

I tossed him the opener from the table beside me. He caught it as if he were cold sober. He opened the beer, stood facing the wall, took long drinks. When the bottle was empty, he opened another, went on facing the wall of the fine old room.

"He wanted to test his mettle, find out if he was a fighter, brave. He wanted to be in battle. We all do, it's part of us. It's not good, maybe, but it's true, and we have to face it."

I got up and got my own beer. "A juvenile game in a fake world. He didn't know what battle was. Listen to that tape, Frank. Jantarro pulled some kind of operation that got him killed. Billy was there, but panicked and wrote to you. Then he got a brainstorm. He knew Jantarro was important to the CIA, so he fed them a yarn, put himself right in the middle of international intrigue. Made himself a big man and got ironclad protection too. He must have felt clever as all hell."

Frank went back to the bed with his beer. I opened another. They were past tasting bad, had no taste at all. Only something to hold. The night outside was still black, but the cool odor of dawn on a hot day was reaching into the room, the faint sounds of an awakening city.

"The CIA didn't really believe his yarn of enemy agents, never worried that much. They hid him and checked it out, but didn't bother with heavy protection. But the killer did worry about him. He'd brought in the CIA, and he'd brought you and me around. That made the killer nervous, more than he or she would have been. The game turned real and ugly, Billy was killed."

On the bed Frank looked down at that last line on its plastic plate. The beer had long ago lost its kick as the slow night dragged on. Neither of us knew how to end it. There isn't that much difference between sleep and death, not in the dark. The fear that this time we might not wake up. Fear and reality, and Frank looked up and said it first.

"He knew, didn't he? He sat in that room drinking beer and talking and knew what was going to happen."

"Yes," I said, but he didn't need me.

"He knew, Fortune! He lied to himself, hid it from himself, but he knew."

Knew he was going to die, knew he could do nothing. Helpless and knew he was helpless, and for some there is no greater horror. Not for most women, helplessness is every day for them. But for most men in the comfortable countries, in the power nations, it is the ultimate horror. Helpless in the hands of the tyrants and the goons, the death squads and the extermination camps, the Gulag and Auschwitz, the superpatriots and the gas chamber, the bullet in the back of the head and the rope. Know you are going to die like a small animal in the jaws of a predator, inevitably and indifferently.

"He wanted to find out if he was brave," I said. "He found out that it doesn't make much difference."

He looked at me for a long time. In the areaway outside the high windows a faint gray light filtered between the dark walls of the city. Then he bent to the last line on the plastic plate. A defiance and a surrender at the same time. Evasion and escape. An escape from reality, an evasion of humanity. The hypochondriac, the pill popper is trying to deal with reality, function as a human being, not escape it all as the pot and cokehead is, the mainliner and the boozer. A retreat into illusion, a giving up of reason, and no Mahlers or Einsteins or Faulkners will come out of it. No one ever worked better with drugs or booze, it only looked like it until morning.

His head was back against the headboard again, his arms limp at his sides, eyes open toward the far wall like a thin buddha. "This country's got no juice anymore. He wanted to do something, and all they gave him was get a job, get a wife, get a family, get a house, and then die. Your life's over before you start, everything's settled. You think about what you're going to do tomorrow, and you realize it's unimportant, meaningless, not even interesting. After you see that, no matter what the hell your age is, it's all the same. Everything is repetition."

If we didn't sleep soon, Dianne Owen would walk in on us all the way from California. The sun would rise. Six million people would move through the city. I drank, he snorted the last dust of his lines. He sat so motionless up against the headboard, so silent, I thought he'd finally passed out. The first thin yellow edged the tops of the windows across the areaway. In the closet I found a blanket, threw it over the couch, took off my shoes at last.

When he spoke his lips barely moved, like a papier-maché figure at some amusement park, "All he asked was something worth doing, a good companion, a decent sex life. Why is it so hard?"

I held my shoe in my lone hand. "Maybe because of what he thought was worth doing, what his idea of a companion was," I said. "Maybe because you have to think about other people."

He lay down on his side and curled into a ball. The sun was on the windows outside, but I wasn't ready to sleep. Sleeping in the same room with another man made me think about the Merchant Marine and the war I missed because of my arm. Yesterday. The older you get the shorter it's been. For Billy Owen it hadn't begun. A fake life ended by someone only too real.

28

The phone stopped ringing. The sun was gone from the areaway. Frank Owen still lay curled on the bed. The Merchant Marine was long ago and yesterday and if you think too much about that you'll curl in a ball and stay there.

The phone rang again.

"Frank? Where—"

"Dan Fortune, Dianne. Frank's asleep. Where are you?"

"Downstairs. Dan, it's three in the afternoon."

"Tell the desk we need coffee, fruit, toast, and whatever you want. Room 32."

I lay on the couch with my lone hand under my head, looked at the windows across the areaway. Windows in a city are like a thousand eyes one on top of the other watching you.

"Frank?"

"I heard. What time is it?"

"After three P.M."

"The police call?"

"No."

When Dianne knocked he let her in. She stood close, her arms around him.

"I'm so sorry, Frank. Do they—?"

"No. He never did a fucking thing, Di, not a fucking thing his whole life."

She sat down. "No, he didn't."

"Where's Nina?" He looked at the closed door.

"She didn't come, Frank. She said we could bury him, she didn't have the money or the time."

His laugh was that high, edgy laugh. "Not even a loving wife to claim his body, tell his kids what a great guy he was."

"He wasn't, and she can't, Frank. He gave her nothing, she has nothing, he'll leave her nothing."

"Is that all the fuck you women think about? Have, have, have? It's everything?"

"Not everything," She lit a cigarette, sat on the bed up against the headboard. "Not today, Frank, please? I came to be with you. It's a terrible thing, I want to be with you."

He sat beside her. "We had a bad day and a worse night, and while we were looking for him it wasn't too swift."

She held his hand. "I know."

She looked at the room littered with empty beer bottles, at the plastic plate with the faint white residue. She squeezed his hand, and when the food came I ate methodically—grapefruit, banana, nectarine, toast, coffee. She had ordered a shrimp salad for herself that almost made me sick. For me it was breakfast time. Our routines program even our stomachs. Frank faced the food for a long time as if he had something else in mind. Cocaine does that to you. Or the death of a brother. Then he ate like a starving wolf.

I called Callow at the precinct, he said he'd like to talk to Dianne and Frank, I could come along for the ride if I wasn't too busy. A lot of American cops think that being funny takes some of the grimness out of their work. The better ones. We left the hotel maid looking stunned as she surveyed our room, and cabbed over to the lower eastside.

"Autopsy's not in yet, but the M.E. says twenty-four to thirty-six hours is now certain from lividity and other tests," Callow told us. "Fingerprint search hasn't turned up any known baddies, or anyone in the case. CIA's cooperating, and they look clean, for whatever that's worth."

We were perched around his desk in a corner of the second-floor squad room. Plush surroundings aren't one of the perks of public service. The appearance of frugality is mandatory in a republic.

"What about Charley Marion?" I asked.

"Iron alibi," Callow said. "He was a thousand miles away the whole two days Billy Owen could have been killed. He got back the afternoon you found the body, got the message from the neighborhood, had dinner with a 'businessman' that night and cancelled the flight Owen was to go on until further notice."

"Cox?" I said.

Callow chewed a nail. "You got any reasons, Fortune?"

"He was hounding Jantarro, wanted him out of the country or in the slammer or both. Maybe he found him first."

Callow drew blood from his cuticle, sucked it. "We thought about it. Some guys get overeager, then have to cover it up. The Bureau investigates itself, Pearce is working on it."

"What's Cox doing now?"

"Says he's going on, even though we hear there's pressure from the Pentagon and the CIA to drop it."

There can be reasons other than dedication to make a man go on in a case that, for him, should be over. Callow wrapped a tissue around his chewed fingernail, flipped open a notebook.

"You knew the decedent well, Mrs. Owen?"

"Yes. He came around pretty often."

"In Santa Barbara?"

"Yes."

"Chasing his brother's wife? A married man too?"

"Ex-wife," Dianne said. "It made it more fun, I expect. Nina gave up caring what Billy did years ago."

"Did she care what you did?"

"I didn't *do* anything with Billy."

"Where were you the last few days? Not counting today."

"In Los Angeles. I have clients there, go down often."

"People saw you there the last, say, seventy-two hours?"

"Some. I drove to Mexico a few days ago."

"Alone?"

"More or less."

"Will the man corroborate your trip and the time?"

"I suppose so. If he remembers."

Frank Owen said, "Picking them up in bars, Di?"

"I like adventure too. Don't play jealous, Frank, it spoils the care-free nightrunner image."

"Are you by any chance trained with weapons, Mrs. Owen?"

"I know karate, self-defense. I've had classes. A lot of women have these days."

"How about using a knife?"

"We were shown ways to defeat a knife attack. Mostly by running like hell."

Frank said, "Di didn't kill him, Detective Callow. She wouldn't have any motive."

"You never know," Callow said, unwrapped his finger to study the tiny wound on his cuticle. "Take you. Your only alibi is Fortune. The two of you were together looking for your brother. What if you and your brother had a reason to kill that Jantarro out in Santa Barbara? But your brother panics, runs to the CIA with his fairytale yarn and they hide him. You have to find him, you get your ex-wife to hire Fortune. That truck attack on you was a friend of Billy's trying to stop you. The CIA was right to think you were a danger to Billy, but you and Fortune conned them, found Billy and killed him. He never used a name on that tape because who calls his brother by his name?"

Dianne laughed. No one else did.

"Why did I want to kill Jantarro? Why would Fortune get involved in murder?"

"Some shady deal. Dope, politics, CIA stuff. Fortune likes money same as everyone else. Right, Fortune?"

"It makes as much sense as anything we have so far."

It fit all the facts of the case. If I didn't know that Frank had been with me the whole time, I could believe it. In the newspapers, in a book, it would make total sense. It showed how hard police work really is, how little we can be sure of what is happening around us, how much fantasy we live with every day.

We left Callow working on another fingernail, cabbed back to the hotel where the maid had put the room in order. On a day you've lost, time is out of joint. It was dinnertime, but the day was still light and my brain told my stomach it was lunchtime. To solve the problem I went out for a walk through the Village and Chelsea and up to Bogie's. Frank and Dianne did not want to take a walk.

"Come get us for dinner," Frank said. "Late."

Dianne smiled at me.

When I came out of Bogie's it was night. Time was back in sync, but the night seemed to hang heavier, as if the last two days had been one long night. In essence, they had. A slow, expensive dinner was the only answer. At the hotel I arranged for a smaller room before I called up to Frank and Dianne.

I took them up to Le Cheval Blanc. It was still there. The owner and *maître*, Fernand, even commented that I hadn't been in for longer than usual. There is no greater sense of importance than being missed by a *maître*. The lamb was pink, the duck crisp, the oysters Monterrey a rare favorite of mine, the Château Beycheville '80 a buy at only fifty percent markup.

"It's knowing stuff like that ruins Frank's dropout act," Dianne said. "What's your excuse, Dan?"

"Even a second-string running back from Nebraska learns something if he's around New York restaurants long enough."

She paid the check. "So you won't have to hide it in your expense account."

In my new room I called Kay.

"Got your message last night. Nice of you to let me know you were alive. Have you decided to move back there?"

"The restaurants are better, but I miss the fog."

"Don't forget the earthquakes."

"There are better ways to make the earth move."

"That could probably be arranged. Shall I pencil you in?"

"Give me a few days."

"The operative word is few."

The police had the autopsy report next morning. There was nothing new. A single knife wound entered under the rib cage into the heart anywhere from twenty-four to thirty-six hours before we'd found Billy Owen. They released the body to Frank, he had it cremated, and he and Dianne flew back to Santa Barbara with the ashes. I stayed in New York.

I talked to Dolph Calin, the CIA men, and anyone around the Avenue B office of Charley Marion who would talk to me. None of them had seen any suspicious strangers, anyone hanging around. Charley Marion had left town. The police checked all flights in from California the three days before we found Billy Owen for any names in the case. None of them appeared, and the descriptions we could give were all far too general and ordinary to be easily recognized by airlines or in New York.

Two days later I got a call from Captain Pearce. He wanted me down at Center Street. Callow was there, they had the file on Pearce's desk. Pearce had the rank, did the talking.

"We turned it all sides up, nothing points to a New York killer. Nothing in the room, nothing from the streets, nothing from a witness."

"He didn't know many people in New York. Not that he'd seen recently, Captain."

"We have to rule out everything we can," Callow said.

I said, "What haven't you ruled out? What did you bring me down here to tell me?"

"A lump of dirt, Dan," Pearce said.

"Dirt?"

Pearce held up a small plastic envelope. I looked at the hard clump of whitish dirt the size of a marble. "The lab people say it dropped off a shoe or boot, maybe fell out of a pant cuff. It's not from New York or anywhere close. It's high in calcium, silicon salts, other stuff like that, has traces of a special kind of crystal with long spikes. It could come from quite a few places, even France, but when they heard where Billy Owen had been living, they got excited."

"From Santa Barbara?"

"Close. It's a particular kind of soil found in and near the riverbed of the Santa Ynez River. It seems that soil has a peculiar composition because the river dries up a good part of the year. In fact, they can even tell what time of year the sample came from. The late part of a dry winter."

I got up. "Like early this year. Thanks, Captain."

"Callow's going out with you."

Callow held up an airline envelope.

His packed bags were in the office, we caught a taxi to the hotel out in front of police headquarters. I packed in ten minutes, paid up, and we were on our way west.

THE VALLEY

29

The 737 from Denver descends into Santa Barbara in a wide circle with a panorama of mountains east, west and north, the narrow coastal plain where the city sits, the vast sea, and the Channel Islands to the south. New York is the creation of man. The hand of nature, of evolution, is covered over, hidden and all but forgotten. In Santa Barbara you can still feel the forces that shaped the planet in the eons before we emerged. For a few more decades anyway.

We went straight to Callow's appointment with Undersheriff Lawson. Lawson led us into his office without a smile. The thin file labelled *Hector Jantarro* lay on his desk as he faced us. He didn't have to open it.

"We went over the case after we got Captain Pearce's call, there's nothing we can add to what we told him. There was no evidence of anything but a drunken accident, we had no reason to doubt the credentials of his family when they came for the body."

"But now you know it was all a CIA coverup. He wasn't a simple Mexican workman, wasn't even Mexican."

"We don't *know* that, Detective Callow. All documentation says he was Hector Jantarro, a Mexican national. His family came from Mexico to claim his body and took it home."

"The CIA hasn't contacted you?"

"Even if they do, we'll need new documentation to alter our official position."

"How about your unofficial position, Sheriff?" Callow said.

"We don't have an unofficial position."

Callow nodded. "The CIA conned you, left you holding the bag, and you'll stonewall it and hope they never admit anything."

The CIA had done just that, and the Sheriff's Department would do just that, and Lawson didn't like it anymore than Callow did. He was a policeman, he liked to do good work. The Sheriff had a whole department to operate, scandal and embarrassment wouldn't help, but Lawson didn't really like it.

"Who he was doesn't change evidence," he said. "It still comes in as an accident."

"Hernan Javier had a lot more reason to be killed than Hector Jantarro," I said. "Javier was hiding, careful, didn't drink much in public, was known for taking care of himself."

Lawson swivelled to take me in. "Why is Fortune in this, Detective Callow?"

"He was hired by Billy Owen's family, he's worked a lot with us in the past. We find him reliable and useful."

"We prefer to keep private detectives out of police cases as much as possible."

I said, "Maybe you should play the tape now, Callow."

Lawson held a hand up toward Callow. "Will this tape be evidence in the Jantarro accident? If so I'll need a statement from you on the circumstances involved. Where it was found, who found it, how it was produced, everything like that."

"It's evidence in a New York murder," Callow said. "What else is up to you. But here's the documentation all made out, signed by Captain Pearce, and the New York D.A., witnessed and notarized. You got a tape player?"

Lawson took one out of a bottom drawer. Callow inserted the tape, punched play, and we listened again to Billy Owen's last moments. Even Lawson was pale. He listened all the way.

"That doesn't sound like Jantarro's death was an accident, does it?" Callow said.

"No," Lawson said, "but how do you know Owen was telling the truth? He was, by your own admission, a notorious liar given to over-dramatizing his actions and importance."

"The killer seemed to think it was the truth," I said.

Callow said, "We think it warrants another look at your accident, Sheriff."

"I agree," Lawson said. "We'll reopen the case, but the tape is only one new piece of evidence. We'll need a lot more than that to make us change our conclusion, and, unfortunately, the trail is pretty cold by now, and the body is gone. Billy Owen may have been our last hope of getting the truth."

"Yeah," I said. "Too bad."

Callow got up. "I'd like to work with your people a few days, if that's okay."

"Of course," Lawson said. "But not Fortune, sorry."

Outside in the afternoon sun I invited Callow to stay with Kay and me in Summerland.

"You're involved with possible suspects, Dan. I've got a motel down by the beach, I'll keep in touch."

At the Summerland house, Kay's car was in the driveway.

I went up to find her in her tower office first. She wasn't there. Downstairs, the living room was empty. She wasn't in the kitchen. I listened, but there was no sound in the house. I got out my old cannon, went along the hall to my office and the two bedrooms. She was in our bedroom.

"Your plane got in two hours ago,"

She sat in a straight chair with the sunlight behind her through the windows that faced the mountains.

"A detective's work is never done."

"Neither is a stud's. Put the symbol away and let's get to the real thing."

"Sounds like a good idea."

She stood. She's tall, and slim, and rounded, and long-legged, and high-breasted, and dark-haired, and she doesn't walk to the bed, she runs. A quick little run that seems to make her smaller as if she wanted to be smaller for me, the way I move more slowly to be taller, more solid for her. There are the archetypes, and we need them, as long as we don't let them get in the way.

We like to undress each other. Even with my one arm. She always kisses my missing arm. The understanding, the acceptance. I touch her long legs, her lean slenderness, all that made her feel un-female when she was a girl. Then the bodies take over and there isn't anything to worry about.

Love and lust and need and delight all around and on and under in warm afternoon sunlight through windows that faced the mountains. Love is what you feel around the lust and the need and the delight, close and near or a long way away. Lust and need is that grip low in the back, in the stomach, in the tight thighs in the thrust forward into and on and under and up. The touch of her lips on your chest, on your belly, on the rigid throb that moves into her and your lips on her nipples and lips and other lips and toes and ankles and neck and belly and wet dark. Delight is what sits back and watches, lies close and feels, moves slowly together and never wants it to end. Love is what you feel before and after and during and what makes you not want anyone else.

Some time later the sun angled low from the west and the mountain side of the house lay in half shadow as the evening cooled. In the kitchen I found two Beck's, a baguette of French bread and a chunk of ripe Stilton laid out under a cloth with a knife and two glasses.

"Tell me about New York."

We ate and drank and I told her about New York.

"Someone from here?"

"Or someone out here recently. Unless the CIA is lying all the way. I don't think they are, but it's always possible."

"What then, Dan?"

"The police are watching that Martin woman, Lee Canton's family is nervous about something, and both Jantarro and Billy Owen worked for Canton. The key is still Jantarro and why he was killed, and I mean Jantarro not Javier."

"You mean the reason is here, not Central America."

"And not politics."

"You're going on?"

"The body's gone, the trail's cold. There's not much the sheriff's department can do. I know more than anyone."

"Then you better be careful." She drank her beer, ate a chunk of baguette and Stilton, watched the darkening sky over the mountains. "Will Dianne and Frank want you to go on?"

"We'll find out."

"Are they back together?"

"For the moment."

"You don't think they can make it?"

"Billy's death scared him. He feels mortal, brief. She feels needed, a safe haven. The wounded warrior and Florence Nightingale. Temporary, on leave, out of the war."

"It won't last?"

I ate some Stilton. "You know the western, *Shane*? It works hard to give the message that the quiet, steady farmer and family man is the 'real' man. But no one leaves the theater believing that. We all know it's Shane, the solitary wanderer, the loner good with a gun, who's the hero. The power, the 'man'."

"Is that what Frank wants to be?"

"It's what he thinks he wants to be."

When it was fully dark, we turned on the light and got up to find some dinner.

30

The fog drifted soft over the freeway and the village, brushed the kitchen windows. Kay slept in, I made my own breakfast. Cold cereal with a banana and a pot of tea.

Alone at an early breakfast window, fogged in, I think of the dawn hours of the morning watch at sea. Nothing but the sea and the ship, the sea and the fog. Then is when it occurs to me that I'm probably no more than a moment in the infancy of a species. A species that might wipe itself out tomorrow, or that could become glorious, even immortal.

Which one, I'll never know.

It's not a thought that Billy and Frank Owen ever had. We cling to our ego, our "I," believe what we want to believe. What Billy and Frank wanted to believe was Shane, the wandering "I" as hero. It's what most seem to want to believe, and that makes the freeway in a fog an adventure. No one slows down. Our love affair with the automobile includes flying free, saddle up and go, don't fence me in. If you don't want to fly, get out of my way. The myth is Kit Carson and the Pony Express, not the homesteader and the freight wagon.

On the west side the sun was trying to break through over the unpainted cottage behind the bare and littered yard. Billy Owen had left no more trace in this shack than his father had in the Nevada mansion.

In the back, Nina and the dark children sang a riding song to golden Taffy. The pony danced with its forelegs, tossed its mane. Nina danced with the pony. The children laughed.

Nina saw me watching. "Frank brought him back in a jug. You want me to cry?"

The thin little boy stood close to her, protective. The sturdy girl danced on with the pony as if no one else were there. Nina touched the boy. He went to the girl and the pony and led them off into the corner of the backyard near the small trailer.

"When's the funeral?"

"Ask Frank. He's doin' it."

"Why didn't you want to come east?"

"I ain't got money to fly three thousand miles to see him dead."

"Frank would have paid. Or Dianne. Maybe you didn't want to come because you knew all along he wasn't going to come back this time."

She looked back to where the children were laughing with the pony as it tossed its head in the sun. "They feel it, you know? They loved him, but they feel the load off us." She looked at me. "Sure I knowed. I always knowed he'd end up like that. One of his lies, big ideas, would get him killed or in jail or on the run. One or the other, and it wouldn't make no difference to me what one it was 'cause for me they'd all be the same. I'd be left with me and the kids all by myself. That's all he'd leave me. Not even burying money. What was I gonna do in New York?"

"Is that what you're going to tell the children, Nina?"

"I should tell 'em lies? Make him look good?"

"He just wanted to do something in the world."

"He never done nothing to make it better for me or anyone else. Not even himself." She smoothed the wrinkles in the loose print dress she wore over long socks and high basketball shoes. Looked down at the dress and herself as if suddenly aware of how she appeared. "Way back, he used to make it better sometimes, but I been on my own with the kids a long time now."

She turned to look at the children and the golden pony together in the far corner of the small fenced yard. They made a solid group. Not happy, maybe, but together.

"Who killed him, Nina? Is there anything you can tell me? Anything he talked about? Something Jantarro was doing? Anyone who was having trouble with Jantarro?"

She went on smoothing the cheap dress that made her look so much older than she was, the old woman's shoes. "I don't care who killed him. It ain't gonna make no difference in my life who it was or why. It ain't gonna make any real difference in no one's life, you know? Not even his."

She walked away and into the house. The thin boy went to the horse trailer and pulled out the pony's saddle. The girl had the halter and harness, began to put it on Taffy. They worked so closely they didn't have to talk, knew automatically what Nina going into the house at this moment meant. She came out with the camera and tripod, smiled at the busy children. She worked over the camera. Checked it, loaded it.

"After the first times I don't figure we ever fucked like he was sober. Last couple o' years there wasn't nothin' at all. If he was home, we'd start out okay, even talk nice sometimes. Come eight o'clock he'd be drunk an' lookin' for a fight."

She finished with the camera, screwed it onto the tripod, nodded to the children who were almost ready. "I know how he felt like he was nothin', but how do you feel for someone who's ruining your life. I mean, how do you feel for him when you're getting hurt all the time. Sure, I knowed how he wants all the time to be what he ain't, but that don't help the trouble he give me. I ain't no saint, you know? I think maybe a saint's someone ain't worried much by other folks."

The children led Taffy to her. She checked the bridle and saddle, tightened everything, hoisted the girl into the saddle. The boy picked up the camera and tripod that was taller than he was. He was stronger than he looked, carried it firmly on his shoulder.

"What will you do now?"

"Same as I always done." She took hold of Taffy's bridle. "Any work I can find, eighteen hours a day for the family. That was okay for me to do, you know, but not for him. He had to be important, get paid what he figured he was worth. I was lucky I got him to marry me. The only thing's changed is I got one less I got to work for."

She began to walk the pony away to start her day's work. I was going to ask her about the children's need for their father, but I didn't. I knew the answer, let her vanish around the shabby cottage leading the pony with the little girl happily riding, the skinny boy bringing up the rear carrying the camera.

31

Only the older woman sat dim on the bed far back in the crawl space under the Victorian on Bath Street. She did nothing when I looked in. Neither asked me in nor chased me out, as if she were accustomed to unknown strangers watching her. Silent and powerless, the stoic fatalism of someone who doesn't know how long she would be allowed to do what she was doing, or what she might be made to do next.

"What do you want?"

The voice was behind me. Gloria Castro in some kind of dark brown and light brown uniform.

"They found Billy Owen dead too," I said.

"Oh, it's you. Owen?"

"Hector's friend."

"Oh. I'm . . . I'm sorry."

She went into the crawlspace room past me, spoke to her mother. The older woman looked at me once, then looked back at the TV screen. Gloria returned, sat on the front bed.

"Did you know his real name was Hernan Javier?"

"Yes, I knew.

"What else didn't you tell me?"

"I don't know. What do you want to know?"

"Who could have killed him."

"It was an accident. Everyone says it was."

"Billy Owen didn't die in an accident, Gloria."

She had a tan-colored name badge. A line drawing of a man with a beard and her name: Gloria. She played with it. Took it off her blouse, pinned it back on straighter.

"If you knew his real name, you knew he wasn't any soldier from Guatemala."

"Guatemala is what he told me. He had enemies from there, that's why the government was protecting him, changed his name."

"Where was he going to get money, Gloria?"

"I don't know about any money."

"He had some plan, some project, some job, that was going to make him enough money to return to his home and be important again. A stake to get back there with enough power to be safe."

"He never said anything about money to me."

"He had enemies from Central America. The FBI was looking for him. Who else was after him? Did he have an enemy here? Did he talk about anyone?"

She shook her head. "He never talked about anything except down there. How important he'd been, how he was going back."

She didn't seem to be aware of what she'd said. Talking by rote, as if someone had coached her, instructed her.

"He was going back without money, Gloria?"

She looked at the door, at her mother silently watching the television in the back. "All right, he said he was going to get some money."

"How?"

"I don't know anything about what he was going to do."

"A job? A business deal? A gift? An investment?"

"Something easy. He laughed, said the money was already in the bank."

"He already had the money?"

"I guess."

It didn't make sense. If Jantarro had already had the money in a bank account, why would someone want to kill him? To steal the money back? Or—?

"Money in the bank," I said. "Is that what he said, Gloria? Whatever he was doing, it was 'money in the bank'?"

"I guess. He had someone by the eggs, and it was money in the bank." She stood. "I got to go to work."

She walked back to her mother, spoke low. When she returned, her voice wasn't friendly.

"My mother wants you to leave. You scare her."

"I'm sorry. Where do you work?"

"Why?"

"I'll drive you."

"Kentucky Fried down on Cliff Drive."

It's how the fast food people make millions. Put kids in cheap uniforms and pay as little as possible. But a summer or part-time job isn't easy for a high school kid, especially if the kid is Latino and a girl.

As we pulled away from the old Victorian house, I saw the pickup truck. It was parked across the street up near the corner in a red zone where it had a clear view of the house. When I reached the first corner it pulled out and came behind us. It had no markings, was too far back for me to read the license, and followed my right turn onto Cabrillo. After I made a left on San Andres it disappeared.

A false alarm? Or did the driver know where, with Gloria Castro in her Kentucky Fried Chicken uniform, I had to be going?

The office of J. James & Co. in Montecito Village was closed. More accurately, it wasn't yet open. People with a pony and a camera go to work early. Elizabeth Henze Martin and J. James did not go to work until 1:00 P.M. Their office hours, discreetly announced on their name board next to the door of number 12, were 1–5 Mon–Thurs (After 5:00 P.M. and Weekends By Appointment).

Most investment firms in California open extra early to match the opening bell of the New York Stock Exchange. Nothing that crass for J. James & Co. and even if her home number was in the phone book, her address wouldn't be. But she would be active in the community, charities and all that. The Montecito Library was across the road. There I found she was chairman of the Fund For The Year Of The Child Reader, address duly listed.

On San Ysidro Lane, it was an old Mediterranean with white walls, a red-tiled roof, blue mosaic tile on the outside walls. Behind a thick hedge and an open gate set between white pillars with the same blue mosaic tiles inset. The name on the rural mailbox was J. James. The gravel drive circled around an operating fountain, white with deep blue tiled interior. The dark wood front door had a barred observation port and an old-fashioned bellpull.

There was no answer to multiple pulls. I walked warily to both ends of the house. It was the kind of place where large dogs appeared. But there were no dogs or people, the four-car garage behind the house at the left was empty. I returned to my Tempo. From the look of it, Elizabeth Martin was more than J. James's business associate. It wasn't a big surprise. She would always go for the boss, and business has a way of making bedfellows.

The Jaguar was parked inside the hedge to the left of the gate where it couldn't be seen from the road. A red Jag, dirty and battered. A pair of pale tan cowboy boots stuck out the open driver's window, the faint sound of western music carried across the gravel. Closer, the music was more insistent, and the acrid odor of marijuana floated to greet me.

"Grow it yourself?"

The boots parted to reveal a round, tanned face with small eyes and thinning hair. "Not lately."

"You J. James?"

"Don't I wish."

He was lying stretched out across the front bucket seats, his feet out the window, smoking the joint and keeping time to the music. The boots and the tan were the only western things about him. His suit was a wrinkled brown gabardine, with a worn white shirt and a yellow and navy blue regimental stripe tie.

"Which one are you waiting for? Him or her?"

Tall and well-built, he was going to fat, his waist thick and soft, skin loose on his neck. "Cop?"

"You worried about the police?"

"In this neighborhood they want to know your business if your car's dirty or your suit needs a press. That's why I'm inside the hedge. I park outside, I have six deputies on me."

"Staking out the house?"

"Me? God, no! Just waiting around." He struggled up to a sitting position, pinched out the joint. "You sure you're not a cop."

"Private investigator. I can't lean on anyone. How about you? What's your interest in James?"

"Not him, her. Liz and me are old friends. Heard she was doing real good so I came up to tap her, but the place's been deserted all yesterday and today. Flown the coop, I bet. Figured this time she was in the legit big time, I'd make a score. Should have known better."

"When you knew her she wasn't legitimate?"

He became wary. "What kind of case you working on? How does Liz fit in?"

"I don't know that she does. Tell me what you know about her, and maybe I can straighten it out."

He looked at the house as if thinking about what he did know, how much trouble it could get Elizabeth Martin into, and how much it was worth.

"All I know is personal stuff and old history you could pick up in the newspapers."

"Old history is what I want."

He looked at his watch. "I could use a couple of drinks, something to eat."

"You know The Pelican?"

"As long as the booze is strong and the steaks rare, it's fine with me," he said cheerfully. "What's your name?"

"Dan Fortune. It's down on Coast Village Road. You can follow me."

"Mark Todd. If you get there first, I'll have a vodka martini on the stem with a twist."

My judgment said he was going nowhere until he freeloaded for all it was worth, but I wasn't about to lose sight of him. We reached The Pelican with the Jaguar right behind me. I even let him go in first.

32

Elizabeth Henze is born in Amarillo, Texas, the year after her father comes home from the army. Fred Henze served four years and three months in what he still calls the "real" war.

"Me and the old Thirty-Sixth. Over the goddamn Arno and up the goddamn mountains. Someone had to show those Nazis what a real German could do."

She is her mother's first child, and will be her only girl. The four years and three months Fred Henze is in the war, Hildy Henze operates a lathe for a local defense plant. She likes the work, and working, isn't happy when the men return and take back their jobs. She never does anything about it. It is so much easier and more comfortable to do what all her girlfriends do, live the life everyone in Amarillo seems to want, the path of least bumps, what everyone agrees is the way it should be. But she never forgets those four years and three months, and whenever she reads about a successful career woman she says she could have been like that if she'd kept at it.

So from the day she is born, Elizabeth is told by her mother that a girl can have a career, should have a career even if she gets married too, is no different from a boy. She learns what Fred teaches her brothers, what special classes teach them, and a few things only girls do: fix cars and plumbing, do electrical wiring, build and use tools, type, dance, twirl. In high school she acts and builds sets, dances and learns the saxophone, plays basketball since she is tall, is a cheerleader and twirls with the marching band.

In high school she also learns new things. From her girlfriends, and television, and movies, and popular novels, and the teachers, and Bobby Travis. The one thing she wants but has not gotten by junior year is to be editor of the school newspaper. The faculty advisor, Mr. Birch, selects the editor, and can choose anyone from the staff or even from outside. But everyone knows that if last year's managing editor was a junior he becomes editor in his senior year. When Elizabeth is a junior, Bobby Travis is the editor and a senior. A tall, handsome boy who has his own car and looks good in jeans and boots and Stetson.

"If you make me managing editor, Bobby, then Mr. Birch'll make me editor next year. I'll be a good editor, Bobby."

"Hey, I don't know, Liz. I mean, we never had a girl editor on the paper. Hell, not even managing editor."

"But I'm the best reporter and editor and you know it."

Bobby grins. "For a girl."

"For anyone," she says flatly. "And that means you, Bobby Travis. I know more and I write better than anyone."

"I guess maybe," he says, and his grin is different. "But what else can you do? I mean, a girl got to try harder, right?"

They are in a booth at the coffee shop after school. They have taken a break from the newspaper, are all but alone. Bobby Travis seems very aware of this, still has that different grin. She is aware of it too, of the different grin, of what she and her girlfriends have often talked about.

"What do you want me to do, Bobby?"

"Hey, I mean, I got to get something out of it, right, Liz?"

She says, "You mean you want to get something into it. Why not, as long as I get the job. Right, Bobby?"

She learns that her mother is wrong, a girl *is* different from a boy. A girl has disadvantages, but certain advantages too, if used properly. Even an edge under the right conditions. She becomes managing editor. In her senior year, when Mr. Birch isn't sure a girl should be editor of something as important as the school newspaper, she convinces him. Despite mediocre grades, her position as editor, with all her other activities, gets her elected student body president and class president, and she sails into the University of Texas as a freshman to be watched.

Fred and Hildy are proud of the first, and, as it turns out, the last of the Henzes to go to college. In her junior year her older brother marries right after high school graduation, joins Fred in the telephone company, and when she is a senior her other brother goes to work on a ranch. At T.U. Liz quickly improves her grades. She works part time for a professor in Bus Ad who runs a co-op, and a biology professor with a private consulting business. As a junior she majors in Bus Ad, does an internship at a local investment firm, and meets Mark Todd.

Two years older, Mark Sylvester Todd is from a different but identical small Texas city. Tall, blond and handsome, just like Bobby Travis, he wears jeans, boots and a Stetson even better than Bobby Travis. He has much better shoulders, and Liz is older now and appreciates shoulders. He also has charm, brains, and ambition, is a big man on campus in the theater, a top student in aerospace engineering, and a fellow investment intern.

Liz signs up for theater. She auditions and is cast in the first show. Mark Todd is the star. He has a girl, but he soon notices Liz. Most men do. Since Bobby Travis, she has worked on that.

"You don't have a lot of talent, but you have a real stage presence." Mark Todd tells her. "Charisma."

"I know," she says. "We work well together. We even look good. You need a tall woman."

"I'm just about engaged."

"That's too bad. I'm free and footloose."

It is no contest. The girl who has followed him to T.U. from his home high school can give him all the usual, but she is not in Liz's class. In charm, brains, ambition and charisma, Liz and Mark are a match, the golden couple, and Mark succumbs before that first play closes. He is not *that* bright, does not realize she is smarter than he is. He will not really learn that until much later. At the time, they make an enviable couple, and that is all he needs.

It is Liz's idea for them to write a theater-movie column for the campus newspaper that is soon picked up by some local weeklies, shopping guides, and 'Things To Do' booklets in motels. This makes them nice money, and they soon learn that a series of plugs for the attractions at specific theaters will be rewarded by grateful exhibitors. Even less frequent plugs will earn them free tickets they can sell on the side.

Mark is dubious. "I've got a hunch it's not so kosher, Liz."

"Of course it is. Who do we hurt?"

"Other movie house owners, I guess. The other movies and the guys who gave us the free tickets."

"They expect *someone* to sit in those seats, can't resell them, and the other exhibitors can pay us too. It's just smart business to get every angle on a buck we can. I mean, we saw the potential, we've got a right to cash in. They wouldn't pay us if they didn't make more money too, so everyone wins."

"Not the guy who runs the theater we don't plug."

"By coming up with the idea we made more people go to the movies. Everyone does win. Anyway, if we didn't do it, someone else would. You got to grab fast or get left out, Mark."

Mark convinces his father to pay for one more year and a masters degree, but even then he finishes a year before Liz will. His father expects him to go to California and an excellent job with great prospects in a large aerospace company. Mark agrees on California, but it isn't aerospace he has in mind. Not at first anyway. He's always got the engineering to back him up, he and Liz agree, but the movies and TV are where the big bucks are, and youth counts.

"Go for broke, right?" he says. "Hollywood, here I come."

"Hollywood here *we* come," she says.

"Hey, you've got a year to be the big star here, finish your B.A. degree." He is earnest. "Why don't I go ahead, set things up. Get a pad, an agent, some contacts. Then you come out as soon as you graduate."

"No way, Jose. You go nowhere without me, buster."

"You don't trust me!"

"Not out of my sight. When you storm Lotusland, can Liz be far behind?"

He laughs. "I never really figured it any other way."

"Good. You'll live longer. We'll get married right after commencement, be in the air by noon."

Three years later they are both sent to prison for selling two ounces of cocaine to an undercover agent at a big Hollywood party where the host claims not to know them.

It begins on a 5:05 flight out of Austin, first class with the blessing of the Drama Department. (They cash in the tickets they got from each set of parents.) A stake, the names of former T.U. drama students who are working, and a strong introduction and recommendation to his agent from the director-in-residence. The golden couple are in Hollywood.

They borrow and buy a house in Studio City once owned by Steve McQueen and large enough for entertaining. They buy a five-year-old Mercedes town car and three-year-old Porsche. Impressive but not nouveau. The agent suggests lessons and coaches. They need a lot of new clothes. They make friends through the former T.U. actors. The agent sends them on calls, Liz lands a few small TV parts, Mark gets a screen test. The test is not a success, but the agent goes out on a limb to get him a featured role in a TV movie. He bombs, is replaced. He has no real talent, she has some but not much. Neither comes across on film. The agent suggests writing.

They run out of money after a year-and-a-half. He gets a job with an aerospace subcontractor in Van Nuys. She finds an opening with a biological consulting firm doing much the same work as the professor at T.U. Their combined pay covers the mortgage, taxes, car payments and food. Not much more. If they are to break through in Hollywood they must go on with the life they're living, even expand their connections. A quieter life is boring anyway. After another year he is arrested for stealing from his boss, she is picked up for shoplifting and bad checks.

Because they are white, married, college-educated, middle class homeowners with no previous records, they are given small fines and probation. But now Mark can't find a job in his field, not without moving to another state, and Liz can only find secretarial work and small Equity waiver stage parts that bring in no money. Mark tries to sell cars to their friends, Liz turns to mail order cosmetics. They borrow from their friends and their agent. One friend suggests a quick cocaine score at this large party. They are caught. No one knows them, the friend is not at the party.

They are still white, a couple, college-educated, own their own home, but they are also on probation so this time they are sentenced to a year and a day. With their age and background they do their time in minimum security prisons. When they get out, the house is gone and the cars. Mark heads back east to get work. Liz stays on in small jobs, still trying for the break in Hollywood. The agent has dropped them, most of their friends vanish, but a few old T.U. grads get her some small bits in TV. Back east Mark is picked up for defrauding an innkeeper, gets ninety days.

Liz is now alone in a small apartment court in Hollywood itself. She continues to make the rounds without success, knows she is never going to make it in show business. She needs a new career prospect, is thinking of going back to college to finish her B.A. in Bus Ad, when she runs into the old aerospace boss who had Mark arrested. He is pleased to see her again, has wondered what happened to her after he had to charge Mark.

"Don't ask," Liz says, smiles.

"I'm not surprised," the ex-boss, who's name is Eric Martin, says. "He's a loser, he always will be. Small time. You're better than that. Where is he now?"

"Back East in jail."

"Christ!" He shakes his head. "I'm sorry, Elizabeth, but how did you ever get mixed up with a nothing like that?"

"It seemed a good idea at the time."

"I suppose it did. But in life, we move on. If we're as smart as I think you are."

"Did you have something specific in mind?"

"Let's talk about it over dinner."

A month later she moves into his big house in Sherman Oaks, he buys her Porsche back. When Mark gets out of jail and writes to say he thinks he has a job in Atlanta, she says how happy she is for him, but she can't come to Georgia, and maybe it would be best to get a divorce. He calls and is sad, protests mildly, but it is clear that under it all he is relieved. Their life, the big ambition, has worn him down. He *is* small time and knows it now. Besides, he has met a woman in Atlanta, and, well, Hey, I hope you hit it big, Liz, real big. You too Mark, she says and really means it.

Liz Todd becomes Elizabeth Henze Martin in the high-powered world of Eric Martin. He has connections in the entertainment industry, offers to get her parts. But she knows now she has no real talent, and that the big money is not in front of the camera except for a rare few, and even then they must own the business too. She decides to work with Eric. He still has the aerospace company in Van Nuys, but it is only part of his holdings. There are two more engineering firms, real estate, the financial interests in Hollywood, and stock investments. She becomes his manager and most trusted advisor, learns all about the world of deals, kickbacks, inflated estimates, padded accounts to take care of important contacts, and cut corners.

There are good and bad days, but Eric Martin always comes out a winner. Elizabeth takes to it as if she's waited for it all her life. She loves the comforts and perks, but it is the excitement she really responds to. The rarefied air of being in the know, of making the world work out exactly the way you want. Power, but more than power. Having and taking. Everything you want. And there is the flaw, the rub. In the world of play hard and loose and a little over the edge if necessary or get left behind, to want is to need. Too much is never enough.

It is some years later. Mark Todd reappears in L.A. with a good job at Norberg Dynamics, the aerospace giant. There are no hard feelings. Mark has his Georgia girl in tow, the couples see quite a bit of each other after Eric Martin learns that Mark's job includes awarding contracts to subcontractors. Eventually a deal is struck. Mark will award contracts to Eric's aerospace companies at a price higher than Eric would charge on the open market, Eric will then inflate costs and expenses, and all the extra profit will be split with Mark. A sweet deal. If you don't take every angle you get left behind, risk losing the game to the more ruthless. A matter of self-preservation, and if being sharp slides over into illegality, you can cop a plea.

Usually, but not always. Norberg spots the fraud, and under pressure from a Pentagon itself under pressure from Capitol Hill, makes a deal with the weak link, Mark Todd, and Eric Martin gets sent away for ten years. Mark gets off with two. Elizabeth has no legal part of the deal, gets nothing. Except fifty percent of the community property in her divorce proceeding. It is not a great deal. Eric had almost everything tied to his business, which saved her another trip to the slammer, but which is as gone as Eric himself. More experienced this time, she has socked away a nest egg, but not a great one. She needs to work and invest and the combination brings her to J. James, Esq.

Gray-haired, distinguished, somewhat older even than Eric, smooth as cream and sharp as Saladin's scimitar cutting silk in mid-air. Banker's pinstripe and black shoes to a high polish. The perfect hair and pink face of a barber every week and more often if required. A man who counsels. Advises. Allows you in.

"I don't usually take on such a small account, Mrs. Martin, and I won't make an exception in your case. But I will offer you a position in my new company, and for an associate I will help."

"What new company?"

"J. James and Company, Mrs. Martin. I have finally been persuaded to offer my experience and modest knowledge to the general public, or that part of it with substantial equity to invest who wish to vastly increase that equity through what is an extremely high yield, but, inevitably, high risk, investment. Ordinarily high risk, that is. With what I have in mind the yield will remain high while the risk will diminish to all but nothing. Does it sound like it will attract people?"

"Like flies," she says. "If you can convince them, and if it's legal."

J. James laughs. "You are the perfect woman for the job, Elizabeth. I sensed it from the moment I met you."

"What do I do, Mr. James?"

"My personal assistant, office manager, investment executive, supervisor of independent investment managers. We will operate coast-to-coast, but concentrate on Southern California for now. There should be enough equity here to keep us busy for the first few years while we shake out the inevitable kinks."

"You've checked my background? Experience?"

"Indeed I have."

She smiles. "I accept. Job and advice. Whatever else."

At last it is the big time for Liz Henze from Amarillo, Texas, now Elizabeth Henze (Todd) Martin. House in Palm Springs. Los Angeles condo in a high rise convenient to the financial center. Limousines. Company jet. Offices and rented mansions in La Jolla, Montecito, Coronado, Malibu, wherever and whenever needed. Country clubs, tennis clubs and yacht clubs. Seminars and investment luncheons. Parties and cruises and private beach houses. Political campaigns for those candidates favorable to investment and growth.

Not marriage, but she is a big girl and marriage has not been too good to her. What she has, coast to coast, is enough.

Feature articles in *The San Diegan, California Magazine*. A mention in *Forbes*, a roundup article in *Fortune*. An interview in *Vanity Fair*. A story in *People*. Interviews on "Good Morning America" and *The Today Show*. The new complete woman.

Fred and Hildy Henze do not understand her, but they smile for the cameras, say, "She's a real busy little girl, our Liz."

Mark Todd, out of jail some years and consulting freelance for small aerospace contractors while running a TV talent agency and acting class, also smiles.

"I don't know anything about J. James," he says to anyone who asks, "but there has to be an angle, right? I mean, hell, that's all me and Liz ever learned."

That's when Mark Sylvester Todd laughs.

33

"It's got to be some kind of scam," Mark Todd said. His fourth martini—on the stem with a twist—washed down the last of The Pelican's best steak. "They have to be long gone. I got the word too late to put the bite on. Story of my life."

"You better talk to the police."

He set the empty martini glass on the table. "Time for me to get back to Lotusland. Thanks for the handout."

"If it is a scam, they'll want her background. Everything you know."

"Not from me, Fortune."

"I've got your name and license number. They'll bring you back the hard way."

"Keep moving and you've always got a chance. Hell, maybe it's all legit anyway. If you see old Liz before I do, tell her for me to hang in there."

Alone, I finished my second Beck's. The police could find him anytime they wanted, and he was right—J. James & Co. could be completely legitimate despite Elizabeth Henze Martin's past. Lieutenant Holley could be dogging her for an entirely different reason.

On San Ysidro Lane I parked again in the gravel turnaround in front of the big Mediterranean. There was still no answer, still no cars in the garage. I walked around the house looking in the windows. Nothing seemed cleared out, not even the study office. The mailbox outside the gate had no more than two days mail in it. If they were gone it had happened within the last day or so. I gave them until five o'clock, then drove to a pay phone in Montecito Village and called Sergeant Chavalas.

"That New York guy, Callow, was in," Chavalas said. "It's still an accident on Jantarro, we haven't a clue on Calhoun or anybody who could have hired him to get Frank Owen. That what you wanted?"

"Almost," I said. "How do I get in touch with the County Prosecutor?"

"You go to his office. Why?"

"I mean right now. I could have a tip for him."

"Is it important?"

"How do I know? It could be."

"Okay, I can't give out his number, but I can call him. What's the tip."

"Tell him I just talked to a guy who used to be married to Elizabeth Martin of J. James and Company, and the guy thinks the James operation could be a big scam."

"James? How come I don't know the company?"

"They're in the county, and you and I don't move in such high financial circles."

"That tells it. What's your number if he wants to see you in the morning?"

I gave him the number of the pay phone. The pharmacy and lunch room was where San Ysidro Road crossed East Valley Road, and I counted six Mercedes, three Jaguars, five BMWs, one Porsche and one Rolls Royce in under four minutes. A society has trouble when the gap between rich and poor becomes obvious, the powers are indifferent, and the rich don't have the muscle to control.

The phone rang. Chavalas's voice was surprised.

"He says come on over now."

The address was less than three blocks away. I wondered what kind of car the prosecutor drove. A large BMW, plus a Nissan 300ZX for fun. I parked behind the BMW. The house was a typical California ranch but larger than average, under gnarled old native holly oaks and ragged eucalyptus. Solid, affluent, impressive, but not a mansion. A home of someone who ran the world, but didn't own it.

He opened the door himself. "Come in."

Led me down an entryway past a sunken living room and into a den lined with law books and diplomas and photos of him with politicians and celebrities. Pointed to a chair, sat at his desk.

"Charley Tucker. Your name's Fortune? A private detective? In this county? How come I don't know you?"

"Dan Fortune. I just moved from New York. New license."

"New York?" He scowled as if trying to understand what New York could have to do with anything. "How the hell do you know about J. James and Company? How'd you get into this? Has James spotted you? What the hell are you after?"

The prosecutor was a tall, thin man in his late thirties. Dark-haired, a full mustache, handsome in a large-nosed way. A strong face. Brisk, quick, on his way up. But nervous now, even alarmed, firing questions without waiting for answers.

"What is it?" I said. "A Ponzi scheme? You're already investigating them?"

"Damn, and damn!" Tucker was up and pacing as if his world had just exploded in his face. "Fortune, if—"

I held up my lone hand. "Elizabeth Martin knows me, but she thinks I'm on something with no connection to her, and I've never seen J. James. I could even have a good witness for you."

"No! God damn it, Fortune . . ." Tucker took a long, deep breath. "Okay, start from the beginning. What are you doing, where does J. James and Company come in? Everything. Not one damn thing left out, you hear?"

I told him almost everything. I didn't know everything.

"Holley?" He shook his head. "No, he's from the Santa Maria station, he couldn't be tailing the Martin woman."

"You're working only out of Santa Barbara?"

He glared at me. "Never mind where the hell we're working out of. That's your only connection to Martin and James? You saw her around Lee Canton, and that's all? You talked to her only about Canton, and this Jantarro and Owen?"

"That's all."

"You haven't found anything to tie her or James to those deaths? Only that she's sold investment shares to Lee Canton?"

"So far," I said. It was getting one-sided, I needed to know things too. "Is Canton part of your case?"

"I can't tell you anything, damn it, except to stay out of the way and don't rock the boat."

"I've told you what I'm doing. I can't stay out of your way if I don't know what you're doing."

Tucker turned in his pacing to stare at me. It was a stare of disbelief that I was there and he was talking to me. But I've been stared at by the best. I smiled. He went back behind his desk and sat down again. He chewed a pencil as he looked at me.

"We've been investigating J. James and Company for nearly a year up here, longer down south. Us, Sacramento, the SEC, the FBI, damn all who else. It's basically a federal case, the U.S. attorney in Los Angeles is running the show, is about ready to move. A slip now, a tip-off, could blow it all, you understand?"

"How are they working the scheme, basically?"

He scowled. "Basically a Ponzi, yes, but with some cute variations. They picked a highly volatile, very high risk, unregulated investment area where it wouldn't be so obvious or unexpected if everything went bust. They got the suckers by promising up to forty percent return on their investment, faked records to show J. James to have made big profits in the past, issued false monthly statements showing everyone doing great on paper. They didn't do much trading, put most of the money in their own bank accounts in the Caymans or wherever, lived high off the hog. If anyone wanted to take cash out, that was when they pulled the Ponzi, paid off with the money they got from new investors. As long as new people invested, they were safe. But once the new investment stopped coming—boom, the end." He shrugged. "My guess is they planned to wait for a sharp drop in some currency, claim to have lost the whole shooting match, go bankrupt, and slip away to collect their loot."

"They couldn't get away with it forever."

"No swindler can, Fortune. But it's a sweet life while it's going on, something can always save them, and even if they're caught they expect a slap on the wrist."

"And they need the adventure," I said. "They like the risk, the danger, the fooling everyone, the life on the edge."

He barely heard me. That much risk and daring and life on the edge wasn't for him. He would like his edge a lot more sure, his risk minimal with no real danger. Just a big score on a sure thing. His arse covered all the way.

"Are they going to get a slap on the wrist this time?"

"From what I've seen, no way. They're preparing an over 200-count indictment on them both as principals, less for the others in other offices. Convicted on all, they'll go away for over a thousand years each."

"Ten to twenty at most," I said. "White collar, they'll pay back a lot of it."

"We're hoping for twenty minimum. I mean, there's over two hundred million dollars involved, eighty million in losses."

"Where does Lee Canton fit in?"

"I don't think he does, except as a victim. We figure he's put a lot of money into the scheme, stands to lose most of it."

"He's not selling to his friends and contacts up here?"

"Some, but we think he's a dupe. That's another way they work the scheme. They get those who've already invested to bring in friends for a cut of the commission. A pyramid on a Ponzi."

"Inventive," I said. "Are you investigating Canton?"

"Not as far as I know."

"And neither Billy Owen nor Hector Jantarro show up in the J. James investigation?"

"If they do, we haven't been told."

The Feds were notorious for not telling locals anything unless they had to. Tucker would know that as well as I did, wouldn't appreciate being reminded.

"Have they skipped town, Tucker?"

He shook his head. "I've told you more than I should have now. But I wanted to make sure you understood how important it is for you to stay out of this, keep your activities low profile, don't rock our boat. Lay off Elizabeth Martin and J. James until I tell you it's okay. Don't even think about them."

"I never heard of them," I said.

We shook hands. His handshake was extra sincere, but there was a film of sweat on his forehead. He was seeing a private gumshoe stumbling around in a year-long federal investigation in his county. It would have given me a cold sweat too, especially if I had ambitions.

He'd already told me more than he knew. Lee Canton was a big victim of the scam, and Tucker didn't know Lieutenant Holley was tailing and watching Elizabeth Henze Martin.

34

Kay watched the sea and the islands with a Beck's in her hand and her feet up. A standard summer evening, the haze thinned out enough over the blue of the Channel to see the long shadow of Santa Cruz Island. She didn't say what she was thinking, but I thought about time and adventure.

"Lieutenant Holley isn't tailing Elizabeth Martin for the fraud investigation," I said, "or isn't working officially. A different reason, or a private surveillance."

"Who gets a private favor from a sheriff's lieutenant?"

Time and adventure. Four hundred years ago, the blink of a cosmic eye if the cosmos had eyes, Juan Rodriguez Cabrillo, Sir Francis Drake, and Sebastian Vizcaino, sailed out there between the islands and where I sat with my beer. For gold and slaves, for glory and adventure, but also to know. If we have a purpose, maybe that's it—to explore, discover the secrets of our planet.

"All Billy wanted was adventure and glory. He never knew how or where to find them except in secondhand dreams."

"Frank, too?" She watched the sun on the channel as if she could also see the tiny ships of Drake and Cabrillo.

"Dianne, in her own way," I said.

"Is it what got Billy killed, Dan? Adventure and glory?"

"Pretty much. But there was a trigger. Somehow he bumped into someone's reality." I told her what I'd learned from Mark Todd and Charles Tucker. "Lee Canton is going to lose a lot of money. Did he know it, get involved in something with Jantarro? Maybe send Jantarro to get his money back?"

"Wouldn't Canton have gone to the police as soon as Jantarro was found dead?"

"Maybe he did. Maybe that's what Lieutenant Holley is doing watching Elizabeth Martin."

"She and James hired a killer to murder Jantarro, sent him after Billy too?"

"Except why wouldn't Billy have just gone to the police instead of running and hiding?"

"Maybe he was going to trap the killer himself?"

Could even Billy Owen have been that stupid? I thought about it as I watched the sea and the shadows of the islands where, somewhere, Juan Cabrillo was buried, a victim of his dreams and illusions too.

"There's another possibility for what Holley's doing. Old Sam Canton would be one person a sheriff's lieutenant would do a favor for."

"Their ranch is in The Valley, and he has two grandsons."

"I'll have to go over there."

Kay didn't like that. "That's money and power, Dan."

"Tell me about it."

Before we could discuss the power of the Cantons, the phone rang. It was Dianne Owen. Frank wanted to talk to me.

"Where?"

"My place, of course. What else?"

"Can it wait a couple of hours?"

"I don't think so, Dan."

I heard that tone in her voice, the slightly hesitant words, the strain. Someone else was there. And not Frank Owen.

"Give me twenty minutes," I hung up and stood up. "I guess detective work's the same everywhere."

"I've got work to do, when you come back we'll eat out."

"It could be a while."

She studied my face. "Is something wrong, Dan?"

"I'm not sure."

"I'll be here."

I stopped for my cannon, took the back roads over the hill into Montecito, along N. Jameson Lane, and over the freeway to Eucalyptus Lane. I parked a block away from Dianne Owen's house in the darkening twilight, watched the house for a time. Nothing unusual caught my eye, I saw no one staked out. Only a rental car with a BUDGET, Riverside Drive, Burbank, license holder parked in front of the house.

A secret intruder wouldn't park so obviously, but I circled to come up to the house along the railroad tracks. The downstairs windows were all open and dark in the warm night. Behind me, the surf rolled lightly on Miramar Beach below the bluffs beyond the tracks. A shadow moved across the lighted living room windows of the second floor. One shadow, tall and thin.

I watched the high window for the substance behind the shadow. It never came, and even the thin shadow disappeared, replaced by a stockier one: Dianne Owen. There was no sign of Frank Owen. The screen door out of the downstairs dining room wasn't locked. Light down the staircase was enough to guide me across the dining room and into the downstairs entry hall.

Above, there were voices. Low key, even casual, and too low to make out any words. The voice that dominated was neither Dianne nor Frank Owen. A voice with an unusual timbre. In the half light below the stairs I couldn't place it. Cannon in my lone hand at the ready, I went up until I could see into the living room with its wide window on the sea.

Frank Owen in a red terry cloth robe sat on a high-backed teak chair in the center of the room. He wasn't talking, his hands were on his knees, and he watched something against the windowless far wall.

Dianne was on the couch wrapped in a voluminous white robe, hands in her lap, stiff and tense and talking, ". . . how can we be sure it wasn't you? Why should we trust any of you?"

She watched the same place on the far wall hidden from me by a large leather armchair. I went up two steps. The black woman sat on the arm of a chair, a Walthar PPK on a side table near her hand. Six feet tall, in a sleek white dress that showed off her hips and breasts and long legs.

"You talked to Nina," Frank said. "You were looking for Billy. Billy and Jantarro. Maybe you found them both."

I realized that their hands were in view because she had told them to keep them there before she put her PPK down. She was being careful but not threatening.

"I was looking for Hernan Javier. I found him too late, had no further interest in your brother. He was a harmless clown, Mr. Owen. We stop clowns if we must, but we don't pursue them."

Her English was smooth and natural, her native language. Educated, but with an accent. Somewhere in the Caribbean. High cheekbones gave her an Indian look to go with the African skin. Her eyes were lighter than they should have been, and despite her youthful appearance I guessed she was in her late thirties. She looked affluent and inviting. She crossed her legs to show a long calf and some thigh through the slit in the dress.

"Why were you looking for this Javier?" Dianne asked.

"Javier was a criminal, and not a clown."

"If all you wanted was Javier, why are you still here?" Frank said.

"Because we wanted to know why he died, who killed him. To be sure we hadn't exchanged one enemy for another."

Dianne Owen reached for the cigarette box on the coffee table. The tall black woman's hand touched the Walthar.

Dianne stopped. "Can I smoke?"

"All right. We'll all smoke until your friend gets here."

She reached into a handbag at her feet for her cigarettes.

I stepped up into the living room.

"I'm already here. Keep your hands away from the Walthar."

She took out a cigarette, lit it, looked toward me and the big old pistol in my hand. Calculated the situation without panic or nerves or heroics.

"Mr. Fortune?"

I nodded. "Nicaragua? From the Gulf coast."

"I was afraid Miss Owen's voice on the telephone might have warned you. But you can put it down, I'm here to talk."

The next player was behind me. Below on the stairs.

"She is, Fortune. Believe it or not, we're all on the same side on this one."

Alan Cox, the FBI man, stood at the foot of the stairs. He had the old mandatory large revolver half-pointed at the floor. I had the black woman, Cox had me.

"Explain it to me," I said.

They knew a Mexican standoff when they saw one. She smoked with a small smile, both hands far from the PPK on the side table. Cox came up a few steps to where he could see us all.

"Ms. Green is an agent of the FMLN rebels in El Salvador, Fortune, she came here after Javier. She—"

"Dolores Green y Vega," Ms. Green said. "Officially, a full representative of the FDR, credentials and all."

The FDR (Democratic Revolutionary Front) was the political wing of the Farabundo Marti National Liberation Front (FMLN) Marxist-Leftist guerrillas in El Salvador. She and Cox were having some professional fun and games, establishing the ground rules. Ms. Green was an undercover guerrilla, Cox was an FBI man, but for the moment we were pretending nobody knew anything.

"No," I said. "Ms. Green is an English-speaking Nicaraguan from the eastern coast."

Dolores Green fanned cigarette smoke. "Born in Nicaragua. But, like Hernan Javier, I found myself exiled in another country where there was work I could do."

"Like exporting a Marxist revolution?" Frank Owen said.

"You don't export revolution like Coca-Cola or cars or cheap blankets, Mr. Owen. It's not a manufactured product you put into a box and ship over the border. Revolutions are made by the conditions within a country. Help can come from outside, but that's all. You helped the French, but France had to be ready. The Mexican Revolution had little effect on the United States."

"It's just an accident that you're a Nicaraguan in the FMLN?" I said.

"Conspiracy, Mr. Fortune? You Americans want it to be so simple. I was born in Nicaragua. My family were exiled by Somoza. I grew up in El Salvador, was educated in the United States, Mexico and Cuba. Our rich have ties with the other rich of Latin America. Our peasants and urban poor are the same from Chile to Mexico. Our revolutionaries have the same enemies, the same hopes of freedom and food for ourselves, instead of coffee and bananas for you."

"Freedom by killing people," Dianne said.

The tall woman walked to the high picture window. "We would prefer political action, but men like D'Aubuisson and his death squads can only be killed."

I said, "D'Aubuisson would say women like you and your guerrillas can only be killed. What decides who's right?"

Frank Owen said, "Was Javier one of those who had to be killed?"

"Yes," Dolores Green said, "but we didn't kill him. That is what Mr. Cox brought me here to talk about."

Cox nodded. "I think Ms. Green has some help for us. She came here looking for Hernan Javier, ran across a few things."

"You came to kill Javier?" Frank said. "Billy too?"

"I've already said we had no interest in your brother," she walked back to the armchair, took another cigarette out of her large black bag. "I came on information that Javier was here and planning to slip back into El Salvador. I came to capture him, or learn his plans so we could capture him in El Salvador and force the government to put him on trial. If they didn't, it would show the world where they really stood. If I could do neither, then I would kill him. But by the time I got here and located him under the name of Jantarro, he was dead."

"How do we know that?" I said.

Cox said, "Because when I spotted Ms. Green I had her back-tracked and found she'd arrived in New York the day Jantarro fell over that cliff. There was no way she could have reached Santa Barbara to help him over."

"He was much more valuable alive, Mr. Fortune. His death is better than nothing, but it has no positive use."

"As a matter of fact," Cox said, "our CIA friends would have had much more reason to kill him to prevent him returning to El Salvador and standing trial. If they got wind of his plan to go home, or if they spotted Ms. Green on his tail."

"I don't think they did," Dolores Green said. "They were caught off guard by Javier's death, had to improvise to cover. If they had wanted him dead, they would have planned a better way."

"So who the hell killed him and Billy?" Frank swore. He still sat in the chair with his hands on his knees as if he'd forgotten his body existed, hadn't noticed the guns were gone.

"That I can't tell you. What—"

"What the fuck are you here for then?"

"Let her talk, Owen," Cox said.

Dolores Green sat, crossed those long legs again. "What I can tell you is there's no evidence of anyone from outside except the CIA contacting Javier, and every evidence he was expecting a lot of money from someone. Enough to buy him immunity from prosecution back in El Salvador. Enough for the most non-political opportunist in my corrupt homeland to look the other way while he got his power back."

The sound of the light surf on Miramar beach across the railroad tracks reached into the room. Traffic on the freeway and cars on Eucalyptus Lane. Voices out walking in front of the house.

"What does that mean?" Dianne said at last.

"It means," Cox said, "that Jantarro was expecting a large sum of money from someone, and that's who killed him."

"It means," I said, "the money had to come from a local source. Some deal or scheme Jantarro was pulling here."

"It means a hyena remains a hyena," Dolores Green said. "He was corrupt at home, he was corrupt here. The CIA could hide him, protect him, but they couldn't change him."

I said, "You think he spotted an opportunity and went after it even at the risk of blowing his cover. At the risk of losing his CIA support."

"A freebooter is always a freebooter, Mr. Fortune. That is something you learn in an underground war."

"But you heard nothing about where the money was coming from?" Cox asked.

She shrugged, looked at an elegant diamond-studded watch. With her speech and manners, she was not from any peasant family. A patrician daughter of landowners and politicians who had chosen the other side. She stood up.

"With Javier you can be sure of one thing. It would not have been honest work."

"Money in the bank," I said. "That's what he told Gloria Castro. Someone he had by the *huevos*."

Dolores Green said, "That is Javier. May I have my pistol?"

I gave her the little PPK. She dropped it into her handbag, nodded to Cox.

"Thank you for the courtesy, Mr. Cox. Perhaps one day I can return the favor."

"We happened to have the same goal in this one," Cox said. "You'll leave the country tonight? L.A. and out?"

She nodded, then turned to me. "We know who is right, Mr. Fortune, by looking at history. A tiny minority of Europeans have always owned and ruled us. But even with a ruthless oligarchy, we were self-supporting until the nineteenth century U.S. expansion. Then *you* turned us into one vast coffee and banana plantation where we could not even grow our own food. If your control was threatened, you 'arranged' a change of government. You crushed all rebellions against your local rulers with the troops you trained for them, with mercenaries, with your own troops if you had to. What the poor people want has never been of any interest to your government or businessmen. 'You stole our countries fair and square,' to paraphrase one of your own senators."

Frank Owen said, "You think the Soviets'll be any better?"

"The Soviets will not own us. There is a large difference between the influence of Cuba and the USSR, and the ownership of the United Fruit Company and the U.S. Marines."

"We're so close," Dianne said. "Can't we help each other?"

Dolores Green seemed to think about helping each other almost sadly. "The trouble with stealing a country is that as long as those you stole it from still exist you can keep it only by maintaining the force that got it for you in the first place. The moment those you stole it from have the power, they will take it back from your innocent descendents, even from generations who were born in the country. Those people will suffer greatly, but there will be nothing they can do. We are taking our countries back from United Fruit, the coffee barons, Standard Oil and the CIA."

She walked to the stairs down.

Frank Owen said, "You're educated. You look rich, classy. How did you end up on the other side?"

She came back up the stairs only far enough for us to see her aristocratic black face. "That anti-Nazi child of *Die Weisse Rose*, Sophie Scholl, said that all people in a dispute should join the side they consider righteous, not the one they were born in, whether it was family or country. I joined the side I think righteous. That is what your brother did not do, Mr. Owen. All he cared about was fighting, it didn't matter what for."

Cox waited in the living room until the rented car started outside, faded away toward the freeway south.

"My job was Javier, that part's over. Good luck."

"Thanks for the help," I said.

"Look me up when you're in Washington. We're not all as narrow as we're made out sometimes."

Then he was gone too.

35

Frank Owen said, "You believe any of that, Fortune?"

"Shouldn't he have arrested her?" Dianne said.

I sat on the couch, closed my eyes, leaned back. Every year the days get longer. And shorter too. You get tired, slow down, and yet the days go by too fast. Sometimes I think the only constant is paradox.

"With Javier dead, what Cox is doing makes sense." Talking with your eyes closed is a strange sensation. As if you're alone in a great void. "Arrest her, and it embarrasses the CIA and State. No one has anything to gain by a fight now. They want her out of the country, she wants to get home. Throw a blanket over it."

"Bureaucrats," Frank said. "I need a beer. You two ready?"

"I'll take one," Dianne said.

I nodded, listened to him cross the room and go down the stairs from my self-imposed darkness. I sensed Dianne watching me, but she didn't speak.

"He's living here with you?"

"Yes."

"On again? Or a fling?"

"I don't know."

Frank came back up. The bottles and glasses clinked as he climbed. I opened my eyes to take my glass and bottle, watched him return to the same high-backed chair, sit with his beer and shake his head.

"In a way you have to admire that Dolores Green," he said as he poured the beer, "but it's all bullshit. There isn't anything to fight for worth a damn anymore. VCRs, hottubs, stereos, home computers,

TV shopping so we can buy without getting out of bed. Microwaves and everything in the freezer. It's getting so no one'll ever have to leave the house. We're exhibits in a zoo, and we put ourselves there."

I'd closed my eyes again. That sensation of a great, black void. "Maybe you're right, but she was right too. Adventure for adventure's sake is dead. A hobby, an empty game."

"There are things to do, Frank," Dianne said.

"New frontiers? What? Space? Christ, those astronauts are puppets of tubes, space suits, computers, teams of experts, and experts to help the experts."

"I was thinking more of poverty, hunger."

"That's bullshit too. No one in the rich countries gives a damn, and for the leaders of the poor countries it's politics." He drank his beer, scowled. "Why should we believe Cox and that Green woman. They could have made a deal to cover the CIA."

"We don't," I said. "We believe ourselves. Everything from that tape to the Santa Ynez Valley dirt to Gloria Castro and Jantarro's character backs Ms. Green's story. The bottom line is that Javier, or Jantarro to us, was in hiding, the CIA wouldn't have used him. If he had a deal going, it was on his own."

"With someone here?"

"Who spends time over in the Valley," Dianne said.

"Who Jantarro had by the balls," I said.

Frank Owen went down for more beer. When he came back he stood at the picture window in his red robe looking out at the oil rigs like aircraft carriers.

"I'm going to find who killed Billy and bring him in."

"Alone?" Dianne said.

"With Fortune if he wants to go on."

"That's something," she said.

"Tomorrow," I said.

He finished his beer in two long gulps. "In that case I'll take a shower, get some sleep, see you in the morning."

He disappeared into the bedroom. Dianne sat with her beer, not looking at me. I drank my beer. More Anchor Steam. It's a first rate beer. Not quite as good as another California beer Kay had introduced me to, Sierra Nevada Ale, but that was hard to get, and sometimes you take what you can get. Most of the time.

"You hired me to help him and keep an eye on him. To tell you where he was and what he was doing. Because you never really let go even though the divorce was your idea. What now? Start all over? You think Billy's death is going to change him?"

The shower started running somewhere on the far side of the bedroom. She listened to the sound, seemed to be seeing something in the silence of the living room.

"I got the divorce, but that doesn't mean it was my idea. I only made it official. Frank wanted out, you can't have a one-way marriage. At least I can't, and I don't know if he'll change or not."

"Then?" I said.

She still listened to the sound of running water behind the closed door of the bedroom. She was seeing Frank Owen in the shower, naked, the water pouring down his lean body.

"We have our fantasies too, Dan."

36

The lion lies in the high grass in the corner of her bedroom. It has a great black mane. Three females pace nearby. Cubs bite at their heels, are cuffed tumbling. She stands naked in the shadow of the jungle. Monkeys and birds scream, snakes slide across her feet. She stares out at the lion. Then it stands and she sees the tight sack of balls between its haunches, the wet penis extended and enormous. Swinging back and forth like a thick red rod as it walks massive toward where she hides.

She and her best friend Mariah have been to the football game. Mariah, giggling, has whispered to Dianne that the second string quarterback is looking at her. He is a tall boy with long hair to his shoulders, a thick chest, tight pants with buttocks and bulge. A junior named Chino. Mariah's boyfriend, Greg, tells them later that Chino has asked who Dianne is. Greg says Chino isn't too swift, but if Dianne wants to they'll double date so she can look him over closer. Dianne says why not, and that night sees the lion for the first time.

Chino does not work out. The date is a disaster. He is a dense lout who expects her to fawn over him, and at the same time is obviously scared to make a move on her. He talks big but does nothing, clings almost desperately to public places where he can be seen.

"You know how to make babies, Chino?"

"Hey, what talk is that. Listen to the music, okay?"

She laughs at him, ruins the date, and does not see the lion again for many years.

Her parents are older than those of her friends, a firmly conservative couple who bring their two children up to be what they are supposed to be. Her brother Max goes East to earn an MBA, join a large company her father's company supplies with OEM switches, and return to be vice president in her father's company as they begin the changeover to electronics. Max is discouraged from marriage until he can afford a proper car, house, children, adequate insurance, and wife. Max dutifully complies.

Dianne also complies. As a girl, she does not go East. She attends a small local college, is encouraged to find a nice young man immediately after graduation. She will raise a family, sail serene at his side through a smooth life. It is a plus if she chooses a husband who can join her father and brother in the company, but it isn't mandatory, her father is not a martinet. She is expected to choose soon, even before her graduation, so the wedding can actually be announced at the commencement as her mother's was. A double sign of her success.

She chooses a young man she's known for years in church and community, who's been away at West Point. The last two summers they have seen much of each other. Richard is steady, reliable, proper, believes what their parents believe. He is not handsome or especially tall, but he isn't ugly and he has a fine future in or out of the army. He is also about to graduate, the families approve, and so they are married.

They spend the first two years in Texas. She fits in well with the other army wives. They are people like her parents, have the same views of such things as the tragedy of Vietnam when the army wasn't allowed to win—when the country betrayed its soldiers—and the new Communist threat in Central America. But it is hot, and dull, and in the second year she finds the rigid structure, the narrow circle, the elitism, stifling.

Later, she knows that the change didn't begin with any of those things, but with the total male orientation.

"Boys get to do what they want, girls pick up after them," one of the older wives says. It is not welcomed by the others.

Richard is what he is supposed to be. Elite, patriotic, hard-working, dedicated. He serves his country, the rest of the world is *them*.

Civilians are *them*. In the officers club minorities are *them*, except the few who are officers and so different. He is a disciplined lover. At least twice a week at bedtime or after a party. She learns that women, too, are *them*.

"Why can't women be line officers? Go into combat?"

"Where do you sleep, go to the john? We live in the open. When you get your period, do we stop the war? What happens if you're captured? The enemy rapes you, gets you pregnant?"

"The enemy does things to men. What's so bad about getting fucked. It happens."

"You think we want our wives fucked by enemy soldiers?"

The third year they are posted to Germany. She is excited, eager. Richard has his first independent command. Germany is new and different. Richard works hard: a bastion of his country on the front line.

Its black mane like a dark satanic halo, the lion moves through the moonlight reflected from the deep snow of the forest outside the leaded windows. She is naked. Her heart pounds. Spears and battle-axes hang on the walls. Her eyes are wide as he looms over her. The swelling balls in the dark pouch between its corded leg muscles. The long, wet, red rod as thick as a tree branch that swings before her. It blocks out the light. On her back her legs spread wide. Open, wet, her hips thrusting. She moans, writhes, slashes her nails into raw hide, bites as the thick, pulsing rod tears her open, fills her bursting.

They have gone on holiday to The Black Forest. In civilian clothes Richard is smaller. It is winter, the snow is deep. He wishes he were back on duty. She knows this and he spoils it but not so much that she wants to leave the dark, medieval aura of the forest and the villages and the Gothic churches and almost hidden castles. A forest that has not changed for thousands of years. The same forest where the barbarian tribes swarmed out of shadows to massacre a Roman army. Vandals, Goths, Franks, all hair and furs and horned helmets.

The old church is deep in the darkness of the trees. Smoke drifts across the snow-covered land. The light is thin through stained glass in the gloom of Gothic arches. Somewhere monks chant plainsong that take her back a thousand years and more. The song and their footsteps echo from the stone and hollow spaces. She understands religion. The medieval need. The weight of darkness, of ignorance, the ultimate weight of no control, of helplessness. In the forest death is tomorrow, death is every day, death is now—sudden, arbitrary, without cause or explanation. The answer is religion, and death has no horror. Men who die without reason kill without reason. No guilt, no immorality. Kill as a bear kills what moves across its path.

Outside the church in the snow and dark trees she wears a heavy robe of skinned animals. The trees are thicker, the dark heavier, the faint odor of smoke fearful. She is alone and lost, fears the smoke but finds it. A shaggy man and two growling dogs huddle over the small flames. The man motions her to the fire. She crouches in the warmth. He hands her hot meat. She eats. She lies down. He takes her. They sleep in the furs. Two men appear from the forest. They spear the man at the fire. One of them grabs her. She bites and kicks. The other man laughs. The men fight. One cuts the head off the other with a single blow of an axe. She lies down for the winner, opens her legs. They cut up the bodies, feed them to the dogs. At dawn they take the furs and the weapons and leave with the dogs.

In the old Inn that night she sees the lion the second time.

Richard decides on a military career and after another year they return to Texas. Dianne is no longer like the others. She does not fit in with the wives who are like her parents. Richard still does what he is supposed to do. Richard will now always do what he is supposed to do. It is what he wants to do, second nature, part of him. She joins a local theater, looks for work, talks to the army wives about their rights. The older wife is not there any longer, the other wives call her a feminist and stop asking her to lunches. She wants to change them, ruin their smooth lives. She wants to annoy their men, hurt the army, destroy the country.

By now she can't imagine why anyone would want to join the army, male or female, but she fights for the right of a female to join the army. She joins a feminist protest at the gates of the Texas base. The Colonel's wife talks to her. She tells the Colonel's wife that the army, the country, and the Colonel are sexist, that women have a right to do anything and everything. The Colonel talks to her himself.

"When a man is fighting for his country, Dianne, he needs to know his woman is backing him up at home. Doing her part."

"I am doing my part. I'm fighting my way for women. I need to know my husband is backing me, doing his part."

"Feminist views are disruptive. Bad for the army."

"So I shut up?"

"You aren't helping Richard's career."

When she joins a protest for the rights of Mexican squatters on army land, Richard knows it is time for a divorce before she ruins his career as well as the smooth lives of the other wives and the country.

"We don't think alike anymore, Dianne. You've changed."

"You don't think, Richard. You'll never change."

Dianne moves to Los Angeles and tries to break into movies or any other acting career. She does not have the talent, has become strong enough to know that and face it. She goes into the talent business with a large agency, soon opens her own talent agency. When the irresponsibility and ego of actors become a bore, she branches into public relations. She finds she is good at PR, adds advertising, and is a full-fledged business woman. The final step is to move her agency to Santa Barbara, devote it to handling female owned and operated firms, and break with her parents who have barely spoken to her since the divorce.

The lion stands in the path of moonlight from the sea to her bedroom. At her high window she looks down at each muscle etched by moonlight, corded with power. She raises her arms and her breasts swing and point. The curve of her belly hollows, thrusts out the mound below with its dark hair. The bull slashes into the moonlight, hooks its vast horns. The lion roars. The earth shakes to a clash by night. Raw wounds open in the grass, trees fall, the night itself is trampled, ripped. The bull is gone. Her flesh is hot, she cannot breathe, her thighs and the wet opening wait for the triumphant lion.

There are many men after she leaves Richard. Affairs and liaisons and companionships that last from weeks to months and once almost all year. One night stands. Weekend flings in mountains and beach-houses. From-party-to-his-place passions. After-meetings-to-her-place unwindings. Blind dates. Even a pickup or two. It is fresh air after her parents and Chino-the-substitute-quarterback and Richard. All seem necessary at the time, none leave any memories or regrets. Not even the one that lasts almost a whole year.

His name is Roy, he is in charge of advertising at one of her client companies when her office is still in Los Angeles. He asks her out many times, but she always has someone else far more interesting. Until they meet at a convention in New York where she knows no one, has no personal contacts, and lets him take her to dinner and the theater. He knows New York well, they have a fine time for the next three days. He isn't handsome, or tall, or athletic, or especially attractive. But he is intelligent, humorous, knowledgeable, admires her a great deal and knows how a free and independent woman wants to be treated. After Richard, and the men since Richard, he is wonderful to be with.

Roy has never been married, living with her is a totally new world for him. He dotes on her. A female is a miracle to him, a discovery, a whole new landscape. He delights in her, can't get enough of looking at her naked. He is a gentle lover, but strong enough and constant. Every night she lets him. He won't force her, not ever. He is patient and always ready, but it is up to her. She learns much more about advertising from him, but he never puts his work before her unless it is an emergency, and then he makes up for it with dinner out or a weekend in Puerto Vallarta. He helps in the apartment, cooks as well as she does.

She leaves him after the year. She has many reasons, the main one being her desire to move back to Santa Barbara, but she has to tell him there are other reasons or he would come with her, commute the ninety-odd miles to his company.

"I've just fallen out of love, Roy."

The physical attraction has gone, the excitement has faded.

"It happens, Roy. I'm sorry."

No one's fault, the chemistry simply changed and left them friends but without the passion. She needs to be alone for a time. She needs to look for the passion that will last. There may not be any such passion, but she has to at least look.

"You too, Roy. You deserve more than I can give you."

He is devastated, but accepts her decision. He returns to his total devotion to his job. But he has come to know the beauty of a woman and she hears less than a year later he has married a real estate woman he met a week after she moved up to Santa Barbara. She laughs when she hears this. Poor Roy.

She enjoys doing what she wants to do without having to worry about what anyone else wants. One of her new activities is the Montecito YMCA and aerobics. Still in her twenties, she has been too busy to notice her body except in bed. Now she notices a faint thickening, and short and sturdy as she has always been she can't take any thickening.

The aerobics class is almost all women, but sometimes there is a husband or a boyfriend. The men are usually older, late forties to sixties, and there is usually only one at a time. The older women defer to him, the younger women smile and giggle as he does the aerobic steps. The instructor both smiles and defers, is always pleased to see him. Men are difficult to get to come to a class of women.

Sometimes there is more than one man. If the new man is younger, the older man begins to do all the exercises he has rested through or skipped when only the women were there, matches the younger man. If the new man is older, then the man already in the class works just enough harder to show he can do more than the newcomer. If they are both young men, then both do more than is required by the instructor, exercises and moves only the youngest of the women can do. Dianne realizes that this is only in a class where all the others are women. In a class of all men, it would happen only with the "leaders." Those who had already acknowledged the "leaders" would not have to do anything more than they usually did.

In her beachhouse bedroom she sees the lion the third time.

She meets Frank Owen when he comes to tell her to stay away from his married brother. There is much of Chino-the-second-string-quarterback in him, only he is a man not a boy, knows what Chino had not had time to know, what Richard will never know, what Roy was too nice to learn. He is nothing Richard or Roy were, everything Roy and Richard weren't. She marries him.

The lion returns to her bedroom every night at sunset. Its tread shakes the earth. She is filled with fear. She is filled with need. She sees her cubs from the great lion. They have its haunches and mane and whipping tail, her face and breasts and slim belly. She licks her dry lips, opens her legs as she does every night when the earth shakes. He breaks into the dark bedroom all yellow eyes and fangs and towering shoulders and tight testicles and the enormous long thick wet red rod that will fill her from her fearful toes to the smiling eyes.

37

"Do all women feel the same as Dianne?"

Kay lay close to me in the bed. The dim shadows of the white walls and dark beams of the bedroom in Summerland. Lay touching me her whole slim, full, round length.

"With me it was a stallion. It's there."

"How far would she go to capture her lion?"

She was silent in the night. "You mean could she have thought that with Billy gone Frank would be different?"

"Is it possible?"

"Not very. She's too smart to think Frank would become someone else that easily."

I said. "Is fear always a part of it? Of me?"

Her lips touched my throat. Her breasts on my chest. "How do we know? There's all kinds of fear, Dan. I suppose a woman, way down deep, wants to be a little afraid of her man. Afraid of something: his power, his strength, his violence, his wandering, his wanting another woman. The thrill, the response. I want to feel a little 'taken,' I suppose. Most of us don't really want to ever be forced to do anything, but there's a small need to think you could force me if you wanted to. You could take me."

"But I better not try?"

"Try. But not too hard or often."

As I went to sleep I remembered that with lions it is the female who does the hunting.

Frank Owen waited on the low wall in front of Dianne's house, the light surf on Miramar Beach a low rumble in the cool morning sun.

"Another try?"

"Could be," he said. "We always got along when it was hot."

"You're going to have to do better than that."

"That's the problem." He got into my Tempo, snapped on his seat belt. "What I have to do."

We took the freeway into town, and police headquarters on Figueroa.

"Come on in," Sergeant Chavalas said.

He waved us to chairs. He looked his most Latino, black hair, trimmed mustache, short-sleeved white overshirt.

"What the hell did you do to Charley Tucker? He's been walking on nails, riding the sheriff and us to find some guy named Todd."

I told him what I'd done to Prosecutor Tucker. "What are they doing on Jantarro?"

"What can they do? The trail's cold, we don't have any motive or evidence for murder except a tape by a dead man who could have been crazy or so scared he'd say anything."

"They're giving up?" Frank said. "They know Billy was murdered."

"No, they'll keep it open, but don't expect them to push too hard, and it's not my case. Your New York guy, Callow, went home this morning early." He shrugged. "On my end we're at a blank wall with Murch Calhoun. Not a whisper about who could have hired him."

"Lee Canton and his foreman hire carpenters."

"That's a heavy charge on a prominent citizen. You have anything to back it up?"

"No."

"Neither do I," Chavalas said. He found something very interesting outside his windows. A jacaranda tree long past blooming. "I looked into it, especially on McElder, but I didn't do any better than you did. They said you'd already asked about Calhoun, they'd looked at all their records. They even showed me the records. No Calhoun."

He did his job.

"Why McElder especially?"

"He gets around the whole county. He lives over in the Valley. He's got a record of violence and skating the edge."

Frank Owen said, "He worked with Billy and Jantarro too. Was he out of town when Billy was killed?"

"He and Canton both travel so much, go up and down to L.A., even over to Bakersfield, no one can say where they are when."

"You mean," I said, "if they wanted to cover their tracks, they could."

Chavalas nodded. "The trouble is a motive, even a reason. Jantarro and Owen worked for them, period. Low level work, gofer and muscle. Jantarro didn't even work that hard. The CIA and FBI are sure no one at Canton knew who he was, not even Billy Owen."

"What about J. James and Elizabeth Martin?" I said. "Any sign of a connection to Calhoun? Between them and Jantarro?"

"That's not my investigation. Tracing Calhoun I didn't run into them. Jantarro and Billy Owen I couldn't say, but what the hell could there be? I mean, that's two different universes."

"There's a bridge."

"Lee Canton again? Jantarro spotted the scam, they had to stop him talking?"

"It's a motive."

He examined the nonblooming jacaranda through his window. "I'll talk to Tucker and the sheriff. We'll be pretty low priority."

"Just a spic and a crazy cowboy?" Frank Owen said.

"Something like that," Chavalas said. "We'll have to wait on line behind the FBI, SEC, and a U.S. attorney."

I said, "You could find out what jobs Canton Construction did the last year or so. The bigger projects, anything Canton had a large stake in."

Chavalas shook his head at me. "The New York cops always do your work for you too, Fortune?"

"How do you think I make a living?"

He smiled. "Okay, I'll get everything Lee Canton did for a year. Buildings, business, the works. That it?"

"You said McElder has a record of violence, skating on the edge of the law."

"Public intoxication, disorderly conduct. Mostly fighting in bars, drew fines and suspended sentences. A couple of thirty-days on the work farm. Over in the Valley they've got more: illegal hunting, threatening neighbors, wife-beating, one assault with deadly weapon rap that got him a year not so long ago. They should have a file on him over at the *News-Press*."

Frank Owen stood up with me. "When you checked into that redneck, did you happen to run across the name of Nina Owen?"

"No," Chavalas said. "You have anything to tell me?"

"She didn't come east, she doesn't care about a funeral, she didn't cry," Frank said. "She couldn't care less. Maybe she cared about something or someone else."

Chavalas kept his voice neutral. "Okay, I'll check into her."

The library was a block over and a block up.

Santa Barbara News–Press, October 14, 1980
RAPE CHARGES DROPPED
SANTA BARBARA—Charges have been dropped against a Santa Ynez man accused of raping his wife.

Kenneth Don McElder, 14 Ridge Rd., Santa Ynez, was released yesterday when his wife, Muriel, refused to testify against her husband. She told Superior Court Judge Molsen it had all been a misunderstanding.

Mrs. McElder, of the same address, said that she and McElder had been fighting, she had driven to Santa Barbara and checked into The Oasis Motel. McElder followed her, forced a key from the night clerk, and let himself into the unit. Thinking he was an intruder, she screamed and struggled with him.

The clerk called the police who found the couple naked, the woman crying in the bed that she'd been raped. McElder was violent and abusive, was taken to jail overnight.

In court, McElder said he had come to apologize and take his wife home, but had lost his temper when the clerk wouldn't give him a key. He admitted he'd been drinking, forced himself on his wife when he found her in bed. Mrs. McElder said she realized the true facts when her husband explained, and refused to press charges.

"How can you rape your wife?" McElder said upon his release.

He pleaded guilty to misdemeanor assault against the clerk, paid a fine and damages, and the couple returned home.

Santa Barbara News–Press, June 17, 1982
MAN GUILTY OF USING DOG AS WEAPON
SANTA YNEZ—A man who ordered his pit bull to attack a neighbor has been convicted of assault with a deadly weapon—the dog. Kenneth Don McElder, 37, was found guilty in Superior Court yesterday and sentenced to a year in jail.

McElder accused the neighbor, Wilson Dunn, of calling the police repeatedly when McElder fired his rifles and pistols at targets on his land, carried the weapons in a threatening manner off his land. "He better mind his own business," McElder said, and later went on to say, "It's my right to carry my rifles anywhere I want. I shoot my weapons anywhere I damn please on my own land."

Santa Barbara News–Press, May 23, 1987
DEATH OF FORMER RESIDENT UNSOLVED DESPITE A HUNDRED WITNESSES
SANTA YNEZ—For two years, the identity of whoever gunned down David McElder in the Montana hamlet of Sage Hill has remained a secret despite over a hundred people who saw the slaying.

The Montana-born McElder, who lived for six years on a farm outside Santa Ynez, returned to his native Sage Hill only four years ago. Neighbors here aren't surprised, either by his violent death or the town's silence. "He was a thief and a bully and sometimes you can push decent people too far," says Wilson Dunn who had had many run-ins with McElder and his brother Ken over the years. "Lies," says Ken McElder, who still lives on the Santa Ynez farm. "Dave and me never let people tell us what we got to do, that's all."

Authorities in the rural Montana village say they lack evidence to file charges in the shooting that occurred in the middle of an angry crowd near the lone tavern. Over 100 witnesses admitted they saw the shooting but not the shooter because they were diving for cover. "They're all guilty," says Ken McElder. "They were all scared of Dave."

Both McElders were born in Sage Hill, Dave in 1942 and Ken in 1945. Their father, Donald McElder, was an Army sergeant who died in World War II, the boys grew up on a mountain ranch with their mother and two uncles. Both joined the army as teenagers, both were given less than honorable discharges. Ken McElder laughs. "The army don't take to guys who don't like taking orders."

In Sage Hill they tell a different story, say that Donald McElder and his wife's brothers were known thieves and poachers who lived in a mountain hideout and worked as hired bullies for large local ranchers. They say Donald McElder joined the army a jump ahead of the sheriff, died not in battle but in a tavern brawl in Australia.

"More lies," Ken McElder insists. "My father was too much man for the army, and Dave was too much man for that town. That was the real trouble."

Whatever the truth of the past, there is little doubt the streets of Sage Hill emptied whenever the six-foot, 280-pound Dave McElder appeared, usually carrying a gun. On the morning he was shot, he was free on bond after being convicted of wounding an elderly barber. He strutted around town armed and shouting threats while his lawyer asked for a new trial. A crowd that had wanted his bond revoked for carrying a rifle gathered at the tavern, surrounded his truck when he came out with a six-pack of beer. Gunshots rang out, and Dave McElder was dead.

In Sage Hill, two years later, no one has been charged with the shooting, the authorities are ready to close the case. In Santa Ynez, Ken McElder says, "They do, and they got me to deal with."

38

There was no telephone number for Sam or Morgan Canton. The number for Double C Ranch Enterprises got me a switchboard. The words personal and detective got me a lawyer. The words J. James and Elizabeth Martin got me Morgan Canton. Lieutenant Holley's name got me directions to the ranch house.

We wound up to the top of San Marcos Pass and the turn-off to Camino Cielo where I'd found Hector Jantarro that first day. The road mounts in a series of looping turns with the whole narrow coastal plain spreading out below through the summer haze. When I was a boy going to Saturday afternoon movies, Tarzan lived up on the top of an escarpment with a hazy, sweeping view just like this. Racist, sexist, nobly male Tarzan. Our childhood heroes are given to us by the society we live in.

Over the summit the Valley opens north and east, with the campsites on the Santa Ynez River off to the right, Lake Cachuma directly ahead. As we drove down, the arms of the lake made by the last and largest dam in the river reached to the highway on the right, the dusty live oaks and brown wild oats rose on the hills to the left, and the rest of the Valley slowly opened up to the west. We passed the Solvang fork, drove straight on by Los Olivos and joined the freeway just south of Los Alamos.

As Connie Ochoa found fifteen years ago, the entrance to the ranch was easy to miss. I was almost past before I saw the intertwined "Cs" and the Canton name. The blacktop road was as narrow as she had said, the arch with the Double C brand was brick now, with locked gates. Frank Owen used the gate telephone to state our business. The gates opened. The horse path still paralleled the road to the ranch house set down among the brown hills with its view of the sea. Two younger men on horseback followed us along the slopes to the house. The man who waited on the veranda was Morgan Canton.

"You haven't been here long, Mr. Fortune?"

"Some months."

"From New York?"

"Sorry," I said.

He smiled. "I like New York whenever I go there. But it is a different world."

In his late sixties now, he wore a dark blue business suit and tie with the gray Stetson and tooled cordovan western boots. A solid, muscular man whose deeply creased eyes and leather face didn't seem to belong in the town suit. The good, simple, honest rustic in his Sunday best. He probably worked on the image, but the suit had cost as much as my whole wardrobe, the boots could be as expensive as my Tempo, and he'd grown up as familiar with a balance sheet as a horse.

"No," I said, "I don't think it is. Not anymore, if it ever really was."

The two younger men sat their horses between the whitewashed old house and the garage with its pair of Mercedes and the red Corvette and silver Rolls Royce. The boy I'd seen at Lee Canton's office, Sam II, was the younger. The older would be Morgan III, close to thirty now. They seemed more than ready to step into their father's expensive boots.

"My father might agree," Morgan Canton said. "He'll talk to you himself."

"In his office here?"

If he wondered how I knew his father had an office in the house, he didn't show it. Then, in a family with the power to have sheriff's lieutenants do them favors, he probably knew all about me and everyone I'd talked to by now.

"He never leaves it these days," he said. He nodded to Frank Owen. "Just you. Your friend can stay in the car."

There is an odor in a room where an old person lives and sleeps. Not of decay, but of staleness, of the slow change and movement of air and light and dust. A narrow bed stood against a wall of the small office. Sam Canton wasn't in it. He sat in what had to be the same swivel chair at the same desk Connie Ochoa had faced him across fifteen years ago. Change comes slowly in the manor houses. Everything was there: leather, old wood, books, ledgers, old photographs, paintings of ranch life. The chair still made no sound, but there was now a computer on the desk. He looked at my arm.

"The war?"

"An accident."

"That's hard on a man." His pale old eyes studied my face to see how hard the loss of my arm had been, how hard it might have made me.

"I was young."

"That'd be even harder."

"I didn't die."

At ninety, he seemed much smaller than Morgan or even Lee. No longer broad or solid, his face lean with hollow cheeks. The mustache was still thick, but as white as his thinning hair. His hands were folded in his lap, the dark skin like parchment, veins knotted. He looked his ninety years, as much as anyone looks ninety instead of eighty-five or ninety-five, but he didn't act them or sound them, his voice low and slow but still firm. He still swiveled slowly in the chair with that perpetual need for motion when he talked or even thought.

"Fortune's English." It was a statement not a question. At ninety, Sam Canton didn't ask questions. If he ever had.

"It was Fortunowski. My father changed it."

"People did that a lot. Never understood it."

"Neither did my grandfather."

"Your name. That's what counts when it comes down to it. What a man makes with his name, passes on."

As Connie Ochoa had realized, he shaped a meeting to make you say what was necessary for him to be able to tell you what he wanted you to know.

"That's why you got Lieutenant Holley to tail Elizabeth Martin? To protect the Canton name? Why you sent your grandsons to check on Lee?"

"Your name is your continuity, Fortune. In this county, this state, the Canton name means honesty and integrity and hard work. All of which my son Lee has a tendency to overlook. That made him an easy target for that woman and her paramour. Holley is an old friend. I asked him to look into what Lee was playing with this time. When he told me, I knew James and Martin for what they were. I told the Sheriff. It turned out the Federal authorities were already investigating."

"But you asked Holley to go on watching."

"To prove my son wasn't involved except as a victim." The old man swivelled. "I understand they expect to make arrests soon. But Lee won't be one of them."

"Prosecutor Tucker's a friend too?"

The smile was thin on his almost mummified face. "Sometimes. You can't be sure with ambitious men."

"They have their own interests," I said.

Without the smile his face was as neutral as a mask. "Are you ambitious, Fortune?"

"Not what you mean by ambitious."

He swivelled. "Tucker says you've been told to forget J. James and Company. Now you know Lee had nothing to do with it all."

"Now I know," I said.

"Then that should finish our business."

"I didn't come to talk about J. James and the scam. I came to talk about Hector Jantarro and Billy Owen."

The silence in the small dark wood office with its musty odor of old leather and older books and still older human flesh was the kind of total silence I've heard inside ancient deserted monasteries in Europe. Only the far-off horse noises, distant voices in argument, the slow almost soundless swivelling.

"Who would they be?"

I told him who they were, and what had happened to them. How the CIA and FBI were both sure that whatever Jantarro had been doing that was "money in the bank" had no connection to the CIA or his past. How whoever Jantarro had by the balls had to be local. The swivelling stopped. The voices outside seemed to be gone, the sounds of the horses. The silence of a tomb.

"Fifteen years ago," I said, "you told a young lawyer named Connie Ochoa that the strong survive, that men build, protect and defend, and women have children to pass it on."

The swivelling began again, slow and rhythmic. "Who else have you talked to?"

"Is that what you taught your sons and your grandsons? That their grandfathers came to an empty land and built an empire with honesty, integrity, and hard work? Or did you tell them about the long lariat, wet stock, the Indian massacres and Mexican murders? About railroad rights-of-way, public grazing land, and government contracts? Fences and water rights? About how hard work has a lot to do with building an empire, but honesty and integrity have very little."

The parchment skin tightened across his fragile bones until his lips disappeared. "Lee is a fool, but he's a Canton, and people tell lies. You're listening to liars."

"You named him for Leland Stanford," I said, "who built his empire on Chinese coolies, helped murder small ranchers and called them outlaws. The men who really stole The West. Not the footloose loners chasing the rainbow and the other side of the mountain. Why settle for a farm or a horse when you can grab a whole state? Why buy if you can hustle, why hustle if you can steal, why steal if you can make the rules? The man who makes the rules gets the gold, and everyone works for him."

He heard me, but was like the character in an opera who stands at the side of the stage and sings his own song totally unconnected with what everyone else on the stage is singing. Or maybe I was that character, singing my aria to no one.

"A wetback and a redneck," he said. "What could they be to my son except hired help?"

"A wetback who was a bigshot cop in a country where the cops and landowners make the rules as they used to out here, a private empire builder down on his luck looking for a stake to be a power again. And a redneck who was really a middle-class dropout caught in the whole macho thing: nobody tells a real man what to do. An ambitious hustler and a fool. Just your meat, but Lee isn't you, and maybe he couldn't handle them."

He knew exactly what I was saying to him, but in his head he was somewhere else where he considered not questions but answers.

"That Martin woman and James," he said. "It would have to be them. Those people had to have spotted their fraud."

"Martin and James deal and hire lawyers. They're the Yankee pedlars, the snake oil pitchmen. They want all they can grab, just like Cantons. But they're not Cantons. They don't kill."

At ninety, he reacted more slowly to the unexpected, the way an old bull is slow to meet an attack from a new direction. But a man fights with his brain, and, unlike the bull, once he has seen the danger responds with undiminished power. The atmosphere of the office changed. His swivelling became faster. Even the sounds of horses and voices seemed to return from outside. His old eyes fixed on me from the dark parchment face.

"You better leave now, Fortune."

I stood up. "Thanks for talking to me. In a way, I came to get you to help your son by helping me, but that won't happen will it? That would weaken the empire."

"You'll go on with this?"

"I think so, Mr. Canton."

"It's a free country. Every man does what he wants to do."

I watched him swivelling slowly behind his desk in the shadowed light. "Louis Brandeis said we can have a democracy, or we can have great wealth in the hands of a few, but we can't have both."

Morgan stood on the veranda as I passed, then went back into the house. I got into my Tempo beside Frank Owen, drove away. I watched the crests of the rolling brown hills. The grandsons weren't in sight.

"Well?"

"I expect he's on the telephone right now. Or Morgan is. The ball's rolling."

"What ball?"

"The ball to stop us going on."

He looked out at the brown hills all around us as we drove, the dusty live oaks that had been here for centuries.

"You think these Cantons are dangerous?"

I looked out at the vast spread of rolling hills. "For cold-blooded, hard-nosed, ruthless, rapacious power, no one has ever matched the Anglo-Norman, and never will."

39

In the triangle between the forks of the highway through the Santa Ynez Valley are the narrow back roads and the hamlets of Ballard, Santa Ynez, Los Olivos. Dusty, rural ranch country. But this is Santa Barbara County so the horses are Arabians, the cattle Black Angus, the irrigated farms alfalfa, premium wine grapes and other expensive and intensive crops. Fine restaurants and a Grand Hotel, the ranches of the wealthy and famous. The substantial suburban homes of the less rich but still affluent. Rural, but a long way from rustic.

The house at 14 Ridge Road was neither rich nor suburban, grew no grapes in its littered yard, raised rusted pickups not Arabians or Black Angus. There was an avocado tree among the twisted old oaks, but it was choked in the hot afternoon by high weeds and wild oats. Ramshackle, the frame house was the same weathered gray of the garage and two rundown outbuildings. A third outbuilding, well-kept and painted, had dog runs behind it. Around the whole place was a sturdy redwood fence eight feet high and topped by three strands of barbed wire.

"Christ," Frank Owen said. "It looks like a fort."

"McElder's castle," I said.

A bell was mounted on the gate. I rang.

The two pit bulls came around the house low and snarling, like two creatures from another planet with their slavering jaws open as they hurled themselves at the fence. We both jumped away, not so much from the danger as the sheer ferocity. The dogs stopped short of the fence, stood braced and powerful, growling somewhere low in their massive chests.

The voice said, "The fence keeps them in and people out. You're police, I hope?"

He sat at the steering wheel of a Jeep that had come up without us hearing it over the dogs. "Name's Wilson Dunn. He's at work, I suppose."

"Private detective, Mr. Dunn."

"Too bad." Dunn was a short, wiry man with a tanned, craggy face and lively pale blue eyes. In his early seventies, his white hair made him look older, the strong, weathered face made him look younger. "She won't answer the bell when he's away."

"Afraid of strangers?"

"Afraid of him. He's afraid of strangers. Men like McElder are basically cowards afraid of death, life, other people."

"You know him well, Mr. Dunn?"

"Know him? I've been cursed, bitten, shot at and threatened with worse. I know Ken McElder."

"Can we go somewhere and talk?"

"On my way to Mattel's Tavern for a beer. You can come along and buy me one."

The back road made a steep descending curve out onto Highway 154 just west of the old stagecoach stop. Under its trees, the rustic tavern is on a frontage road east of where 154 rejoins U.S. 101, and the three-street town of Los Olivos is around the corner. Once it was the end of the railroad line from the north where passengers trans-shipped to the stage coach over San Marcos Pass into Santa Barbara. After the railroad came down the coast, it became a well-known country inn for travellers inland, and only a few years ago still had rooms and detached cottages for hardy weekenders who could survive the unheated nights.

"What do you want to ask me, Mr.—?"

"Dan Fortune. This is Frank Owen."

"Owen? Do I recall an Owen being around Ken McElder?"

We were at a corner table where Wilson Dunn seemed at home with his mug of draught beer.

"My brother Billy," Frank said. "Someone murdered him."

"I'm sorry, Mr. Owen." He looked at each of us. "You think it was Ken McElder?"

"Has he been away recently? A couple of days about three weeks ago?"

"He's always away. He is a man who does exactly what he pleases and boasts of it."

"Would he kill, Mr. Dunn?"

Dunn drank. "It would depend, first, on the orders of his superiors, and, second, if he felt personally threatened. I did time in the army before and during the war. There is a type who thrives in the middle echelons of the military. Sadistic bullies to those below them, totally obedient to those above them. The enforcers of the rules. The army is always right, but even more than that, *their* captain or colonel or general is always right. Yet they are also dominated by animal cunning, and will turn on anyone if personally threatened."

"That's McElder?"

"Completely. He will do what his personal superior tells him to do, up to and beyond murder. But will also always think of his own hide first."

"You've made a study of McElder."

"Sheer self-preservation. I'm the only one in the Valley he knows he can't bully. I expect it's saved me a great deal of trouble. Intimidation is how the McElders survive."

"If he was all that," Frank Owen said, "why did he leave the army? Get a dishonorable."

"The only possible way. He was a weapons instructor, was accused of being too harsh on the men, too brutal, too much by the book with no margin for error. He could have gone to prison, but there were some embarrassing circumstances about his superior officers so he was simply kicked out."

"He's a weapons expert?"

"Has a collection in his kennel office that would shame an Argentinian General."

"Knives?" I said.

"Every possible type. Commando gear, an assault armory. He never goes out without a rifle, has threatened most people in the area, and any campers or tourists who cross him."

"You mentioned Billy Owen," I said. "How about a man named Jantarro?"

"There were always men riding to and from jobs in his Bronco or a pickup. He liked to stop home, pick up beer and sandwiches he had Murial make for them all. Poor Murial. She's one of those women who think McElder is the way men are supposed to be. In the past she tried to break, seems to have given up now."

"You know McElder's boss?"

"I know the Cantons. Not my kind of people, and Lee's a Canton just a little dumber. The grandsons I don't know, but I expect they'll do their duty." He looked at the clock. "Two's my limit. Still time for a couple of hours in my garden."

He left with a wave, and I left Frank Owen and a third beer to find a phone to call Sergeant Chavalas in Santa Barbara. He had a rough preliminary report on Canton Construction's jobs for the last year. "The company itself was general contractor on a hospital up in Monterey, a school and highrise up in Santa Clara County, a couple of restaurants in the North County. They subcontracted on another hospital, school and six commercial buildings, and built two local condo developments."

"Anything look bad? Unusual?"

"The normal arguments over cost overruns, unnecessarily tough regulations, inspectors being arbitrary and not showing when they're supposed to, but nothing in the records looks bad. They had a big year, profits look normal. Up in Monterey they did say there seemed to be a report they can't find. They're looking into it, but they figure it's just an internal screwup."

"What kind of report?"

"On the hospital sprinkler system."

"Where are the local developments?"

They were both in Goleta out beyond Isla Vista. Frank Owen gulped his beer and followed me out to the Tempo. We drove back to Santa Barbara over the pass.

"Pick up your car and check out those housing developments."

"What are you going to do?"

"Talk to a lady about a motive."

40

Through the gate framed by the white pillars with the blue mosaic tiles, the elegant old Mediterranean on San Ysidro Lane still looked deserted. Nothing moved, and no one was staked out on the road or behind the high hedge. But Elizabeth Martin's red Mercedes 450SL sat in the gravel drive in front of the house.

For a long time there was no answer to my rings.

Then I heard the click of high heels on those large red clay tiles the rich who built these old mansions had liked so much.

Her voice came from inside the heavy door, "Yes?"

"Miss Martin? Dan Fortune."

"Who?"

"The private detective who met you with Leland Canton. I talked to you about Hector Jantarro and Billy Owen."

"Oh, yes. I'm sorry, I'm really quite busy."

"It's about murder, Miss Martin. It could involve you."

Behind the heavy dark wood door with its wrought iron bars over the observation port she was silent. I heard a long sigh, and then the lock clicked and the door creaked open.

"I call you Daniel, right?" She turned away. "In the living room."

Her high heels echoed through the long entry hall of polished tiles with a hollow emptiness like a museum. She wore all black and charcoal gray. Reserved and proper, if not demure. There was no way Elizabeth Martin could be demure, not even in a chaste gray dress, black pumps, her blond hair combed into a severe pageboy, small pearl earrings and a single rope of pearls at the closed collar of the dress. The reliable businesswoman, a female of propriety. What didn't fit was the cigarette she lit as she waved me to a couch. And that she seemed too restless to sit down herself, stood against the mantelpiece, the cigarette hanging from her lips, smoke rising into a half-closed eye.

"What do you want, Daniel? I told you I know nothing about a Jantarro or Owen. Nothing at all about Leland's business beyond his investment with us and in general."

"Maybe Jantarro and Owen knew about you," I said.

She went on leaning against the high white marble mantel in the large but warm living room with its solid old furniture even my amateur eye knew was all authentic antiques from some early nineteenth-century English masters. It all glowed with a soft, sheen that only comes from two hundred years of hand rubbing.

"Tell me what you want, Daniel."

"Where's James? How long have you been living with him?"

"Why? Want to take me away from him?"

"You know better than that."

There was a flash of the strong sensuality I had seen earlier, the sexual game. "I don't interest you, Daniel?"

"You'd interest any man. But there's someone I wouldn't risk losing, and we both know I'm not your kind of man."

"What is my kind of man, Daniel?"

"J. James and up. Montecito. The Yacht Club. Real estate holdings," I said. "He's gone, isn't he?"

"Gone?"

"Flown the coop. Run for cover. Taken it on the lam. Cut for the county line. Grabbed the cash and high-tailed it. Off in a cloud of dust. Whatever colorful phrase you want to use."

She waved away the cigarette smoke, "Why would he do any of those?"

"The real question is why you didn't go with him? What kept you here?"

She turned away, reached up to put out her cigarette in the ashtray on the mantel. "He travels fastest who travels alone."

Her back to me, she tamped the cigarette over and over until all vestiges of smoke were gone. Then she left the mantelpiece, sat on an elegant high back wing chair, her head laid against the purple velvet upholstery, her arms flat on the chair arms. "Have you been investigating us all along, Daniel? The talk of murder and Leland a smoke screen? For that old man Leland has to impress so much? That would be it, wouldn't it? The Cantons. I told Jack we shouldn't let Leland get in so deep."

"I haven't been investigating you at all. I'm still not."

"Then?"

"Stumbled over it." I told her about Mark Todd, Prosecutor Tucker, old Sam Canton and Lieutenant Holley. "Who came? The Sheriff? Tucker? Justice?"

"No one came. We were in Los Angeles. When it was time to come back up here Jack said he had business, told me to go on ahead. Of course, I did." Her smile was a shade bitter. "I was here perhaps an hour when the man called. Polite but cool, very cool. An assistant U.S. attorney. They were in our Los Angeles office. Jack was gone, they warned me not to leave the country."

She sat there staring ahead like Cleopatra on her throne just before she took the asp out of the basket and put it to her breast. Her Mark Antony would try to fight it out, probably on a nice tropical island where he could hope to bribe the officials and beat extradition. She would sit and wait. We all use the weapons we have. She would stay as Cleopatra had, but there would be no asp. We don't deal much in death before dishonor today. She would negotiate, throw herself on the mercy, find a new man to pay the lawyers. It was, after all, white collar crime, insider crime, and she could delay it until she was too old to care what they did to her. It would be years before they sent her away, and it wasn't the Justice department she stared at in the fine old living room. It was John James, her Jack.

"I knew what he'd do if it happened, and I'm still stunned." She shook her head in the high chair. "Is it biological, or is it how we're taught? Even a tough, fast-living broad like me? Is there always a

Jack James somewhere for every woman? The one you 'do' for, trust without doubts, believe you're a unit with? Can men and women ever be a unit, Daniel, or do those balls mean it's dominate, rule, and go it alone in the end?"

"I hope not."

She shifted only her eyes to look at me. "Why does that make me think less of you? It shouldn't, you say what you think. I read a story where at the end the writer said the story proved it takes more than big balls to make a revolution. Leland, now there's a weak man. He thinks he's such a powerhouse wheeler dealer, but he hasn't really got any balls at all." Her eyes took on a shine. "Nothing like his father. That old man I could really have gone far with." She suddenly laughed. "Listen to me, eh? Are we all crazy? Men and women? Or just primitive. The old bastard was probably the one who blew the whistle on Jack and me. An old son-of-a-bitch who's father got his start stealing neighbors' cattle, rustling Mexican herds across the border in the dead of night, killing people who tried to make a home on the public land he grazed his cattle on. Son of thieves and murderers who got rich, who ruins my life, and I admire him!"

"A thief," I said, "is someone who steals last and doesn't have the luck and power to keep what he stole and build on it."

"The difference between a casket and a castle is bad luck and bad timing?"

"More or less, and Sam Canton didn't blow the whistle. He would have, but the government beat him to it. He just went on watching you to be sure Lee got out clean. He admires a sharp dealer, but not against his family."

She shook her head sadly. "Jack wasn't quite as smart as I thought. He was so smooth, so slick, so confident. So sure, so gracious to allow you 'in' on his skill and mind. Nothing crude, no athlete in bed. Never too needy. He would allow a woman 'in' on his desire. But, in the end, only Jack was important to Jack." She smiled. "Still, we had a good run. I hope he makes it, beats the extradition. It's white collar crime, I'll be okay. Hell, forty percent of us get off clean, and less than one out of five gets more than a year. Eighty percent get little or no time in jail, and those are pretty good odds, right?"

"With any luck, and the proper humility, you'll draw a fine and probation. Serve soup to the poor for a couple of years."

"You don't approve?"

"Someone else I met in the case said she'd rather live in a world where the rich are the criminals not the poor."

"Perhaps so, but we don't have that world."

I said. "You said you let Lee Canton in deep. How deep?"

The years slipped smoothly into place in her mind like the oiled machine they were. She pulled back, closed up, prepared a smile to ward off unwanted curiosity, cover her tracks, con me.

"Why?"

"I'm looking for a motive."

There was something close to a flash behind her eyes. She had realized the reason for my question, seen a possibility of revenge, even of victory of a kind. And it wasn't Lee Canton she wanted to bring down, it was old Sam.

"He invested over a quarter of a million, expected forty percent profit. We put him off, told him we needed another hundred thousand to build the profit even higher."

"Did you ever pay off?"

"Not a dime. He was so greedy it was simple."

"When? The first investment and the second?"

"The first about a year and a half ago. The second about nine months ago."

"How did he pay?"

"Company check. Good as gold."

"Company money, not personal?"

"I don't think there's any difference with Leland. He lived off the company, charged everything remotely legal to it."

"Did Jantarro or Billy Owen bring the money? Contact you for Canton?"

"No, but—"

She sat in the wing chair, head against the purple velvet, arms flat on the chair arms, and smiled at me like a live sphinx.

"What?" I said.

"When he came up with the extra cash, he joked about we'd better get rich soon because he didn't have a lot more corners he could cut. And in April, about the time you appeared, I got the feeling he was pretty nervous a few times when we had drinks."

I got up. "Maybe they won't throw the book at you."

"I'm really going to miss the excitement, the perks, the goodies, And, of course, Jack." She smiled. "But, then, I expect something will turn up."

She was still there in the chair with her now proper blonde hair against the purple velvet when I left. In the reserved gray dress and simple pearls. Ready to appear in any court.

41

In the evening sun, Frank Owen stood outside the second housing development. It sprawled along the oceanfront north of Isla Vista, an endless series of condominiums tortured into grotesque shapes by the need to give every unit an ocean and a mountain view and command the highest prices. Except the "affordables."

"They're back that way," Frank said. "Farthest from the ocean at the bottom of the slope."

"We wouldn't want to take away the poor's incentive to do better by spoiling them, would we? Nothing unusual at the first development?"

"I'm no construction expert, Fortune. It looked like this one—flashy crackerboxes. All kinds of features like Jacuzzis, atriums, freestanding fireplaces, two-story windows and exposed beams, but put together with cardboard, thin siding, metallized plastic and staple guns. They don't build like they used to."

"They never would have except for cheap labor. Let's look around."

It was, as Owen had said, all flash, glitter and little substance, but nothing seemed wrong. Normal concrete block foundations, decent landscaping, covered blacktop parking areas and paved walks. They were still selling, the office was in the building closest to the sea with the finest view. A saleswoman got to us before we were through the door.

"Hello, my name is Karen, what can I show you gentlemen? We still have a few units for families, a few ideal for singles who can save a great deal by sharing."

"They look expensive," I said.

She looked at my arm and Frank's jeans. "They are upscale units, but value for value we think we have one of the best ratios." Her enthusiasm had dropped as she looked us over, but she had been taught that no one, but no one, is to be prejudged. "Can I show you what is still available?"

She walked us a little too fast through two units, one with everything set up to be shared by two presumed bachelors, the other more for family living. Both had the required ocean and mountain views, plenty of glass, lots of shine. Our comments must have irked her, because she launched into a defense of the great expense, no luxury left unturned.

"There is even a complete sprinkler system throughout the complex as a total safety measure. They don't do that very often even in Montecito."

She pointed up at the sprinkler heads discreetly placed to be as unobtrusive as possible but strategic enough to cover all areas in case of a fire.

"That's the only real feature I've seen," Frank said.

I looked at the sprinkler heads, heard Sergeant Chavalas's voice on the telephone earlier, "*Up in Monterey they did say there seemed to be a report they can't find . . . On the hospital sprinkler system.*" The only one I could reach was over the stair landing. I pulled at it.

"What are you doing!"

The saleswoman stood paralyzed. Outraged, but trained within an inch of her life that the customer can do no wrong. I pulled harder.

The sprinkler head came off in my hand.

Shards of plaster and glue clung to the base. There was no sign of a metal connection.

We sat in the living room of the Summerland house in the darkening night, the last narrow streak of gold between a black sky and a blacker sea, waiting for the telephone to ring.

At the condominium development I'd laid the sprinkler head in the hand of the uncomprehending saleswoman.

"Thanks for the showing, we'll get back to you. Come on, Frank."

The saleswoman still stood and stared at the sprinkler head as we got out of there. At the cars, Frank shook his head in wonder.

"Christ, talk about shoddy work."

"Not shoddy," I said. "They're not badly connected, Frank, they're not connected at all. Glued to the ceiling. Fake."

We both let it sink in.

"What do we do?"

"We call Chavalas from the first phone away from here."

"You think—?"

"Probably all his buildings. Probably other things that don't show. Foundations. Missing joists. Anything and everything to save costs while charging full fee to get the extra cash he needed."

The first telephone was at a Mobil station near the freeway.

Chavalas listened. "Fake?"

"Glued. No pipes at all. Did you hear from Monterey?"

"I will now. Where will you be?"

"The Summerland house."

"It'll take time to contact everywhere Canton built. I'll call you."

Frank Owen drove to Dianne's house, I went to Summerland. Dianne was there with Kay. So was Nina Owen. The two children played in our yard. They weren't as silent anymore, the stocky little girl laughing, the boy smiling at her as she swung on a branch of our avocado, as if a weight had been lifted from them. The weight of the unhappiness of their parents that was more than the loss of a father who had never really been there.

I told them about the fake sprinklers and Lee Canton's need for investment money in the get-richer-quick-scheme that was a scam and made him a total loser again.

"Jantarro was an opportunist who wanted to get back to El Salvador with the money to buy safety and power. He must have discovered what Canton Construction was doing, wanted a share. A big share. Lee Canton's money was all tied up."

Kay said, "Dan, Nina remembered something."

Dianne said, "We were talking about Billy, the past, and—"

"We started talkin' about Billy gettin' killed," Nina said. There was a new confidence in her voice, in her interruption of Dianne. As if she'd begun to realize that it was possible to live on her own. "Dianne said was I sure Billy never said nothin' about Jantarro? I told her like I told you, Billy don't talk to me much the last couple of years. I said, anyway, nobody said nothing about Jantarro to me, not even that McElder when he come to bring me Billy's money from Mr. Canton."

Dianne looked at me as if Nina had said something momentous. "Don't you see, Dan? McElder asked her all kinds of questions about where Billy was, what Billy was doing. Had Billy said anything about going anywhere? Did she know where he was or what he was doing. But nothing about Jantarro. About what Jantarro could be doing. About could Billy and Jantarro be together?"

I saw. "The way McElder and Canton both suggested to me later they could be." Both of them had hinted more than once that Billy Owen and Jantarro could have gone off together, be involved in something together. Why hadn't they suggested that to Nina earlier? "He never asked Nina about Jantarro because he knew where Jantarro was. Because he knew Billy couldn't be with Jantarro. Because he knew Jantarro was dead."

We were all still thinking about it in the twilight living room when Frank Owen arrived. He'd driven to Dianne's house, found it empty, guessed where she'd be. I told him what Nina and Dianne had figured out.

Frank said, "It had to be McElder. Canton isn't that tough. Let's go and get him, Fortune. We know where he lives, he doesn't know we're on to him. Let's get him now."

I sat in my new leather Eames chair. "He knows, Frank."

"We can face him down. There's two of us. I've got my gun at Dianne's place, you've got your pistol."

"The police'll handle it."

"He killed Billy!"

Dianne said, "Sit down, Frank. Have a beer."

"You've both done all you can," Kay said.

Frank said, "You're afraid of him."

"If I'm not, I'm a damned fool," I said. "Sit down, Frank. Have a beer. I've got better things to do than play damned fool games with a crazy damned fool like him for the sake of some damned fool legend. You want to get on your horse and go after him, go ahead. I'm waiting here until Chavalas calls to tell us we're right and he's got the proof."

"Where's your gun?"

"In my desk drawer. Down the hall past the bedrooms."

Dianne was up. She'd been sitting in her favorite spot on the window seat with the last light behind her over the far out Channel Islands. "For Christ's sake, Frank, grow up. He's killed twice. Dan says his house is a fort. What are you proving?"

"If you don't know by now you'll never know!"

"I hope," Kay said, "it turns out to be more than just that you're as tough as a bully."

The traffic on the freeway between us and the sea sounded close enough to be inside the house in the silence of the odd L-shaped living room. Frank Owen didn't sit down, but he didn't walk down the hall to my office. Nina Owen got up.

"It's real dark," she said. "I got to go an' get the kids inside."

Dianne went into the kitchen, came back with five open bottles of beer. "Frank?"

He took a beer, walked to a window and looked out at the black sky. When Nina returned with the two children, we were all drinking the beers and listening to the night and the silent telephone. She got the kids bedded down in the spare bedroom, came back to join us.

"I'm going to go study and work at beautician's school, get a real job. Dianne got me in, and she knows a workin' mothers pool where I can get kid care cheap. I figure me and the kids can hang onto the cottage, if we still goes out with Taffy on the weekends."

"You'll live alone?" Kay said.

"I got to. For a while, anyway."

Dianne was on the window seat again. She looked up at Frank where he still stood at the window looking out at the night and the lights of the oil platforms like the flotilla of aircraft carriers. "How about us? What are our chances? Do we have to live alone too?"

He drank. "You tell me."

"Maybe," Kay said, "we expect our relationships to do too much."

By midnight, Sergeant Chavalas still hadn't called. Kay and I went to bed. Nina took the guest room with the kids. Frank and Dianne opened up the couch in the living room.

It was 2:00 A.M. when I heard the soft noise outside the house, lay in the dark and listened.

42

The front door smashed open.

"Dan!"

With my one arm I somehow managed to push her down behind the bed and grope for the door.

Out in the living room, I heard Frank's voice, "What the fuck—!"

The house rocked with the explosion.

Glass shattered. Lamps toppled. Wood splintered.

In the bedroom bottles fell off the dresser. A large framed abstract watercolor crashed to the floor.

The woman's scream echoed through the sudden silence and the acrid odor of the explosion.

"Fucking—!" Frank again.

A burst of semi-automatic fire—five shots squeezed off almost as fast as an automatic assault rifle.

Through the bedroom door, I slid along the wall of the hall. There was no light. Only the moon silver from the wide windows that faced the ocean.

Heavy breathing, the straining of violent effort. More glass falling and the smashing of wood.

In the moonlight two shadowy figures grappled in the living room. One was Frank Owen, naked. The other was only a shadow. A big shadow with a black knit hat, a blackened face, a black jacket, pants, boots.

The two heaving shadows struggled over a dark assault rifle, holding to it, throwing each other, flailing with legs to trip, to maim, to topple.

Nina Owen stood in the open doorway to the spare bedroom, her hand over her mouth, the children huddled behind her.

Frank was down, still held to the assault rifle as the bigger shadow flung him back and forth across the floor, smashing him into chairs, tables, trying to shake him loose, break his grip on the rifle.

Nina Owen pulled back into the bedroom, slammed the door. The lock snapped. Furniture dragged inside the bedroom.

Along the hall to my office I groped in the dark for the bottom drawer and my old cannon. Back out into the hall toward the living room. Kay beside me.

"The telephone doesn't work!"

"Get back in the bedroom, lock the door!"

I pushed her through the open door. The wires had been cut. By the book. The mercenary raider.

Frank Owen was up on his knees, the rifle still in both hands, and in both of the massive shadow's hands. The shadow kicked, slammed his boot into Frank's shoulder, broke his grip on the rifle.

Frank sprawled backwards over a smashed coffee table.

The shadow fired three quick shots.

Fired at something else in the dark room.

Jumped toward the hallway where I crouched.

I fired.

Missed.

Fired again, my hand sweating on the big old gun.

The shadow grunted and went down. Who the hell was it?

Came up blazing wild shots toward where I had to be. Prone, I fired again, but he was on his feet and coming. I stumbled along the hall to my office. Past the bedroom.

It seemed like hours but only seconds, maybe a minute, had passed.

Kay, Nina, needed time to get out the windows. Push the kids out and jump after.

Past the bedroom into my office, the door open, and jumped behind the door.

Silence.

Soft steps and then a rifle butt slammed against the door of the guest bedroom. A foot kicked. A voice swore. Ken McElder's voice.

"Goddamn! Fuck!"

Another smashing kick with the heel of a boot. A burst of semi-automatic fire through wood. Another four shots.

"I'm comin' in for you, bitch!"

I waited against the wall behind the open door of my office.

Silence. No more kicks or rifle butts or shots. Somewhere in the hall he waited for me to come to the rescue.

I waited behind the door.

A floorboard creaked close outside in the hall. A shadow crossed the faint line of moonlight between the open door and the jamb. I could almost hear his eyes move as he stared into the dark office where I had to be, the assault rifle up and moving right, left, looking for that patch of darker dark that showed where someone stood. Waiting for that movement across the faint moonlight in the office.

She spoke.

"Murderer."

Kay up and out of the shadows behind my desk. Pale in her nightgown like a ghost from some Victorian novel. *The Woman In White*, He came into the office, rifle up. So close I saw it was an A-15, the semi-automatic civilian version of the M-16 assault rifle. Saw every detail of its dull black metal surface, the carrying handle, the muzzle sight aimed at Kay, the bulky bulletproof vest he wore, the grenades looped to his harness.

Raised my old cannon as he passed beyond the door and shot him twice in the side of the head.

Shot him again where he lay sprawled face down after slamming off the wall where his blood and bone dripped from my first two shots.

The whole house vibrated with silence.

"Dan?" Her voice shivered.

I bent, touched him. He was dead in his spreading blood on my office floor.

"Go next door, call the police."

"I don't have to."

Only then was I aware of lights in the other houses through the windows, the voices calling across the night, the sirens coming closer.

In the living room we found Frank Owen still naked, kneeling beside the couch, his left arm hanging down dripping blood, his right side bleeding. On the couch Dianne Owen was unconscious, bleeding from the nose and head and chest.

The deputies found a thin commando dagger in McElder's boot, four grenades on loops, and another assault rifle on the floor of the living room, its clip empty. His Bronco was parked at the corner in the shadows under a large palm. The pit bull was tied to the steering wheel. They had to send for Animal Control before they could approach the Bronco.

It had three more assault rifles in it, a case of grenades, and stacks of full clips for the rifles.

They took McElder's body to the morgue, Frank and Dianne Owen to the hospital. Nina Owen had been hit through the door in the fleshy part of her left arm, the silent boy had an ugly head wound where a bullet had grazed. They went to the hospital in the 911 ambulance, the little girl clinging to her mother. Kay and I got off with nothing more than cuts and bruises.

Sergeant Chavalas's call came while the deputies were still questioning us. He was at Lee Canton's Montecito house, asked the sheriff's people to bring me with them.

Sheriff's cars stood all around the big white frame house on Featherhill Road that had lights in all the downstairs windows. The single city police car belonged to Chavalas who came out to meet us. They told him about McElder's attack on my house.

"You okay, Fortune?" he asked.

I nodded. "What did you find out about Canton's jobs?"

"The sprinkler system in the Monterey hospital was attached to short pipes that went nowhere. The rest of the systems in all Canton's

269

buildings were either short-piped and not hooked up, or the heads were just glued or nailed up with no pipes at all. The more he found he could get away with, the less he put into the systems. They've found some substandard footings, expect to find whole ones missing. Foundation waterproofing charged for but never done. Below spec stuff everywhere. There had to be inspectors on the take, they're going over everything Canton Construction did."

"What does Canton say?"

"Nothing." He looked toward a morgue wagon waiting in the driveway, lit a cigarette. "He was dead when we got here."

"Suicide?"

He smoked. "McElder. Before he went after you and Owen and the others. The wife heard it all, hid upstairs with the kids. She was so scared of McElder she didn't call 911 for over an hour. We might have stopped him getting to you."

In a living room twice as big as our rented one, but smaller than the one in J. James's mansion, Mrs. Leland Stanford Canton sat in an enormous, ugly, conversation pit sectional of two couches, a loveseat and two armchairs all upholstered in a gaudy salmon color. She was an emaciated platinum blonde in a pale blue skirt and blouse and navy linen jacket, washed out blue eyes, nervous hands that twisted together. The sheriff's people stood around her, with Undersheriff Lawson seated facing her.

"The kids are at her sister's, the Cantons are on their way," Chavalas said. "I guess the sheriff wants to nail down all he can before the lawyers show up."

"You knew something was wrong in your husband's business, Mrs. Canton?"

"Not really, Leland never talked about business to me, I don't understand it. But . . . but I knew he was nervous, upset, and I did overhear things he and . . . and . . . McElder talked about on the patio sometimes. You see, the kitchen windows open on the patio, and if I'm cutting and arranging flowers, or making something special Dolores doesn't know how to cook, they don't know I'm there, and—"

"What did you overhear, Mrs. Canton?" Lawson said.

"What? Oh, yes, I'm sorry. This . . . this . . . has been a terrible . . . shock. Leland—"

"Of course." Lawson was solemn. "But if we're to get to the bottom of this tragedy, we need to know its roots."

She nodded. Well-trained in good manners. "I knew he was concerned about money. He had put me on a strict budget the last year, said we couldn't afford a new car, or anything. Our cash position was difficult, but that we could buy ten cars in a year or so. I assumed he'd made a good investment the way my father used to, that we would soon have plenty of money."

"Nothing specific about this investment?"

"Only once. Mc . . . Elder talked about doubling the profits on everything for Lee, and Lee seemed pleased. He told McElder he wouldn't regret it. Then, perhaps sometime in April, I'm not sure exactly when, Leland was agitated, and McElder said he shouldn't worry. 'Not to worry,' I think were his exact words, he had it all taken care of. Something to the effect that they would have a party and send him off. That someone would believe someone else named Billy and make it easy."

"And tonight? You heard nothing about why McElder—?"

She looked around at them all in total incomprehension, the way I imagined Lee Canton had looked at Connie Ochoa fifteen years ago. "He came in dressed in that black vest, with a rifle. All black, even his face. That silly hat, a knife in his boot, and those things hanging off him. Leland took him into the library. I was frightened, I listened at the door."

"What the hell are you doing?" Lee Canton says.

"They know. That fucking Fortune and the brother."

"Know? Know what?"

"Your goddamn investment in that scam, the sprinklers, the rest of the shit."

There is silence in the library behind the closed door.

"I'll call my father. He has the lawyers. We'll beat it. Get out of that halloween costume and put those weapons—"

"Fuck lawyers," McElder says. "They got to guess it was me put the rock to that wetback thought he was so smart and tough, and me that snuffed Billy. We're talking gas chamber, you stupid bastard."

"Don't be crazy. If we don't panic, all they can get us for is fraud, and I can beat—"

"Asshole!" McElder rages. "You couldn't beat your dong! You blew the whole fucking thing not knowing the goddamn CIA was behind the wetback. So Billy panics, calls them in, and they hide him. His jerk brother shows up, goddamned one-armed Fortune gets into it, we've got to stop Billy before he talks, and it goes to hell with the FBI, cops, and Fortune all after us."

"And so you plan to fix it by killing Fortune, the brother, their wives and children? Everyone you think knows? Maybe the FBI too?"

"The FBI and CIA are out. It's all here. After tonight, no one knows."

"You're stoned, Ken. Drunk. Listen to me—"

"Stoned, you shithead? You bet I'm stoned. High as a fucking eagle in heat, but it's not drugs. I don't need drugs, Mr. Canton, sir."

There is another silence. When Canton's voice again reaches his wife outside the door, it is different, strained.

"I took you on when my father kicked you out. I give the orders. Put those weapons away. Go home. We'll beat—"

"Fifteen years. I don't know how the fuck I stood your puke for fifteen years."

"Ken—!"

"Nothing personal Mr. Canton, sir. It's just that you know all about it, and it's my butt."

The shots come and Mrs. Leland Stanford Canton runs upstairs to lock herself in the bathroom. After a time she remembers the children, rushes out to get them and lock them all in the upstairs office. It is an hour later before she walks shakily down and into the library.

"He . . . he was still alive," she said. "He whispered to me, 'Not enough profit if . . . if. . . .' and he died." She looked around at us all. At some point while she told what had happened, all the Cantons had arrived. She looked at old Sam. "I don't think he knew I was there. He just whispered. To himself, I suppose."

"It's all right, Louise," Morgan Canton said. "We'll take her now, Lawson. If you want anything more, you can talk to her after the funeral."

"Where is he?" Sam Canton said.

"In the morgue, Mr. Canton," Lawson said. "There has to be an autopsy, I'm sorry."

Morgan said. "Let us know when we can bury him."

"The man who did it?" Sam Canton said. "McElder?"

"Dead, sir." Chavalas told him about the attack.

The old man looked at me. "Thank you, Fortune."

"It didn't help anything, Mr. Canton."

I didn't tell them it had been Kay who really got McElder. At least the two of us. And simple fear. Inculcated habits are hard to change even when you want to.

"Maybe not."

"Except it saved a messy trial. Fraud and all that."

"That disappoints you, Fortune?" Sam Canton said.

"Doesn't it you? Justice not done?"

"Not especially," the old man said.

"He wasn't man enough, was he? He didn't get away with it."

The two younger Cantons, Sam II and Morgan III, growled in unison, "Listen you, we—"

"Out," Morgan Canton said.

The two younger men were surly, but left, with old Sam ahead and Morgan escorting Louise Canton.

Chavalas gave me a ride home. Kay was waiting. We went to bed without looking into my office. Tomorrow we could clean up the blood, look at the damage. Tonight we lay together. Talked, not even trying to sleep.

43

Frank Owen was released from the hospital a week later. Dianne Owen died.

Frank took it hard, wandered around with his left arm in a sling, drinking and snorting up a storm. Dianne had left instructions she wanted to be cremated and scattered at sea. They scattered Billy's ashes at the same time, and a week after the memorial Frank piled his backpack and suitcase into his old Porsche and drove south for Mexico.

Nina Owen was treated in emergency and sent home with the little girl. The boy stayed two days in the hospital to be sure. Nina started at beauticians' school. With Taffy and the camera on weekends, she could just about get by in the Westside cottage until she got a real job.

Chavalas and Lieutenant Holley spoke for me at the hearing on McElder. Justifiable homicide in self-defense. They returned no charges, liberated my license, and gave me a pat on the back that didn't make me feel any better. No one spoke for Kenneth McElder except his wife.

"He didn't have any friends," she said. "Only his brother, and he's dead too. He always said today's friend was the enemy tomorrow. You couldn't trust anyone except yourself."

The news stories were short, focused almost entirely on the attack on my house, the two earlier murders, and the widow. "He wasn't easy, he didn't know his own temper sometimes, but he was my husband, and a woman should love her husband. He could be mean, I don't deny it, but men are like that. McElder was a real man. He was my man. What do I do now?"

I wasn't called for Lee Canton. That inquiry was fast and quiet, without publicity and only the barest details in *The News–Press*. Kenneth McElder had gone on a murderous rampage to cover his earlier murders that were caused by irregularities at Canton Construction. Sam Canton convinced everyone there was nothing to be gained from revealing more of the story since Lee was dead. The funeral was private.

Elizabeth Henze (Todd) Martin accepted Morgan Canton's offer of legal help if and when she was indicted. There would be no need to mention the late Leland Stanford Canton at any trial.

John James had still not been located, although Chavalas told me they had him traced to Guyana, when Frank Owen came back, rented a room near us in Summerland, and got a job tending bar in one of the newer hotels in town.

"She was with me everywhere I went," he said over the bar when I went in to talk about my money. "She died because of me and Billy, I was running away. But you can't run away from it, Fortune, and back here I can at least help Nina out."

It was mid-morning on a sunny August day, no one else in the bar except the manager adding up last night's receipts.

"I miss the hell out of her," he said. "I kept coming back, didn't I? We just couldn't make it work. Was Kay right, it never can work with a couple of free people?"

"That isn't exactly what Kay said."

He dried a glass, looked at two young women in bikinis who came in from the pool. "After Billy was killed it was like we had it back. But it always changes."

The two women were in their early twenties. Hard thighs and tight buttocks and small, high breasts. Long, loose dark hair as they sat at a table, looked at me and Frank. They didn't look at me long. Frank called to the waitress, smiled at the two women.

"Christ, I wish I'd killed McElder!"

"He's dead, does it matter how?"

"It matters to me. Okay, so I'm a cowboy at heart. Why not? They were men, strong and independent."

The waitress had brought the two women pina coladas, and they watched us over them as Frank's voice rose. I needed a beer. Frank got it, sat back on his stool behind the bar. He smiled at the two women. The manager didn't smile at him, looked at his watch as if timing how long Frank had been talking to me.

"McElder paid that Calhoun to run me down?"

"The part-time hooker who talked to the man on the phone listened to a recording of McElder, said it sounded like him."

He nodded, only half-listened to me. "The West was real, Fortune. Better than we have now."

"Real, yes. Better I'm not so sure." Beck's is nice beer too. A lot better than they had in the old days. "You know who your westerners really were? Lee Canton, Ken McElder, and Murch Calhoun. Drifters, thieves, pimps and bullies. The nameless cowboys who herded the cattle were just low-paid workers with long hours who got out of it as soon as they could or lived alone in bunkhouses all their lives like sailors on the old sailing ships."

"So a lot of it's a legend. Maybe we need legends."

"Someone does," I said. "Myths and legends hide the real world, the real power. It's one way those in power get others to do what they want. In your romantic Old West the power wasn't with the cowboy or the gunslinger or the honest sheriff or the brave U.S. marshal. It was with the railroads and cattle barons and town builders and government suppliers. Pour a beer."

He got another Beck's, poured. The two women finished their pina coladas and left. Frank Owen watched them go. He wanted to go with them, banter, make small talk, take them home, have a ball. He didn't want to listen to me. Fuck him! I'd had to kill a man because of him and his juvenile brother and their fantasies and I was going to have my say.

"Footloose and fancy free, do what you want. That's great to a point. But freedom is *for* something. Freedom for nothing is empty license, self-indulgence. Being 'free' of all demands, all obligations, is to have nothing. To be behind the wheel with nowhere you have to go, no one you have to answer to, nothing you have to get up for, is to be a zero. To have nothing you have to do is to have nothing to do."

The manager stared toward us. People crowded into the bar for lunchtime. The manager looked at his watch. Frank flipped a finger at the manager, poured a beer for himself.

"Work every damned day for that manager in a place like this? If that's what I'm supposed to want, give me the open road. If that's what a woman has to mean, I'll pass."

"Keep moving," I said, "and you'll never die, right? Like Billy and your father. Never commit to anything."

"Billy never had a chance. Buck wanted more than grubbing for money, found it with Helen, then my mother destroyed it so he took the only way out a man could."

"Your father was a self-indulgent coward afraid to try for a real life because he might find out he didn't want what he told himself he did. Afraid he might find he didn't want his great love enough to leave his comfort for her. Afraid his wife might not really give a damn if he left. Afraid things might not work out with the love of his life. Afraid of the responsibility of doing something about his life. It was easier to be a proud, solitary, lonely, misunderstood tragic hero. The only El Dorado he really wanted was a lazy life with no demands."

Near noon, the lunch crowd settled into the tables and booths. The manager had finished with the receipts, greeted the more important customers at the door. Two more waitresses had come on duty, one of them, a small brunette, smiled at Frank. He finished the beer he'd poured for himself, nodded to me.

"I have to go to work. You're wrong about my father."

He took his empty bottle and mine, dropped them into the trash behind the bar, and went down the bar to wait on three businessmen who'd just come in. They all had Bud Light. It's something I'll never understand. I suppose I'll always be a stranger in my own country. Frank brought me a fresh Beck's.

"Send me your bill. When Dianne's money is settled, I'll pay you what she owed you."

"After the war," I said, "I moved around. Me and the Beat Generation. They had one thing right over the Sixties—life is a trip, not a space. What they had wrong was they went on the road alone and wondered why it fell apart for them. You can't take the trip alone, not in the little picture or the big. Isolation doesn't mean freedom, it just means isolation. Your problem is you don't share the small with a woman or the big with the world. It's not sex, it's not even companionship, it's just part of being human. Alone, your trip won't mean shit, not even to you."

"She's dead, Fortune. What do I do about that?"

"You don't care about Dianne. A sentimental pose like your father's suicide. You feel sorry for yourself. There's nothing to fight for or even live for except today's kicks and the next high. Have *fun*, goddamn, 'cause it's all nothing and only fools believe it isn't. Go it alone on coke and booze." I put my money on the bar, stood. "Billy never stopped being eighteen, and neither did you. The only one castrating you is you."

As I walked out into the noontime sun of a Santa Barbara August, I felt sad for Frank. Not for Billy, his pain was over. Frank had a long time left to do nothing.

The beach and the sea were across the wide boulevard. The rim of the Pacific. We began on the rim of the Mediterranean, are finishing on the rim of the Pacific. Maybe the real finish. As a species, getting there was always more important than the destination, the trip not the arrival. It was the battle not the victory that made us rulers of the planet. Now that there was nowhere to go, would we end here? Could cowboys learn to look inward at the real jungle, the real war?

I got into my Tempo and drove toward Summerland and Kay. It wasn't a question I could answer. Not alone anyway.

THE END

**Read the first chapter
of the next exciting Dan Fortune mystery**

Chasing Eights
**by Dennis Lynds
#15 in the Edgar Award-winning Dan Fortune mystery series**

The dark was motionless even with a sea wind that blew through the palms and old oaks. Night is not our time. We need light so we can see and touch and not have to imagine the dangers hidden in the shadows.

I had heard the sound that wasn't wind or imagination. The big Victorian house set back from Toro Canyon Road near Via Real had shown no life since I'd arrived. It was all gray towers and gables and turrets with a widow's walk on its main tower. Most of its windows were closed and curtained in the last light of evening. There were no cars in the driveway. A plain house with no one home. But unless Angela Price's husband was lying to her, behind the windows covered by drapes and vegetation imported to Southern California from every semitropical of the world, was a professional poker game.

It wasn't the game I listened for. Not from the big shadowy Victorian, but from across the road where two smaller houses were darker. What could have been two muffled shots, footsteps in the brush.

I waited five minutes, circled to cross the blacktop road away from the sea and freeway, came up on the small house through trees and the chaparral. They were both little more than cinder-block shacks, one darkened and neat with curtains, the other a tumbledown half-ruin in overgrown weeds.

He stood behind the tumbledown house.

A wolf face in the brief headlights of a passing car. Skin grooved like leather, a graying mustache, a dark windbreaker of no color. A western hat and worn jeans. Eyes reflected straight toward me. The one sweep of light and then only a skinny shape, a shadow rigid in the night. I moved closer. When the next car passed, its lights swept emptiness.

Cars moved in a steady drone on the freeway, passed on Toro Canyon Road and Via Real. I moved on to where the Latino had been standing. The body lay between the broken house and a rear shed. A heavier texture in the night that made me stop before I fell over it. In the beam of my flashlight he had no face.

Old Captain Gazzo in New York told me you never get used to it, you only withdraw into some private nightmare where it is always midnight. Death is difficult enough, violent death is, in the end, impossible. Gazzo drew the shades down on his office windows, kept them down for the next twenty years, so he wouldn't see all the bloody bodies lying shattered in the dark glass like color negatives. They become you, you become them, and you never get used to it.

A pool of dark liquid, bone, and tissue where his head lay in the weeds. Without half a head he couldn't be alive, but I took his pulse, checked his heart and breathing. There was no heartbeat, no pulse, no breath. He had no eyes to look into. A short man, thick and muscular, with brown skin and black hair worn long, in a dark blue pin-striped suit, pale blue shirt, blue-and-red tie. His black half boots had tassels. Shot in the back of the head at close range. He had been on his knees, dirt on the pin-striped trousers. A heavy gun placed against the skull, red marks on his wrists where they had been held behind his back. There were rings on his fingers, a stickpin in the tie, a gold Rolex watch, but his wallet was in his hip pocket as if he wasn't used to wearing a suit yet.

The driver's license was in the name of Santos Torena. The pistol was in his pants, a snub-nosed Colt .38. I put the wallet and pistol back, searched around him with my flashlight. The body was still warm, the weeds were trampled, but I found no clear footprints. I had seen enough death to know I could do nothing for Santos Torena, so I went back across the blacktop to the Victorian. It was still dark and silent as if nothing happened out in the night.

I walked around the place, listening for voices. Poker is unlike other forms of gambling. There is no edge to the house, so it cuts the pot for its share. You play only the odds, the others in the game, and yourself. If you play perfectly, the way you know you should, you will always win over the long run. But human beings do nothing perfectly, even less act always the way they know they should, and so poker is a game of tension, of frustration, of anger at yourself. A game of self, and it cannot be played in the silence of blackjack or roulette, the isolation among crowds of horse racing. It is a game of talk, of laughs and curses, of long explanations of why one did or did not, of analysis of past hands tonight and weeks ago, of what could have happened and might have been.

I heard the voices, climbed the steps of a side porch. Through the white curtains on French doors the players sat in a room beyond the one next to the porch. Eight men around the green felt table with a dealer's slot. The angle gave me four faces, two backs and only the hands of the dealer as the cards went around.

A tall man with horn-rimmed glasses and a black-and-white checked shirt under a black vest sat next to the dealer. He wore his glasses on a cord, his long red hair ragged as if cut with a knife. His eyes watched the cards of the other players, and the other players themselves.

Underweight and gray-faced, a balding man in his forties sat in a blue blazer that hung too loose on his bones, a red-striped button-down shirt, bow tie. He looked at his hole cards, scanned the cards of the others with pale eyes that saw little, seemed to look out through the bars of a cage.

The third, a little man in his seventies with the precise face of an accountant, held his hole cards tight to his chest. Steel eyes that studied both his up and hole cards over and over, calculated the value of his hand rigorously. He would be a man who folded a great deal.

Between the old man and the balding one with the caged eyes, the fourth player was who I had come for. Angela Price had described her husband well. Forty-two, a whisper over six feet and two-hundred pounds. Maybe fifteen pounds overweight. Thick dark blond hair that had been golden. Erect, his chest out, belly in under a proper white shirt and blue tie, blue three-button suit with vest. The posture of an athlete, the clothes of a successful business man. A confident expression to the blue eyes as if aware of people watching him.

But Jack Price wasn't an athlete, and he wasn't confident. It was there in the belt that cut into his waist, the shirt that bunched out of tight pants. Pale, thick fingers almost like the fingers of a baby. The tightness of everything because he would not admit he was overweight. And the face. A soft face, puffy and smooth, the nose and chin too small. Behind the confident expression there was a flicker in the blue eyes. He was a man who would always feel someone was watching him.

In the room there were only two who would take money from the game over the long run. The thin man in the checked shirt who studied the cards of everyone, and the owner who cut the pot. The others never really looked at what anyone else held, played as if they were alone with their cards. Too busy with other problems. Too eager and too distracted at the same time. They played at poker, the game not the result.

I walked through the trees to my Ford Tempo parked up the road. I looked at my car telephone. In my work the rule is tell the police everything, it's the law, you need them more than they need you.

There are exceptions to every rule. Santos Torena was the man my client's husband was supposed to meet tonight. I couldn't help Torena. I needed to know more of what was going on before I talked to any police. You owed a client that much.

I called Kay. The machine answered. I left a message – the job was going to take longer, eat without me.

Meet the Author
Dennis Lynds

A raconteur and Renaissance man, Dennis Lynds changed the mystery form and along the way created colorful private detectives who consistently won awards as well as the hearts of readers. He was a tall, lanky man with a nose the size of Gibraltar and a generous nature that made him a soft touch for friends, panhandlers, and his children. He published some 40 novels under various pseudonyms, won awards such as the Edgar, the mystery world's highest honor, and received accolades from legendary authors like Ross Macdonald. "A novelist of power and quality, . . . one of the major imaginative creators in the crime field," Macdonald wrote of him.

The New York Times named several of Lynds's novels to its Best Mysteries of the Year lists. Remarkably, two of them written under different pseudonyms appeared on the same list – *Silent Scream* by Michael Collins and *Circle of Fire* by Mark Sadler.

Amused, Lynds said that none of the *Times* editors realized he was both Collins and Sadler. "I don't think they ever figured it out," he explained. And he never bothered to tell them.

Seldom does an author change the course of a genre once; rarely twice. Lynds is credited with being the writer who, in the late 1960s and early 1970s, propelled the detective novel into the Modern Age. His most famous pen name was Michael Collins. With that name, he created the opinionated Dan Fortune, the star of one of America's longest-running private detective series. The first book, *Act of Fear*, won the Edgar Allan Poe Award for Best First Novel. "Many critics believe Dan Fortune to be the culmination of a maturing process that transformed the private eye from the naturalistic Spade (Dashiell Hammett) through the romantic Marlowe (Raymond Chandler) and the psychological Archer (Ross Macdonald) to the sociological Fortune," according to *Private Eyes: 101 Knights* by Robert Baker and Michael Nietzel.

At heart, Lynds was a rebel. Two decades later, he rattled mystery critics and changed the field again, this time by introducing literary techniques into the genre, beginning in the late 1980s with *Red Rosa, Castrato*, and *Chasing Eights*, and continuing well into the 1990s with *The Irishman's Horse, Cassandra in Red*, and *The Cadillac Cowboy*. Other authors followed, proving the flexibility and durability of the suspense world. "No one could accuse [Lynds] of reworking the same turf in his novels. . . . His last several books have pushed the private-eye form into some fascinating new shapes," according to *The Wall Street Journal* in 2000. *The Los Angeles Times* commented, "It takes style to bring that off. Bravery, too, of course."

Lynds also published mainstream novels, short stories, and poetry. Five of his literary short stories were honored in *Best American Short Stories*.

During World War II, he was a rifleman and carried books of poetry in his knapsack as he fought across France. He was a strong swimmer, so when he and fellow infantrymen were surrounded by Nazis, he plunged into an icy river, leading them to escape. He earned two Purple Hearts and a Bronze Star. Later he graduated with a degree in chemistry from Hofstra and a masters degree in journalism from Syracuse. A lifelong New Yorker, in the mid 1960s he finally left the East Coast's bitter winters to settle in the warm sunshine of Southern California. He was married three times, to Doris Flood, then Sheila McErlean, and finally to Gayle Hallenbeck Stone Lynds. He had two daughters, Katie and Deirdre Lynds, and two step children, Paul and Julia Stone.

Dennis Lynds died at age 81 in 2005. Jack Adrian wrote in *The Financial Times*, "Unusually for a mystery writer – as a breed, they tend to favor things as they are, rather than as they might be – the American author Dennis Lynds, politically, came from left of center. This did not mean he preached bloody revolution. He wrote to entertain." Entertainment was something Lynds never forgot, that and to be generous to his friends.

Obituaries celebrating his work appeared around the globe. In a typical understatement, he commented near the end of his life, "I had a good run." His career had lasted more than fifty years.

A Dangerous Job
#14 in the Edgar Award–winning Dan Fortune mystery series

by Dennis Lynds

Originally published as *Castrato* under the pseudonym
Michael Collins

If you live in New York City, you know you're going to change your address, phone number, and job more than once. That was as true in 1989 as it is today. And it was in 1989 that iconic private detective Dan Fortune made his final move, leaving New York's towering skyscrapers and old brick alleys for Santa Barbara's swaying palm trees and sandy beaches – and Kay Michaels. Fortune was in love, real love, in fact he was so in love with Kay – a tall, beautiful model – that they'd moved in together. "Kay's a woman, not an actress," he explained.

But before he can really settle in, Fortune finds Santa Barbara isn't the paradise that locals like to believe. A young man named Billy Owen is missing, and Dan is hired to find him. Billy always wanted to be a hero, a white knight who rode in to save the day. In truth, he's part of a gun-running operation in Central America, and he's the black sheep of his family.

His older brother, Frank, is looking for Billy, too, but the only clue is the murder of Billy's shadowy Latin friend. When someone shoots at Fortune and tries to murder Frank, it becomes clear that Billy's latest mission of glory has put him in over his head. Fortune faces danger on all fronts – from a ruthless, wealthy family to the FBI and CIA.

When Billy turns up dead, the mystery deepens, leading Fortune from New York's bohemian Chelsea neighborhood to California's

Santa Ynez Valley and a seemingly forgotten world where the old unwritten codes of the cowboy still stand.

"A tautly crafted mystery." – *Publishers Weekly*

"The most ambitious of the series . . . engrossing." – *Kirkus Reviews*

"Finely honed prose, suspense, and bits of reflective philosophy . . . crackling with excitement." – *Library Journal*

"His best yet." – *San Diego Union*

"It's refreshing to encounter [Lynds's] uncynical, unjaded private detective Dan Fortune living happily in Santa Barbara with his lady friend Kay . . . [Lynds] combines superb characters and excellent plotting to produce an exciting mystery." – *Booklist*

###

www.ingramcontent.com/pod-product-compliance
Lightning Source LLC
Chambersburg PA
CBHW061542170626
46811CB00001B/58